Methodical Illusion

To Matt,
Thank you for taking
one of my sisters-in-flight.
Sylvia -Fasten your seatbelt!

Methodical Illusion

Rebekah Roth

KTYS media

Methodical Illusion is a work of fiction based on historical facts. Some names, characters, places, events, and incidents may be either the product of the author's imagination or a compilation of persons the author has met. Any resemblance to actual events, locales, organizations or persons, living or dead, may be pure coincidence and beyond the intent of either the author or the publisher.

Second Edition

ISBN 978-0-9827571-3-0

Library of Congress Cataloging-in-Publication Data
Roth, Rebekah
Methodical Illusion
Fiction
2014954848
ISBN 978-0-9827571-3-0 (soft cover)
Library of Congress Number: 2014954848

To contact Rebekah Roth:
www.methodicalillusion.com

KTYS media
www.ktysmedia.com

Printed in the United States of America

Dedicated To:
To those who lost their lives
September 11, 2001

The 343 NYFD Firefighters
The Passengers and Crews of
American Airlines Flight 11
United Airlines Flight 175
American Airlines Flight 77
United Airlines Flight 93
The first responders from all departments
The surviving family members who lost loved ones
The occupants of the Twin Towers

"You never find yourself until you face the truth."
Pearl Bailey

Endorsements

"*Methodical Illusion* is an important book. For the first time, it brings the inside knowledge of airline and FAA protocols of a 30-year flight attendant to bear on cutting the Gordian Knot of two of the most difficult and disturbing *un*answered questions of 9/11: What *really* happened to the planes and the passengers? It won't be long before you're inside Roth's characters as they uncover and connect real dots and are forced to a shocking conclusion that may take us all a giant step closer to the Truth."

 -Barbara Honegger, former White House Policy Analyst and Dept. of Defense Senior Military Affairs Journalist, 2000-2011

"OF ALL THE THEORIES CONVEYED TO ME OVER THE YEARS, AND OF ALL THE SOMETIMES FANCIFUL NOTIONS REGARDING EVERYTHING FROM REMOTE VIEWING OF THE SET-UP TO DIRECTED ENERGY FULFILLING THE MISSION, AND HOWEVER WILLING I MAY BE AND MAY HAVE BEEN TO EMBRACE CERTAIN ASPECTS OF THEM, THE FACT IS REBEKAH ROTH'S "METHODICAL ILLUSION" MAKES THE MOST SENSE BY A QUANTUM LEAP. IT IS SO POWERFUL THAT I SUSPECT A NUMBER OF COMPLICIT PARTIES ARE VERY WORRIED THAT THEIR "METHODICAL ILLUSION" IS ABOUT TO UNRAVEL AND JUSTICE MAY AT LAST BE DONE."

 -John B. Wells, Host, Caravan to Midnight

"Rebekah Roth's Methodical Illusion is both an entertaining page-turner and an important historical document. Like Philip Zelikow's 9/11 Commission Report, Roth's book is a work of fiction. But unlike Zelikow's novel, Methodical Illusion reveals rather than conceals the truth about 9/11."

 -Dr. Kevin Barrett, Editor for "Veterans Today" and Host, Truth Jihad

"Rebekah has written a thrilling book that is sure to be both entertaining and informative. She presents the salient facts of 9/11 in an intriguing and interesting way. Rebekah uses her knowledge of flight attendant procedures and does a brilliant job of unraveling the enigma of the cell phone calls, why, when and where they were made."

 -KK, American Airlines Pilot (ret)

"Masterfully written using an elusive yet perfect blend of intrigue and fact, Rebekah Roth offers a gripping account of indispensable factual details of the most horrifically historic event of our lifetimes. The events as seen and described through the eyes of a seasoned airline professional will certainly cause turbulence to your otherwise clear-air normalcy bias. It is very important history and elegantly written."

 – Douglas J. Hagmann, Veteran Investigator, Host, The Hagmann & Hagmann Report

Forward

"I first learned about Rebekah Roth when hearing her being interviewed on Hagmann & Hagmann and then again on Caravan to Midnight. It was readily apparent that she knew from an insider's perspective exactly what she was talking about. The interviews were riveting and answered many question about the anomalies and the total failure to follow well defined and required in-flight protocols which only a professional would know. The day her book arrived I sat down and read it through cover to cover. Her many hours of in-depth research have uncovered the truth and shed much light on the mysteries of that day. The reader will find many of the who, the how, and the why questions answered. For those who have yet to emerge from the cognitive dissonance it will be a journey they can take along with Vera in her quest for the truth.

For Airline pilots and flight attendants 9/11 and the subsequent implementation of the Patriot Act effectively destroyed most of the command latitude and much of the allure of those professions. Crewmembers were now considered and treated as a potential "terrorist" when reporting to work. TSA lackeys were given authority to search sacrosanct flight bags containing the required navigational charts and flight manuals. It was invasive, humiliating and deeply insulting especially in light of the fact that no competent pilot, let alone incompetent "hijackers" could accomplish what was claimed to have been done with those aircraft. Yet the "official" story must be reinforced at all costs.

Rebekah Roth has succeeded in weaving the real events of that day into a novel which is entertaining, technically accurate and informative. Methodical Illusion is a journey with Vera which every American should take."

Brent D. Capt UAL (ret)
21,000hrs, DC-3 B767 + A&P
Pilots for 9/11 Truth

Introduction

I enjoyed a nearly-thirty-year airline career, working as both a flight attendant and an international purser. I was trained as an emergency medical technician and served as a volunteer firefighter.

My expertise and training as a flight attendant allowed me to research the events of September 11, 2001, with an insider's knowledge that eventually led me to discover details and answers to some of the most haunting questions surrounding that infamous day in our history.

I enjoyed a very exciting life both in the air and on the ground, and because of that I was encouraged by co-workers to write a book. As I began to do that, I discovered that ten of the accused 9/11 hijackers were still alive. Several of them were also airline employees employed with Saudi Arabia Airlines. They had had their identifications stolen years before 9/11. At least four of the accused hijackers threatened to sue the U.S. government and the FBI if they did not stop using their names and identities. That discovery, along with the U.S. government's refusal to discontinue their false accusations, ignited my curiosity.

After thousands of hours of research, using official government documents, print and video media from 9/11, and several books, I discovered that there were also at least two women involved in the 9/11 event. Using my personal knowledge of in-flight procedures, FAA hijacking protocols, the state of Massachusetts, and cell phone technology, I discovered yet-to-be-exposed details concerning the planes, the passengers, and the perpetrators, all of which are woven into Methodical Illusion.

This book is the result of my extensive research. It is based on real life events. It is written as a novel to protect me and my family from the repercussions that inevitably occur when one gets too close to the truth. I am now considered by many to be a foremost expert on the events of September 11, 2001. I invite the reader to contact me with any questions through my website www.methodicalillusion.com.

Rebekah Roth

"To learn who rules over you, simply find out who you are not allowed to criticize."
Voltaire

one

The left hand reached toward the Bible and centered itself firmly on top of the leather-bound book as the camera froze there momentarily, allowing much of the gold embossed lettering to be visible between the fingers. Vera stopped packing her suitcase and stood reverently glued to the television screen. She reached for the remote and turned up the volume just as the camera slowly pulled back to reveal Joel Sherman lift his right arm to the square. There, in the Oval Office of the White House, stood the soon-to-be-President of the United States standing next to his radiant wife, Mica, who was holding the Bible upon which his hand now rested. In front of them stood the Chief Justice of the United States Supreme Court, dressed in his black robes with his right arm also raised to the square. The words of the oath of office echoed from the Chief Justice to President Sherman and then into Vera's mind. ". . . to the best of my ability, preserve, protect and defend the Constitution of the United States, so help me God."

Vera exhaled with a sigh of relief. The country had gone through such turmoil over the past few years. Immediately after the elections in 2012 and even before the President was inaugurated for his second term, evidence began to come forward regarding the Benghazi attacks, in which the U.S. ambassador to Libya and three others had been killed. By February, it had become quite clear to the public that the President and the Vice President had been running a secret arms operation through Libyan rebels to the resistance in Syria. Not only was that operation illegal, but it was patently treasonous. Rumors to such effect had been circulating for months following the embassy attack on September 11, 2012, but the media had a tendency to ignore most of the salient points, and the Republican Party didn't seem to have the stomach to pursue the matter after their crushing defeat at the ballot box in November. About the only thing the Republicans could muster was to replace their leadership in the House by naming Joel Sherman as Speaker. In January, certain Al Qaeda leaders were captured by the Mossad trying to arm the Palestinians with many of the weapons they had obtained from the United States. The evidence they provided could no longer be ignored and the Mossad had a peculiar way of persuading the United States media to publish everything they were uncovering.

Following the exposure of the ever-expanding IRS scandal, where the President had used the agency to target his enemies, the political fight was in full bloom. The Republicans sensed blood in the water and, since they controlled the House, threatened simultaneous impeachment of both the President and Vice President. The Democrats circled the wagons and dismissed, ignored, or obstructed every attempt to comply with House investigations and subpoenas. The stalemate that ensued stretched well into the fall and essentially shut down all legislative progress having to do with governance. The people became more and more frustrated with the mounting problems that Congress failed to address. The status quo likely would have continued indefinitely, but for the daughter of the President's top senior advisor. In a moment of defiant independence, she slipped past her Secret Service detail while visiting Cairo and was kidnapped by Al Qaeda. Ironically, they transported her to Libya and threatened to kill her unless her mother testified before Congress about the Administration's conspiracies as they related to the Benghazi attack. Her mother threatened a full scale offensive in retaliation, but quickly relented, knowing the

President had little or no support for such an action. Shortly thereafter she went before a House oversight committee and revealed so much corruption and illegal activity on the part of the administration that even the press was dumbfounded. She apparently was testifying under some type of immunity agreement, but that detail had never been clarified to the public. Of course, the beheading videos of the Western journalists that were sent to the New York Times, along with the daughter's video pleading to her mother to save her life, was what persuaded the president's advisor to testify before Congress.

After that, it was all downhill for the President. Many of the less-progressive Democratic senators could no longer support the Administration. The press, with the exception of a few brain-damaged commentators on MSNBC, began to call for impeachment, and the public's voice wanted it sooner rather than later. In October, the House of Representatives filed fifteen articles of impeachment for high crimes, misdemeanors, and treason against the President and Vice President. The former Secretary of State, who had resigned in January after the election, was arrested and indicted on similar criminal charges. The debate in the House lasted three weeks due to the abundance of charges and a desire by nearly every House member to be on the record voicing their opinion. In November, the House voted overwhelmingly in a bipartisan manner to impeach both men. Only twice before in the history of the Republic had a President been impeached, but neither time was he convicted in the Senate and removed from office. Never had both the President and Vice President been impeached at the same time. The conviction of both left the door open for several constitutional issues regarding succession. The Supreme Court ruled immediately that if both were convicted in the Senate, the Speaker of the House would become the President. With the overwhelming evidence against both men, the Senate was persuaded to try them simultaneously, yet separately, and to schedule the votes one right after the other—the Vice President first, then the President, to avoid any confusion as to who would become the next President. Of course, if the President was convicted and the Vice President was not, the Vice President would immediately be sworn in as the next President.

Their trials began in November and lingered on until the Christmas recess. They resumed again in January and consumed the entire Senate calendar. Witness after witness was called, and the public watched intently on television as each revealed, in detail, the depth of the Administration's involvement in these heinous crimes. New revelations were exposed, but by this point it was clear that Joel Sherman, the Speaker of the House, would become the next President of the United States. Testimony wrapped up on Thursday, January 30. The following day, the Chief Justice, who had presided over the trials, made clarifications to the law and a vote was scheduled for the following Monday. The outcome was no surprise. Every Republican and every single Democratic senator who was planning to run for reelection, along with a few more moderate Democrats, voted to convict both men. The vote was 74-25—with one abstention—to convict the Vice President and 73-25—with two abstentions—to convict the President. The now-former President posed arrogantly in his chair as the Chief Justice excused himself to be transported to the White House to swear in House Speaker Sherman.

An air of calm came over Vera as she muted the television so as not to have to listen to the commentators' reactions to this historic event. She hoped that this change would bring a renewed peace to Washington and that the political process could begin to care about the people again and focus its attention on the country's problems, which had been neglected for so long. She folded the last of her clothing for her trip to Japan, rechecked her cosmetic bag to make sure all the necessary items were present, and zipped up her suitcase. No matter how many times she had flow to Asia there was always a sense of excited anticipation as she reached for her uniform blazer and checked to see if her wings were pinned on straight.

The airport terminal seemed crowded for a typical Monday afternoon. Lines extended into areas that were usually only occupied on busy weekends. Vera casually noticed the long lines, but after nearly thirty years as a flight attendant, she was not at all fazed by the large crowd. As she rolled her suitcase toward an unmarked stainless steel elevator, she couldn't help but notice a well-dressed, handsome man standing near a gift shop. His fashionable Italian suit and his impeccably-styled dark hair bore a striking resemblance to her late husband, Jeff. Sadly, the instantaneous attraction she felt in seeing this man dissipated rapidly—and with a twinge of pain, as she remembered their last moments together.

Jeff loved his Harley, and every Saturday morning, rain or shine, he took off on it and returned feeling invigorated. He never had a specific destination in mind nor an exact time to return, but he did have a unique name for it: "Windsweeping." Vera used Jeff's weekly ritual for her own special time of renewal—a brisk walk along the beach with their golden retriever, Kelli, followed by a long, hot bubble bath.

On one of these ordinary Saturdays, as she was wiping the mud off of Kelli's paws, a state highway patrol car pulled into their driveway. Vera's heart froze as the officer slowly climbed out of his vehicle and walked toward her with a stoic look on his face, born no doubt from experience, but which needed no explanation.

"Mrs. Hanson?" he politely inquired.

She nodded, not taking her eyes off of his face. Though his expression had not changed, its message was screaming out "disaster." Kelli barked a quick almost-puppy-like yelp as the officer spoke. "Your husband, Jeff, has been in a very serious motorcycle accident. I am here to inform you and to transport you to Evergreen Eastside Hospital as quickly as possible."

Vera's last moments with Jeff were short. He never did regain consciousness, although she was certain he knew she was there as he took his final breath. The doctors had allowed her to be by his bedside once they realized there was nothing more they could do for him. She had always been thankful for the miracle of making it to his side before he died, but that memory always commenced the cycle of pain in which she now dwelt. The details of exactly what had happened to Jeff that day were never clear enough for Vera to have had complete closure. Jeff was the most safety-conscious person she had ever known, which is why the state patrol officer's words swirling in her head—". . . the other vehicle . . . black . . . no other injuries . . . no witnesses . . . not sure how or what had happened . . . no investigation would be possible"—never made complete sense to her.

She shook her head as if to clear all the unpleasant memories and quickly fingered in the four-digit security code to open the elevator door. Distracted by her memories, Vera had apparently forgotten to swipe her company ID card. She leaned forward, swiped the card clipped to her lapel, then again punched in the security code. Again nothing. She waited, her eyes trained on the elevator door, wondering why it wouldn't open. After several moments, she was convinced the security code had been changed while she was on her days off. The security at the airport had gone out of control after the terror attacks of September 11, 2001. Everything changed—the codes, the procedures, the federal aviation regulations, and nearly all company policies. The changes had become so all-encompassing and capriciously implemented that it became nearly impossible to know all the policy directives that the federal government used to control both the flight crews and the traveling public. Vera wasn't certain that terrorists had any knowledge of the constant changes in the airline industry. She was pretty well convinced, however, that they could take command of any airport terminal simply by driving up to the curb and opening fire with machine guns in the ticketing area.

Suddenly, the elevator door opened and a 757 crew with their luggage rolled out together, chatting about the weather and hoping that their flight would arrive on time. They were headed to Las Vegas and sounded far more excited about their layover than working the trip. Vera stepped into the empty elevator, rolling her suitcase and tote bag ensemble behind her. The doors closed and down she headed into the bowels of the airport. "Wow," she thought to herself, "what kind of security do we have here?" She wondered if terrorists knew that this very elevator would open up one floor below the terminal, right onto the tarmac. Could a terrorist, dressed as a pilot, simply wait like she had waited for a crew to come up, then walk into the employee elevator, ride down, and be right on the tarmac with the jets? She considered talking to a supervisor about her security concerns, but immediately changed her mind when she recalled how several of her flight attendant and pilot friends had shared similar concerns with company supervisors shortly after the 9/11 terror attacks. Their unease with some of the procedures and practices was not taken seriously. On more than one occasion, they were told that they were being paranoid or racially profiling passengers and were ushered out of the supervisor's office. Vera recalled how one of the flight attendants had been so upset that she had gone directly to the FAA. When she finally got to the correct office to voice her apprehensions, the man behind the desk, an Arab, quietly listened, then reassured her that there was nothing to worry about and politely showed her the door. A few weeks later, that flight attendant was called into her supervisor's office and told in no uncertain terms to keep her security complaints to herself.

She was advised that the next time her superiors found out she had gone to the FAA or any other federal agency, she would be terminated.

When the elevator stopped, the doors opened to a crowd of ramp personnel and flight crews, some on break, others just waiting for the elevator, and a few punching in at the nearby time clock. To the untrained eye, it looked like organized chaos. Vera easily navigated her way through the crowds and greeted all the employees she knew. The hallway walls were cinder block, heavily painted over in the company color scheme du jour. Presently the wall colors matched the airplanes—gray with a wide red horizontal stripe. Tacked here and there on the wall were framed travel posters that promoted one international destination or another. The floors were tiled with old industrial linoleum, heavily scuffed from the ramp rats' black boots and the wheels of the crews' rolling suitcases. Vera wondered when—or if—the company ever cleaned the floors. She had been in that part of the terminal at all hours of the day and night and hadn't once seen a cleaning crew. The place was dingy, dirty, and a far cry from what she knew most people imagined her glamorous life to be whenever they learned that she was an international flight attendant. Whatever prestige might have been associated with her job had been sucked right out of the air the moment she stepped foot out of that elevator.

Her flight to Tokyo wasn't scheduled to depart for several hours, so she headed to the crew lounge area to relax and to mentally prepare for the long journey ahead. The paint in that room seemed to leach out of the cinder block, and it was difficult to know if the entire room had ever been painted at the same time. A large bank of vending machines filled one wall. One side of the spacious room offered old chrome furniture resembling kitchen tables of the 1960s. The mismatched chairs, made of metal, vinyl, or wood, had torn fabric seat cushions. Along another wall were broken-down sofas separated by dark wooden end tables, most of which were heavily scratched. The lighting was poor and, with no windows to the outside, the room took on a dreariness that exuded the atmosphere of a time capsule. Defying the gloomy ambiance, the lounge was abuzz with activity. Flight crews in uniform or in street clothes were both coming and going. Others were reading flight schedules, magazines, and books on almost every imaginable subject. The lounge was really no more than a waiting room, one which never welcomed you in nor made you hesitate to leave to work your flight. It was just how the company wanted it to be—serviceable, but with no hint of the company's marketing slogan about proudly providing passengers with stellar service.

Vera found an empty table in a corner of the room, cleared off the newspapers spread out across the top, and settled in for her three-hour wait. Moments later, she noticed Grace Lewis enter and glance around the room. She caught Grace's eye and motioned her over.

"Hey, Vera, it looks like am I'm on your flight to Tokyo this afternoon," Grace said as she situated her suitcase against the wall and sat down across from Vera.

"Great! I'm the purser on the flight leaving at two for Narita," Vera smiled. "But what in the world are you doing flying to Asia? I thought you were exclusively the Paris and Amsterdam queen."

"Sick leave make-up," Grace sighed. "I called in sick for two Paris trips, so this Tokyo trip is my best bet for making up the lost time. It's worth twenty-five hours, right?"

"Twenty-five hours and forty-five minutes, to be exact," Vera confirmed. "Glad to have you on the crew, Grace. I haven't flown with you since that Paris flight when you couldn't stop talking about some hot guy you met at the bar. When was that, about a year ago?"

"Ah, Khalid," Grace filled in. "Yes, I'm still seeing him, and

I've introduced several flight attendants to some of his friends. I've become known as the 'Middle East Matchmaker.'"

"Oh, really?" Vera questioned, raising an eyebrow. "That's news I didn't know. Are any of these lucky women on our crew?" Vera was intrigued to hear that Grace had been carrying on with this Middle Easterner for far longer than her usual three-to-four-week stint with any new guy. "How often do you fly to Paris, Grace? I thought those trips went a little above your seniority."

"Oh, I'm able to hold Amsterdam, and I found a guy five years senior to me who likes to trade my Amsterdam trips for his Paris flights," Grace explained. "I get to Paris at least three times a month now, sometimes four. But sometimes Khalid flies to meet me in Amsterdam. He loves to introduce his friends to flight attendants, so I'm usually dragging three or four lonely-heart crew members out on my layovers. I'm sure you must know some of them, but none are on our trip today. These guys have so much money, they pay for everything, and it's not uncommon for one of them to shower a new acquaintance with incredible jewelry by the end of the trip."

"Wow," exclaimed Vera, "they give out that kind of jewelry? Any strings attached?"

"Honestly, most of these women are so blown away by the lavish expenditures that they continue seeing these guys every time they fly to Europe. Who wouldn't?" Grace asked with a smile, her own fingers adorned with three gorgeous rings and her wrist with a stunning diamond tennis bracelet.

"Well, I can see we'll have plenty to talk about on the way to Tokyo," Vera remarked. "Will you be up for dinner and a beer at the infamous 'crew lounge,' Grace? I'm sure you've heard all the wild stories about that place, even in Europe."

"Oh, you must be reading my mind. I haven't been to Japan in almost a year. I'll stay close to your side, if you don't mind. I wouldn't know where to go or what to do. Dinner will give me a chance to finish telling you all about Khalid."

Grace wasn't known for her intellectual prowess. Most of her co-workers recognized that what came out of her mouth bordered on comedy—and not because she was particularly funny. Everyone, however, noticed her attachment to the finer things that money could buy. Grace would often show up for dinner wearing outfits worth thousands, and she was always adorned in more jewelry than most people would ever find appropriate. As she reveled in the attention, she would often toss back her long flowing hair and proclaim with a smile, "You know me, dressed like a whore on holiday." Everyone seemed to take her self-deprecating comment in stride, for they knew that Grace's evenings were filled with going to places her crew member friends would only be visiting in their dreams. Her lifestyle, her attraction to money, and the stories about the men who could provide her with such excess would surely supply Vera with a very interesting evening in Narita.

two

By the time the flight arrived in Tokyo, Vera had put in one of her typical twenty-four-hour days. The added time she spent commuting from the West Coast to Detroit—just to work the flight—compounded her fatigue. Normally, she would head right to her hotel room and straight to bed, hoping to recover sufficiently for the flight home the next afternoon. But tonight she needed to summon up enough energy to take Grace out to dinner and finish hearing about her Middle Eastern boyfriend.

As the purser for the flight, Vera was the last crew member to deplane, after having checked through the cabin to ensure that no passengers remained on board. Typically, by the time she arrived at the small blue-and-yellow bus for the ride to the hotel, she had to stand and hold onto the metal pole behind the bus driver. This time, though, Grace had saved her a seat, which Vera quickly slid into. Then she turned to Grace and asked, "So, are you too wiped out to go out for dinner?" Before Grace had an opportunity to respond, Vera continued, "The 'crew lounge' is always lots of fun. You never know who is going to get too much alcohol on board and start pole dancing while taking off her clothes. Last month, a very senior gal got hammered and stripped down to her waist. She had recently had a boob job and was quite proud of her new assets. She went from one pilot to the next, imploring them to take a feel and asking them if they felt real. Then to top it off, she stood on the bar and shook them for the entire lounge to see. Of course, the men all loved it and encouraged her every move. But word—along with a few explicit pictures—quickly traveled back to her fiancé in Florida. Let's just say, she's now going to be so occupied moving out of his house during her days off she will only care about her boobs if they can help carry something."

Grace picked right up where Vera left off. "Was this who I think it was?" she asked, almost jumping out of her seat. "Damn, it was Jane, wasn't it? Her boyfriend flies the 747-400 to China, and his house on the beach in Florida is a total palace. Oh, my, she's going to wish she had made do with a Wonder Bra. Her boyfriend comes from old money and it's big old money."

Vera just smiled. Not one to promote what was commonly referred to as "airline rumors," she never gave out names when starting or repeating stories about co-workers. "You know me, Grace, I never remember names. That's been my personal policy since I started my career. The best way is to stay neutral, while still providing the story with legs. I figure at the speed these stories make their way through the company and around the world, everyone will eventually get the names of the guilty parties from someone other than me."

"With stories like this one, Vera, it doesn't matter how exhausted I am. I have to see this place for myself, so the next time I hear about some shenanigans that one of my co-workers is involved in here in Japan, I'll at least be able to visualize the surroundings," Grace smiled and gave a slight nod and a wink in Vera's direction.

The bus pulled up in front of the sprawling three-story hotel, and the flight crew began to slowly file down the narrow aisle and out the door. The first ones out of the bus were already standing at the front desk eagerly waiting to receive their keys by the time Grace and Vera stepped onto the pavement. Fortunately the line moved quickly. Once Vera had her room key in hand, she turned to Grace and said, "Okay, it's now just after four o'clock. I want to shower and check my email before we head out. Let's say we meet here in the lobby at five-thirty. How does that sound?"

"Oh, I'll be here. I am staying in 394. Call my room if I'm not here exactly on time. I wouldn't want to miss this opportunity for the world." Grace pulled her suitcase and garment bag from the long line of crew luggage the driver had brought into the lobby and turned to find the elevator.

"Will do," Vera called out as she headed off in the opposite direction.

Grace found her room, closed the door behind her, and immediately began to wonder what she would wear. She hoped she had packed the right shoes and jewelry to accent her sexy blue silk top with the brand-new linen pants Khalid had just given her on her last trip to Paris. She turned on the faucet in the bathtub as hot as it would go, and hung her chosen outfit on the retractable clothesline to steam out the wrinkles. Then she looked at herself in the mirror. The combination of long hours and dry air had taken a toll on her usually smooth and flawless complexion. She had just the thing in her suitcase—a dōTERRA essential oil-based facial scrub and cleanser. She'd have a quick facial, take a long hot shower, and try to relax until it was time for dinner.

The lobby was filled with several 747 crews when Grace met up again with Vera. They were fortunate to have been on one of the first flights to arrive at the hotel. The restaurants in the neighboring area were all small, with just three or four tables— barely large enough for a party of four. They were family-run places that offered simple Japanese cuisine, such as dumplings called gyoza, tempura, and tonkatsu, all served with the standard bowl of miso soup, rice, and pickled vegetables. The beer was always ice-cold, which tasted especially refreshing after a long flight.

The two women walked out of the lobby toward the narrow street filled with cars, trucks, and bicycles dashing and darting through traffic as if choreographed by an unseen conductor.

Vera pointed through the traffic towards a two-story, white stucco building with a red awning above the door. "There it is," she beamed, "the infamous 'crew lounge' that you've heard so much about. I personally prefer to not eat there. It's not that the food isn't any good, but it's always so crowded that dining takes too long and detracts from the whole experience." Vera turned and looked down the street in the opposite direction. "There," she said, pointing to a navy-blue-and-white curtain hanging above a small glass doorway in a quaint wooden building. "That cozy little mom-and-pop place has the very best food, and it's probably not too busy yet."

"I'm game. This is your call, Vera," Grace piped up. "As long as I can get an ice-cold beer, I will follow you anywhere."

Vera thought for a moment. Then she replied, still pointing at the blue-and-white curtain, "Let's eat there, then head over to the 'crew lounge' for some excitement later."

At the first possible opening in the traffic, they darted across the narrow street, nearly being hit by a truck that seemed to come out of nowhere. They walked in single file along the cement-tile sewer cover that doubled as a sidewalk, then ducked in under the dark-blue cotton curtain that hung above the doorway.

"Cone bon wah," the small man behind the counter greeted them, bowing in their direction.

"Cone bon wah," Vera chirped back, smiling. "That's 'good evening,'" she whispered to Grace, aware that her Japanese was at best rusty and at worst nonexistent. They seated themselves at a table for two in a darkened corner of the small room. Before they could situate their chairs, the owner's wife was at their table, serving them each a glass of ice water and a steaming hot washcloth tightly rolled on a bamboo tray. "Cone bon wah," she smiled, bowing slightly in their direction.

"Ni Sapporo beer-roh," Vera ordered, holding up two fingers, in case her Japanese wasn't quite perfect.

"Beer-roh, ni," their waitress confirmed, pointing at each of them. "Beeg-oh," she motioned with her hands, indicating the larger bottle of beer so popular in Japan.

"High, beeg-oh," Vera responded, laughing at the exchange.

Grace giggled at Vera. "You speak pretty good Japanese."

"I know enough to eat well, find a cold beer, and not go home with any strange Japanese men, but that's about it," Vera admitted, embarrassed that she didn't know more of the language after all her years of flying to Japan.

The waitress returned with two very tall beer bottles and two tiny glasses, placing them in front of the women and bowing again.

The two tired and thirsty flight attendants filled their glasses, raised them in unison, and together offered, "Cheers!" After downing the entire glass of beer, Vera suggested they order some gyoza. Grace nodded her agreement as she finished off her glass.

The owner stood behind the bar—the grill and cooking surfaces behind him—watching the women carefully for a sign that they were ready to order. Vera caught his eye and with a smile raised her hand. "Two gyoza, doe zoe," she said, as she again held up two fingers. He nodded in acknowledgment of her order. Grace poured a little more beer into her glass and then filled Vera's.

"Salute," the women said in unison.

Over a tonkatsu dinner, the two discussed the most recent airline news. The company had been granted a new route to Milan and another to Helsinki. Hopefully the news of several upper-management changes would have very little effect on flight crews. The juiciest gossip was that someone in upper management had been fired after a homosexual encounter with a vice cop in a public restroom. That story had hit the national and cable news networks, which reflected very poorly on the company. The man in question had been an executive vice president for over fifteen years, and the revelation shocked everyone, especially since he and his wife had five young children and were devout Catholics.

"I flew with a gal who used to be his neighbor when he lived south of Seattle," Grace bragged. "She told me they lived on a cul-de-sac and their backyards were separated by a six-foot cedar fence. One night she stepped out onto her upstairs deck, which overlooked both of their yards, and caught him in his hot tub with another man. He happened to look up at that moment and spied her watching him. After that, he avoided all contact with her. If he saw her coming down the terminal, he would duck into the men's room or even hide in a storage closet. Wow, he finally got caught," Grace giggled.

Vera raised her eyebrows. "Interesting. Shocking, actually. I had no idea. I always thought he was a little different, but I could never quite put my finger on what exactly it was about him that seemed so odd."

"Well, enough of company business and gossip," Grace interjected, ready to direct the conversation to her own personal saga. "I still have to fill you in on the latest from Paris and my Khalid."

"Oh, yes, you must tell me absolutely everything about him," Vera demanded with a chuckle. "Let's pay our tab here and walk across the street to the 'crew lounge' for another beer, and you can tell me all about your adventures in Paris with this new Prince Charming you're so crazy over."

The winter evening had turned cold, and as they stepped outside they simultaneously adjusted their scarves and collars. "Good thing it's a short walk," Vera said.

The "crew lounge" was busy as usual. A large table of American men—mostly pilots from either their company, FedEx or UPS—seemed to be the loudest focal point in the room. The bar was also filled with flight attendants, some younger gay Japanese men, and a few junior reserves from the Honolulu base.

And as Vera expected, the entire place was deafening. The walls seemed to vibrate with a mixture of loud laughter, thunderous music, and non-stop talking.

"Let's grab that small table by the window," Vera pointed and began to lead the way. Grace followed, keeping her eyes wide open in hopes of seeing everything and everyone as they moved past the bar area. A young Japanese girl rushed to their table carrying two ceramic plates of spicy crackers mixed with peanuts. She hurriedly bowed as she set the plates in front of them. "Beer-roh?" she asked.

"High," Vera nodded, appearing to bow in response, "Nee beer-roh, doe zoe."

Before they even sat down, Grace began to tell Vera about her Paris love. "Khalid is so handsome," she started in, reaching into her purse for her cell phone. "Here he is." She handed the phone to Vera. "He is truly a prince—well, maybe not really. I'm not sure. But he acts like royalty. He has impeccable taste in clothes and his watch is something only a king would wear. He knows about fashion and buys me the hottest new designer clothes and jewelry he finds from all over the world. When I arrive, he takes my uniform and has it dry cleaned. He has my shoes professionally shined, and his valet serves me fresh-squeezed orange juice with a splash of champagne while I take a bubble bath. It's really incredible, and it's all taking place in romantic Paris. My layovers there are more like a fairy tale than anything else. His car is a Maybach. Vera, do you know how much those cars cost?" She continued without allowing Vera to even attempt an answer. "Khalid has the best of the best of everything. He spoils me so much. I'm a princess when I'm in Paris."

"Does he work?" squeezed in Vera, hoping to discover something a little more substantial about this man other than the size of his bank account.

"Work? Not that I'm aware of. He has never mentioned any

type of work or business, and he's always available, no matter what time I call him," Grace replied, giving very little thought to her answer.

"Where's he from?" asked Vera, growing more curious than interested.

"From?" Grace repeated, as if she had never wondered the same thing. "From? Well, I don't know, I've never asked him," she admitted. "I guess that didn't really matter to me. Anyway, he is just super-rich and so amazingly smart." She pushed her left wrist toward Vera, flashing her diamond-and-ruby tennis bracelet. "Fifteen-point-five total carats," she bragged, as she slowly rotated her wrist under Vera's inspection. "It's platinum, not white gold. The guy definitely knows his stuff."

"That's the most incredible bracelet I've ever seen," Vera complimented. "What was the occasion?" she asked.

"Occasion?" Grace questioned. "I guess he just really likes me." She sheepishly smiled, but offered no legitimate response.

"Well, how many of our lucky co-workers are now dating friends of Khalid?" Vera inquired.

"Oh, wow, at least a half-dozen by now," Grace chimed in, proud to have some idea of the answer this time. "These guys are real charmers. I would love to introduce you to one of them. Would you consider picking up a Paris or Amsterdam trip this summer or fall? Late summer and early fall are really beautiful times to visit Paris. I know Jeff was a great guy and all, but isn't it time you start thinking about adding a little romance to your life? That's one thing these guys really know—romance." Grace hesitated, waiting for Vera's response, hoping she had not crossed a line, yet knowing that if she had, she could blame it on the alcohol.

"Well, Grace, that's nice of you to offer, but I'm not sure I'm ready for a rich Middle Eastern lover at this point. I'll keep it in mind in case I need some new jewelry. I realize I can't remain a hermit forever," she smiled.

The music grew louder as more crew members filed in, laughing, talking, and some of them singing along with the music. Karaoke was always fun at this place. Many of the crew members came here to drink enough beer so they could summon the courage to perform on the lighted stage in the corner.

Out of nowhere, Grace piped up and said, "Vera, I think these beers have gone to my head. All of a sudden I'm spinning. We had better get back to the hotel." Grace began slurring her words. "I'm not sure if I can walk on those little smelly sidewalks all the way back to the hotel without losing it."

Vera took Grace by the arm, paid their tab, and walked behind her, keeping one hand on her shoulder all the way back to the hotel. She remembered Grace's room number and walked her to her door. "I'll see you in the morning," Vera said softly. Grace laughed and mumbled something unintelligible as the door closed behind her. "Oh, that crazy unregulated Japanese beer," Vera thought to herself as she found her way back to her own room.

three

The transition in the White House was fraught with the kind of problems one would expect when an unelected President assumes the country's helm. Regardless of his plans for moving the country forward, President Sherman's efforts to heal a broken nation took precedence. In many ways, he was uniquely qualified for this herculean task. Joel had endured a tough childhood. His father died when he was ten, and his mother raised him and his two brothers on a school teacher's salary. As the middle child, Joel learned quickly how to solve problems and make peace. In high school he excelled in two areas—academics and athletics. As a result, he was awarded two separate scholarships to Stanford University—one to pursue his love of physics and the other to play football. Unfortunately, his football career concluded at the beginning of his sophomore year with a season-ending leg injury.

He wanted to enroll in the ROTC program, but Stanford, being the liberal bastion of brilliance that it was, had eliminated that program in the late sixties. With extra time on his hands, Joel was able to take flying lessons through the university, and by graduation he was instrument-rated on two different multi-engine aircraft. The Air National Guard jumped at the opportunity to take a Stanford physics graduate who was already a licensed pilot and teach him how to fly jets. Within a short time, he was flying F-16s on selected weekends and throughout the summers for the Air Force.

His stint with the Guard also allowed him to return to Stanford's MBA program. He could round out what he felt was a perfect educational blend of science and business. By the time he graduated from the business school, Joel had made enough friends and contacts to easily launch a career with The Boeing Company, where he rapidly climbed the corporate ladder to become the liaison between engineering and marketing. It wasn't many years later that he was being considered for a position on Boeing's board of directors. While he and Boeing's CEO were conversing, their discussion turned to politics and the possibility of Joel running for a seat in the House of Representatives from Washington State. That simple turn of events changed Joel's life forever. He ran for the congressional seat in the next election cycle and, with Boeing's help, won easily. From there, he advanced into House leadership positions, and after only twelve years in Congress, he found himself elected Speaker.

President Sherman's first order of business, as outlined in the Twenty-fifth Amendment, was to select a Vice President, who would then have to be approved by a majority of both houses of Congress. Due to the angst created in the government by the impeachment proceedings, his advisors strongly urged him to select a moderate nominee who could easily pass a confirmation vote without any controversy. That was not how Joel felt, but under pressure he selected Lon McClean, a longtime Republican senator who had a reputation for being a Republican in name only. Despite being acceptable to both sides of the aisle, McClean narrowly won confirmation.

For the next several months, President Sherman filled Cabinet positions and top governmental agency posts. It took longer than usual since he had no benefit of a transition team and had to make the necessary changes while still running the government on a day-to-day basis. His schedule kept him busy and tied to the White House. Yet all the while he felt a compelling need to bond with the people of the nation—to give them confidence in his ability to lead them through this time of crisis.

By May, he had begun to accept invitations to speak at major openings of corporate offices and industrial plants in various parts of the country, where the business climate exemplified conservative principles of investment and risk rather than government handouts. He felt that his presence set a tone for the type of change he wanted to make during his Administration. In all cases, he was well received, and his encouraging message of American grit and ingenuity was beginning to receive some positive press.

Vera's normal routine was a three-day trip to Asia, which she took three times a month. She hadn't given much thought to the changes taking place in the country, but it seemed to her that the general chaos was subsiding. With her hectic schedule and the time-zone changes she constantly flew through, resting when she could and avoiding television news was her normal way of life. Vera's and Grace's schedules didn't usually allow them to see much of one another except in passing in the Detroit crew area. In early July, Grace made a point of scheduling another trip to Japan just so she could catch up with Vera and take another shot at the 'crew lounge,' hoping to be there when something exciting occurred. It turned out to be an uneventful trip and time passed quickly.

"Ladies and gentlemen, we have just begun our descent into Detroit, and ask that you check your documents. Make certain your customs forms are completed and your immigration papers are filled out correctly. Please include them with your passport for review by the customs and immigration inspectors." As Vera finished her landing announcement, Grace quietly sidled up behind her, waiting to draw her attention.

"Vera, I still really want you to think about flying a Paris trip with me before the summer is over or at least early in the fall."

"I'll give it some thought, Grace. I have a bunch of vacation time coming up over the next four months, so I can easily pick up a shorter trip. What's Paris worth time-wise?"

"Sixteen hours and forty minutes in the summer," Grace offered. "That will be great. You'll have a wonderful time, especially if I have the chance to introduce you to one of Khalid's friends."

The plane landed and taxied to the international terminal. Vera watched out the window, as the jetway started to move toward the aircraft. "Flight attendants, doors for arrival, please," she announced in a calm, clear voice, then stood up to disarm the emergency chute at her door. "Cross-check doors, please," she announced to the crew. She then dialed an 'all call' through the interphone system to each flight attendant station, waiting for each to reconfirm that all doors and their corresponding emergency slides had been disarmed.

Vera's door popped open. A small group of agents, interpreters, customs officials, and immigration officers stood at the entry. A red-haired woman in a dark navy suit, who Vera thought looked strangely out of place, stepped inside. She was obviously looking at crew name tags in search of the flight's purser.

"Hello, Vera," she announced in a very business-like tone. "I'm Julie Farr, from in-flight services. I need to debrief your entire crew. Please call the crew and let them know to come immediately to first class after all the passengers have deplaned. I will also need you to call the pilots and request they leave their luggage stowed and come directly to the debriefing area."

Vera did as she had been instructed, yet her mind began to race. In all her years of flying, she had never experienced a debriefing of any kind following a normal uneventful flight. Such an occurrence was beyond unusual. All she could think about was something bad must have happened. Had there been terrorists on their flight who she was not aware of and whose intentions had been aborted? She searched her memory of the events on the flight and couldn't recall anything out of the ordinary. As the last passengers stepped off the aircraft, the flight attendants began filing into first class and one by one took a seat. They spoke in hushed tones, inquiring of one another if anyone had any information about the debriefing. The pilots were the last to join the group, looking just as puzzled as the flight attendants. Vera did a quick head count: four pilots and sixteen flight attendants. She reported her count to Ms. Farr, who was now standing at the very front of the first class section and looking visibly shaken.

She nodded a thank you in Vera's direction and began to make her announcement. "I am here to inform you that there has been a very serious incident in Las Vegas. One of our own 747s has crashed into a hotel resort." She hesitated then continued, "Ahem, please excuse me. This has been an extremely difficult thirty minutes. We are not sure at this moment what has happened or even the extent of the devastation, but it is a disaster for the company. As some of you may be aware, President Sherman and the First Lady were scheduled to be in Las Vegas. They apparently arrived late last night." Tears began welling up in her eyes and her voice grew weaker. "Right now, we don't know how they might be affected by this tragedy. We don't know what has happened, but we have lost a plane, a flight crew, a major Las Vegas resort, and quite possibly the President of the United States and his wife. I wish I had more details for you."

Before she could continue, Captain Smith interrupted, "Do you know who was piloting the aircraft?"

"We do not have any details at the moment, it happened while you were on descent and I have been reviewing fragments of information on my way to meet your crew. Crew scheduling is reconfirming the names of all the crew members who had checked in for the flight, so we might not have that information for several hours. Of course, after they reconfirm, they'll notify the families before any information is made public. There will be a company information hotline set up as soon as any information is available. You can access that on the company intranet. Please do not share any information, when it becomes available, with the press. Our public relations spokesperson will handle all communications, so we ask all of you to please keep the particulars private—within our airline family."

The flight attendants sat in stunned silence, looking at one another in disbelief. Aircraft incidents, especially crashes, were always a concern. And although they were usually not spoken about except at yearly recurrent training class, they were always on the minds of both flight attendants and pilots. Any crash or any loss of crew members, no matter which airline was involved, was like losing a family member. The airlines, in a strange way, were like one very large family. Even though there were different companies, the lifestyle of all their employees was the same. Similar schedules, hotels, passengers, even lack of sleep connected everyone in the airline industry, giving them a strong sense of unity experienced in few other professions.

Questions ricocheted in each of their minds as they sat in shocked silence: Were the President of the United States and the First Lady killed? What had happened? And whatever it was that happened, how did it happen? Were many people on the ground killed? Was it a terrorist act? How many people in total were dead? Who were they? Who were the crew members? These questions and more floated around in a vacuum of answers, creating a tension that began to build inside the hearts and minds of everyone present. Suddenly, Julie's head jerked, as if she were hearing some new information in her earpiece. All eyes focused on her with anticipation, which dissipated some of the building pressure. "Yes, yes, oh, good, that's good, yes, yes, I will, thank you."

The crew watched and waited patiently for her to speak. "The company has just learned from the Secret Service that the President was not in Las Vegas. Apparently, a last-minute emergency meeting with the Speaker of the House early this morning kept him in Washington. He sent the First Lady along as scheduled last night, with her contingent of assistants and Secret Service agents. We still do not know her status.

"I am so sorry," she continued, sniffling and carefully wiping her eyes. "This is really breaking news, and we are quite uninformed. I was sent to notify you of the incident, but I really have little to share, as you can see. If you are stopped inside the terminal by any passengers who may have seen the report on CNN, please tell them you have just flown in from an international flight and you know nothing. Remember our motto: "Let the press be damned!" She tried to smile and sound strong, but failed to keep her voice from cracking. "We just ask that, as employees, you do not speak to anyone about this incident at this early stage. The company wanted you to be informed of the accident, and we wanted you to hear the news from us and not from our passengers or CNN. You are free to deplane to go home or to catch your commuter flights. Please check in with the special employee hotline for updated information regarding the names of the crew members when it becomes available."

Vera offered a box of tissues to Ms. Farr. "Thank you," Vera said, "for giving us the news about this accident. I'm certain the entire crew appreciates the way you handled this difficult situation. It's never easy to be the bearer of bad news, especially news as tragic as this."

"This has been one hell of a morning, as you might imagine. I wish I had some details to give you, but it's just too soon. We've had a very difficult time receiving any information from the general office or out of Las Vegas operations. As you know, information never comes quickly. It is important to get the correct information to the families of both passengers and crew. We're trying to at least meet all of our international flights to let the crews know that this incident has occurred and to reinforce our desire to have nothing said to the press. Dispatch is swamped and crew scheduling is going crazy with phone calls asking about the working crew."

After completing all of her purser responsibilities, Vera was the last crew member to deplane. She wasn't looking forward to walking alone to customs and immigrations after the horrible news that had just been shared. Her thoughts were still in turmoil, and she felt the moment approaching when she needed to talk the confusion all out. As she reached the door leaving the jetway, she was pleasantly surprised to see Grace standing there waiting for her. When they saw each other, they began firing questions at one another, not realizing that neither of them was listening. When it dawned on them, they both fell silent, which somewhat eased the anxiety they were feeling. As they walked together to the customs hall, they took turns saying exactly the same thing and reassuring one another that answers needed to be forthcoming before they could relax. The news had not reached the customs' agents yet. If it had, they would have been engaged in conversation about the accident and pumping the flight crews for whatever information they were willing to divulge. Instead, the agents hurried the two flight attendants through the line, not even bothering to open their bags or ask them any of the standard questions.

Vera and Grace continued to wonder aloud about the accident as they headed to their respective domestic gates. When they reached the place where their paths would diverge, they stopped and hugged. Grace reminded Vera to call her about a trip to Paris and Vera nodded in compliance.

The waiting area at the gate for Vera's flight to back to Seattle was crowded with passengers and their luggage. A large group was beginning to gather around the flat-screen TV as news about the plane crash in Las Vegas began to break. Vera could see in big bold letters: BREAKING NEWS: PLANE CRASH LAS

VEGAS. There were no live video shots, only her airline's large corporate logo above the announcement. Vera's mind once again raced around all the questions she had asked earlier. She was too tired to think clearly, but she realized that now that the news had broken, she would be a target for questions if she traveled in her uniform. She glanced at her watch and saw she had just enough time to quickly change her clothes. Vera was fortunate to secure the last first class seat on the flight home. After a long Asia trip, it was always a blessing to have the privacy and room to stretch out and relax. She leaned back and opened USA Today. A bold headline announced President Sherman and the First Lady's planned trip to Las Vegas: PRESIDENT SHERMAN AND FIRST LADY TO HELP VEGAS RECOVER. The First Couple were to be the guests of honor at a casino resort opening on the Vegas strip. The Patriot Hotel & Casino was the newest hotel and the first significant construction project to be built on the strip since the Cosmopolitan opened in 2010. The new resort took on the patriotic themes of U.S. history and the men and woman who dedicated their lives to the creation of the country. The Patriot had been receiving a great deal of media attention since Joel Sherman had become the President. This grand opening was to be a huge event. The First Couple were significant supporters of Las Vegas' rebirth as well as the American patriot movement known as the TEA party which began in 2009. Members of this group had been very vocal in their support for the impeachment of the previous President, and they delighted at the prospect of Joel Sherman becoming the President. As House Speaker, he had assisted them by raising money for their candidates nationwide and since his inauguration, the TEA Party movement continued to grow, rallied on by President Sherman, as its de facto leader. The media had done its best to demonize this patriotic movement and its campaign for a smaller, less-intrusive government with lower taxes. When the Occupy Wall Street movement realized that the two seemingly opposite groups were after very similar outcomes, the movements united, creating a forceful collective outcry of Americans that no politician could ignore.

The previous President had verbally assaulted Las Vegas tourism by telling the American public to "not waste money or spend their children's college funds on a trip to Vegas." The economy and tourist numbers were immediately affected by his remarks and the city remained in dire straits throughout the years of his presidency. Some of the outlying casinos had gone bankrupt and were boarded up. Many parts of downtown Las Vegas looked like large refugee camps with people sleeping in the streets under cardboard boxes and plastic tents. Tourism had continued to decline. Record unemployment added to the high crime rate and to wide spread drug abuse. Discarded hypodermic syringes littered the sidewalks and landscaping. Along the Strip, work crews spent hours every day removing discarded drug paraphernalia and beer bottles from the elegant landscaping surrounding the large casinos. The increased drug and crime problem added to the decline in tourism since it was no longer safe to walk up and down Las Vegas Boulevard at night. Murder had become an almost-nightly occurrence throughout the entire metropolitan area. Media coverage in the rest of the country had spread the news about Las Vegas' decline, which magnified the growing tourism crisis. One national news report referred to Las Vegas as "Nevada's newest emerging Ghost Town."

Vera recalled a 747 trip she had flown to Las Vegas nearly a year earlier; the crew van taking them to the Bellagio carried an armed guard. The guard explained to the crew that the route down Tropicana Boulevard had become so dangerous that drivers feared stopping at the traffic lights. She never wanted to go back to Las Vegas again after that frightening experience. Vera read through the rest of the article knowing that as of only minutes ago, things had changed drastically for the city, for the

President, for the country, and for her airline.

The first class flight attendant tapped Vera on the shoulder waking her up after the plane had rolled to a stop at the gate. She had obviously been more exhausted than she had thought. The past 72 hours had taken its toll, and it felt good to sleep the last three hours of the flight home. Her drive home from the Seattle-Tacoma International Airport—SeaTac, for short—usually took about twenty minutes, depending on the time of day. Seattle was well known for its gridlock traffic jams, and the clock was pushing into the commuter hours. It was after exhausting trips like this one that Vera wished she could just take a cab home to Alki Beach.

Kelli was kenneled at the neighborhood dog hotel only blocks from her house. The moment Vera drove up, Kelli sensed it and began to bark until Howard, the kennel's proprietor, let her out. The overjoyed golden retriever greeted Vera with whimpers and doggie kisses. Her stays had become a weekly routine, and although she had adjusted to the kennel, Kelli never lacked for enthusiasm when welcoming her mommy back home. As Kelli waited patiently by her side, Vera paid the boarding fee and chatted with Howard, who wanted to know if she had heard any news of the plane crash that had killed the First Lady. Vera was careful not to divulge any information, as she had been told. Then she realized that she had no details and that Howard probably knew a great deal more than she did. She questioned him about the First Lady, since that information was not available to her when she left Detroit. He confirmed that she had been a casualty. Vera winced. The pain of losing a spouse was something she knew all too well.

Vera and Howard walked outside as Kelli stood wagging her tail at the car door. "Oh, Vera, I wanted to ask you, uh, uh, do you have a new man in your life?" Howard asked shyly, stumbling over his words.

"Heaven's sakes, no," Vera quickly responded. "What makes you ask?"

"Sorry to be so forward, Vera, but shortly after you dropped Kelli off the other day, a tall, dark, well-dressed man poked his head into the office. Kelli was still with me. He asked me to confirm that you were Vera Hanson. I didn't give it much thought and answered that it was you and that this was your dog Kelli. Before I could ask his name, he ducked out the door and was gone. At first I thought he was a new man in your life, but after he drove off, I got a strange feeling about him. I just thought I would ask."

Vera listened carefully to Howard's story, shook her head slowly from side to side as he spoke, and declared, "No, I have no idea who that might've been." She felt a twinge of nervousness as she opened the car door for Kelli. "See you next time," she smiled and waved as they drove away.

Once inside her house, Vera threw on a polar fleece top, grabbed Kelli's leash, and promised her a nice long walk on the beach. Vera and Jeff had bought this house about eight years ago. They had fallen in love with the location, even though the house needed a little work. That didn't stop them from bidding higher than the asking price so they could be the lucky winners in the bidding war. The architectural design was a typical Seattle craftsman-style. The view from the house was nearly panoramic, sweeping from the Puget Sound islands to downtown Seattle. Both the Cascade and the Olympic mountain ranges could easily be seen from most parts of the property, and nearly every window offered a breathtaking view. The Space Needle floated above the skyline, and ferryboats passed to and from the nearby islands, blasting their horns. The many nights Vera had shared with Jeff, enjoying the calming view and gentle salt air, were etched into her memory forever.

Kelli ran ahead the full length of the leash, stopping to bark at Vera as if to say, "Hurry up," then sat and waited for her to catch up. They sat down together on a small patch of grass. Vera patted Kelli's head until Kelli curled up next to her. This was Vera's favorite way to relax after long trips to the other side of the world and back. The salt breeze filled her senses with life, and its cleanliness reverberated through her lungs as if to confirm that life was again worth living.

When they got home, the sun was beginning to set. Its reflection on the glass of the downtown skyscrapers added light and dimension to Vera's view as the sun began to dip below the horizon. Kelli was lying on the kitchen floor, patiently waiting for her after-the-beach-walk treat, her big brown eyes following Vera's every move. After obliging Kelli with a peanut-butter-flavored biscuit, Vera curled up in the window seat in the dining area and took a long, slow sip of wine. She knew she should turn on the television to check for updates on the accident, but she wasn't mentally prepared for the bad news. She was familiar with nearly every 747 pilot in the company, since she rarely flew any other aircraft. Her curiosity finally got the best of her and she reached for the remote.

The emotionless voice of a news anchor filled the room. "The plane, we have learned, was apparently taking off from McCarran International Airport in Las Vegas when something went terribly wrong. For those of you just joining us on this broadcast, we are covering breaking news out of Las Vegas, where a 747 has crashed directly into the newest hotel casino on the Las Vegas Strip, The Patriot. The First Lady of the United States, her staff, and her assistants are still unaccounted for. The President is not expected to address the nation until sometime tomorrow. We will give you further information when it becomes available. It has taken several hours to get video feed in from Las Vegas. Hopefully we will have a live feed to share with you within the hour. We are awaiting approval from the Department of Homeland Security, the FAA, and several other federal agencies to gather and share with our audience pictures from the crash site.

"Again, ladies and gentlemen, we regret to inform you that it is now presumed that the First Lady of the United States, Mica Sherman, has been killed in Las Vegas as the result of a horrible plane crash directly into her hotel." The TV showed a still photo of the Patriot on a split screen with a stock photograph of a 747 with the company's logo clearly visible on the plane's side and tail.

Vera hit the power button to turn the television off. "This isn't normal," she thought to herself. "It's been almost seven hours since that accident happened. Why is there no video of the event and crash site? Surely, there were security cameras that had to have caught something on film. There were tourists with cameras all over Las Vegas day and night. Someone must have pictures of that plane taking off."

four

The phone rang, startling Vera into a state of consciousness. She had fallen asleep on the sofa while trying to catch a late update on the Vegas crash. Dawn was just beginning to break over the Puget Sound, as the morning light began to fill the room. "Hello?" she said, her voice more hoarse than usual.

"Vera, it's Grace. Oh my god did you hear the news?" Her words coming so rapidly that Vera had a difficult time comprehending what Grace had just said.

"The news?" questioned Vera. "I don't know any more than what we heard in the briefing. What is it?"

"Do you remember my friend Amy Baylor? She was the gal I introduced you to a few months ago at the crew check-in desk—tall, blonde, super thin. She was from Biloxi, Mississippi, remember?" Grace quizzed.

"Yes, I do remember her. She flies Europe trips most of the time. I think I was the purser on her first flight to Japan a couple years ago. Oh no, Grace, she wasn't on the Vegas . . . ."

Grace interrupted, "Yes, she's gone."

Vera couldn't quite understand Grace's words, but the emotion behind them explained all she need to know.

Grace began to sob, "Vera, this is so horrible. Amy had met Imad, one of Khalid's friends, in Paris a few months ago. I talked to her the day before her trip. Imad was going to meet her in Las Vegas. He loved to play roulette. When he heard she had a layover in Vegas, he made arrangements to be in town. She was totally convinced that he was going to propose to her. He had been hinting about marriage, and they had been looking at rings when they were both in Paris about three weeks ago. Oh Vera, she's dead, they're all dead." Tears wrapped around each of Grace's words and her sobbing was doing all her talking.

Still holding the phone, Vera opened the door to the back yard and let Kelli outside. "Who else?" She asked.

"I don't know, I don't know. I was so shocked to hear about Amy. She was so happy just a few days ago. I tried, but I couldn't finish listening. The company has that special hotline for us to use to get all the information, but I just couldn't listen to any more of the names. Amy's name was listed first," Grace explained.

"I'll call the number later, Grace. I was just so tired and emotional last night that I fell asleep on the sofa in the living room. I couldn't even listen to the news. I had CNN on for about two minutes when they said they had no live feed and that there were a bunch of federal agencies involved. I knew this was going to be unlike any crash we had ever experienced. The First Lady . . . have you heard anything definitive yet?"

"Gone, Vera, they're all gone," Grace continued. "Her secretaries, the staff, and the Secret Service agents—all gone. Just like the World Trade Center towers, the building is nothing but dust, and there have been no bodies found. The entire Patriot is nothing but smoldering ruins. It's like a bomb went off. There is just a huge crater full of debris. The news report said that some of the surrounding hotels had been heavily damaged as well. They closed McCarran and no word yet on when it'll reopen. It's like the entire strip is a crime scene. It's really weird. Do you think it's because of the First Lady? I'm not hearing the usual information. The DHS said they don't think it was terrorism. They're waiting for the information from the black boxes, once they finally find them."

"That's really strange, Grace. Something must be very wrong." Vera poured a cup of coffee and let Kelli back inside. "It must have something to do with the First Lady and all those Secret Service people who were protecting her. Did you say the building is just dust? Does that sound like a plane crash or a bomb going off?"

"Poor Amy," Grace resumed sobbing, ignoring Vera's questioning. "I tried to call Khalid in Paris, but no answer on his end. I wonder where Imad was staying. I'm certain Khalid would know. I wanted to tell him Imad wasn't going to be able to fly out of McCarran anytime soon. I have no idea when he was planning to return to France."

"Well, I would think that President Sherman would have to fly into there," Vera wondered out loud. "I feel like we're not being told the truth about this. Do you happen to know which aircraft it was—the ship number?"

"No, I don't. I only know about Amy and what I just heard on CNN a few minutes ago. Something isn't adding up right, Vera. Why would they close McCarran?" Grace started to cry again, "Vera, this is like a horrible nightmare. I need to get off the phone and try to contact Khalid again. I might call you later in the day."

"Okay, Grace. You take it easy, try to relax, and just be patient. All the information will eventually come out. Let's hope Imad is found safe somewhere on the other end of the Strip. Maybe Khalid will know more when you finally get in touch with him. Good-bye, girl. Stay strong," Vera reassured her.

Now that Vera was awake, she was tuned in again to the horror of yesterday's news, which had become magnified by the information Grace had just shared. Vera was relieved she would be having nearly a month off from flying. Anytime there was death involved with a tragedy, it struck chords inside her that were just too uncomfortable to repeat. She straightened things up on the sofa then settled into the cushions. "So sad," she said out loud, thinking about how the President felt right about now, followed by a sense of certitude in knowing. She tried to imagine how he could possibly continue to lead the country and perform his duties. She knew precisely how badly he must hurt inside. Thinking about the President's difficult position was beginning to overwhelm Vera's emotions. She forced herself to constrain her thoughts into someplace less stressful. No place in the world was more relaxing than her beach cottage just three-hours away. It had been her plan for several weeks to spend some time at the cottage, which needed seasonal repairs. Now she needed the solitude that the beach offered. She found her address book and made a phone call to arrange for Frank Burton, her favorite handyman, to meet her at the cottage later that afternoon.

The beach house had been left to Jeff when his father passed away, but finding time to take care of it properly had always been a problem, even more so for Vera after Jeff's passing. Every year, the winter storms took a toll, leaving at least a full week's worth of clean up to do. Kelli loved chasing seagulls and running after sandpipers along the shoreline. Vera enjoyed taking long walks and listening to the rhythmic motion of the ocean waves beating against the shore. It provided the perfect background sounds to wash out all the jet noise that lingered in her memory.

As she packed, she debated taking the small television set from her bedroom to watch the news, but decided to bring her laptop and wireless card instead. The cabin had never had a television, which was part of its charm. The laptop would allow her to read the news about the crash as it became available to the public. She knew Grace would be phoning and was certain several other friends and family members would be calling to ask about the crash. There was no question that this particular accident would be on everyone's mind, with the First Lady being involved. She gathered a few things together, set the house alarm, and locked the doors. Kelli knew all the signs of a trip to the beach house and jumped into the backseat the moment the door to the Mercedes was opened.

"Hi, Ms. Hanson. It's nice to see you again," Frank said as he jumped down from his large green four-by-four pickup truck. "It's hard to believe it has been almost two years since we had a look at your cottage." He smiled and tipped his baseball cap. "I've stopped by after storms passed through and have done some quick outside inspections. I knew you were going to need a few new cedar shakes, so I threw a bundle into the truck. We had some real big winds last winter. I lost a few shakes on my own place down the road."

Vera smiled and remembered why she appreciated Frank so much. He was prepared, timely and above all else, honest. "I can also see I'm going to need both of these broken shutters fixed. I just hope there's no water damage inside. Can you believe it's already July and I'm just now getting around to having you deal with these problems? I really should sell this place, but I simply cannot bring myself to do that. It was such a wonderful part of my husband's life. Anyway, let's take a look inside and see what you'll have to deal with in there."

Vera unlocked the front door. "No sign of water so far," she reported. Kelli ran into the kitchen area, where she remembered her food and water dishes were usually set. Frank went right to work making the repairs while Vera dusted the furniture and swept the floors. When Frank was finished, she paid him and left Kelli in the cottage while she made a quick trip to the market. She was looking forward to the approaching sunset and the soothing sounds of the ocean splashing through the surf. All the horrible news that waited for her in her computer could just take the evening off.

five

President Sherman began to stir. His eyes were not yet completely open, but he knew he was not in his bed. He vaguely remembered dozing off in the residence of the White House, but had not quite made it to the bedroom. Just the thought of going to bed without his precious Mica and not knowing where she was physically—or what it even meant that she was dead—made the entire evening seem surreal. When he finally excused himself to be alone, he wandered upstairs and fell asleep on one of the sofas in the great room.

"Mr. President, sir?" A soft male voice was heard in the hallway followed by a light tapping on the door. The President's eyes were now open as he began to adjust to his surroundings. Again, he heard the voice from the hallway, "Mr. President, sir."

"Yes, yes, please come in, Mike," the President answered. Mike McFee was the personal valet to the President and had served him well in the same capacity during his time as Speaker of the House.

"Were you able to get some restful sleep, sir?" asked Mike, as he presented a silver tray with a flowered porcelain coffee service and filled the President's cup.

President Sherman tried to smile, but it fell from his face before his words were able to reach his mouth. "Would you tell the Vice President I'm fine, Mike. I did sleep some in between updates, so I guess there's no longer any need for him to remain here at the White House. I appreciate him stepping up to the plate. If I had needed any medication last night, I would have been much more comfortable taking it, knowing he was here. Tell him when I am feeling up to it, I'll be in touch with him." No information about Mica had been confirmed yet, but Joel's soul was listening to his heart, and its solitary beat whispered to his consciousness that he was now alone.

"Are you sure about that, Mr. President?" Mike offered, breaking the hush that had come over the room. "I'm certain the Vice President would be more than willing to remain here for as long as necessary, sir."

"No thank you, Mike, I'll be fine. I really have no other choice, do I? I think I have just enough time to shower and put on a fresh suit before my morning security briefing. If you would be so kind as to take my coffee down to the Oval Office, I'd be happy to finish it there."

Mike nodded and followed the President into the residence bedroom to lay out his clothing in preparation for what was sure to be another long and very difficult day. The President made his way to the Oval Office via the exterior portico in an attempt to avoid as many people as possible. The awkwardness of the unknown made it difficult for staffers to react to his presence. He knew he would be doing them a favor by keeping as low a profile as possible until there was at least definitive word on the prior day's tragic events. He pushed on the concealed door that opened into the Oval Office and was pleased to see all of his advisors waiting for him. The regularly scheduled security briefing consisted of the National Security Advisor, the CIA director, and either the Secretary of Defense or one of his undersecretaries. On those occasions when security risks were elevated, they would be joined by the Secretary of Homeland Security, a representative from the State Department, the FBI director, and sometimes the chairmen of the House and Senate committees responsible for national security and intelligence. Today they were all present, not so much because of the plane crash, but because of the loss of the President's wife. They all rose as the President entered the room. Each solemnly greeted him with an expression of condolence, being careful not to be too specific, yet precise enough to tender a heartfelt concern for the tragedy they knew orbited around their leader. Normally this briefing tended to be somewhat casual, with the President joining them on one of the couches in the center of the office. Today, however, President Sherman took his seat behind the large, hand-carved oak desk.

"I have a few words to say before we get started," the President began as he leaned forward, placing his folded arms on the top of his desk. "As you can probably imagine, I'm more than emotionally involved in yesterday's event. Being emotionally involved is probably not the best place for the President of the United States to be when investigating the kind of tragedy that took place in one of our most popular cities. Nevertheless, I'm not going to allow how I feel to get in the way of uncovering every detail of what transpired. In many ways, I think you will find that I will demand more of you and your agencies in getting to the bottom of this particular plane crash. You may feel an urge to placate me, perhaps even protect me from details you think I might find unbearable, but I warn you that as my emotions change, I will hold each and every one of you responsible for sharing every fragment of information you uncover. And I will not settle for 'we think.' I must know. Am I clear?"

This tone was quite irregular for the President, yet it reinforced in each of them how important their responsibilities were in arriving at an accurate conclusion of yesterday's event. Each nodded, while keeping their focus on the President.

"Very well, let us begin. Jerald, what do you have?" The President questioned.

As the National Security Advisor, Jerald Reitz was directly responsible for funneling information on threats to the country through his agency and, in conjunction with the CIA, arriving at a threat assessment based on intelligence protocols.

"Mr. President, at the moment we believe that Flight 685 took off heading south from McCarran bound for Amsterdam early yesterday morning. At some point after liftoff and before it completely cleared the airport property, the right wing of the 747 took a violent dip, causing the jet to stall. According to eyewitnesses, the pilot seemed to overcorrect, causing the plane to ascend momentarily then nosedive into the Patriot Hotel & Casino tower. It appears at this time that the initial explosion occurred as the plane was flat up against the tower, causing maximum damage. There seemed to be a significant secondary explosion, which brought the rest of the building crashing down around the 747 wreckage. The NTSB has found the black boxes and they're heading back here to be analyzed. That information should give us an idea as to what caused Flight 685 to experience such an abnormal takeoff. As of now, I'm not prepared to arrive at any conclusion regarding terrorist involvement. If it is an accident, it is very unusual, and the timing, along with the location, is highly suspect. I'll keep you informed as any and all further information comes my way, sir."

"Thank you, Jerald. Ms. Napioli, what do you have to add to this preliminary report?" The President asked.

Jamie Napioli was not President Sherman's first choice for Secretary of Homeland Security. She had been chosen by the previous President as payback for her efforts to pull in votes from the gay and lesbian community during his first presidential campaign. She was not particularly well liked by most Americans. Knowing that she could deflect a lot of heat that came from Homeland Security's actions may have encouraged President Sherman to keep her on in her position. The fact that the National Organization for Women was prepared to launch an all-out attack on him if he replaced her may have been the only asset in her column for remaining as Secretary.

"Sir," Ms. Napioli began, "at this time we have no indication of terrorism. There had been no increase in chatter prior to this incident. We have received no direct intelligence that might indicate this was the work of any known terror group. Interpol is reporting nothing unusual, and no increased chatter has been reported by Israeli intelligence or any of our CIA contacts throughout the Middle East. We, uh, we have to be careful not to offend the Muslim community by saying anything that might indicate that we suspect Islamic jihadists are involved at this point, no matter what indicators we may find. This situation must be handled with kid gloves. CAIR has already phoned my office and my cell phone twice. They are very concerned that we do not wrongly implicate the Muslim community for this incident."

President Sherman wanted to roll his eyes as she spoke. This woman was painful to listen to, and her analysis did not instill in him any level of confidence. She reminded him of some of his elementary school teachers when she spoke. Like them, it seemed she thought that if she repeated her words often enough, it would compensate for her complete lack of knowledge. "Damn it, this is my Secretary of Homeland Security," he thought. "I am going to have to make a change as soon as things settle down." He made a mental note to call his friend Jim Bowman.

"What is occurring on the scene presently as far as recovering bodies? Obviously, I'm concerned with finding Mica, and I want that to happen as quickly as possible."

Jerald Reitz spoke up again. "Once the NTSB concludes their investigation and gives me the all clear, I will personally see to it that the process is expedited and that you are kept directly in the loop. We all grieve with you, Mr. President, and want to help make that process as palatable as possible."

"Thank you, Jerald; I genuinely appreciate your concern. I'm wondering, however, if it would be prudent to remove the jet wreckage to a secure location, where it can be discretely and completely inspected for any signs of potential terrorism." The President made a point to look directly at Ms. Napioli as he spoke. He was sizing her up to determine if her analysis was generated from any level of intelligence or if political pressure was in charge of her opinions. He could see her taking a deep breath to object to his suggestion, but he stared her into submission and she remained silent.

"That is an excellent idea, sir. I will get in contact with the commander at Creech about procuring a hanger. That Air Force base is far enough out of the way and exceptionally secure. Not only that, but some of our best explosive experts are stationed there and can assist the NTSB with their investigation," responded Jerald.

The President glanced over toward Jamie. He could tell that she was currently caught up in her own thoughts. Jamie was indeed thinking, thinking about events over the years that had led up to her taking the helm at Homeland Security and how any or all of them might have combined to play a role in the events at Las Vegas. Her mind continued along the timeline of the TSA's creation and how the methodologies for airport security had changed over the past decade. Following the devastating terror attacks on September 11, 2001, the Patriot Act was immediately enacted to give the government more power. In 2006, a terror cell was discovered by British authorities planning to blow up airplanes bound for the United States by using explosives that would be mixed with liquids. This caused the TSA to limit the amount of liquids and gels brought onboard any aircraft boarding in the United States. The next memorable terror attempt was by a 23 year old Nigerian man named Umar Farouk Abdulmutallab, who attempted to down an Airbus 330 in route from Amsterdam to Detroit, carrying 278 passengers and 11 crew members. Mr. Abdulmutallab told law enforcement authorities that he had an explosive powder taped to his leg, and that he had mixed it with chemicals held in a syringe. Later it was learned, that he had the plastic explosive PETN sewn into his underwear and a syringe filled with TAPN, the combination of which could have become a powerful explosive that would have easily taken the Airbus down. His attempt failed, leaving Abdulmutallab with first and second degree burns and the remnants of a small fire on the wall next to his seat.

Following the Christmas Day "underwear bomber" as he later became known, TSA announced that many changes would take place, but refused to make them public. The idea was to keep the terrorists guessing. The TSA suggested it would place plainclothes behavioral specialists in many terminals, allow bomb-sniffing dogs to patrol the waiting areas, and change the passenger and carry-on inspection measures to be more rigorous. In the days leading up to the 2010 Thanksgiving weekend, the TSA implemented a new policy for airline security. They had purchased several million dollars' worth of a new type of X-ray machine that literally saw through a passenger's clothing, showing a naked view of the person. The TSA announced that all traveling public would now have to either go through a backscatter machine X-ray or be subject to a new form of pat down that compared only to something a person entering a prison might experience. Children, including infants, were subjected to these physically intrusive pat downs as well. The traveling public became outraged. There were protests at many airports leading up to Thanksgiving Day. Cell phone videos documented the invasive pat downs and were shown on both television news and on the internet. The privacy rights of the American public were violated as never before under the guise of security. Following the terror attacks of 9/11, and with each attempt to destroy an aircraft, the TSA would react by demanding more intrusive inspections at airports. Three months following the 9/11 terror attack, the "Shoe-bomber" as he became known, a 28 year old

British citizen attempted to blow up American Airlines flight 63 from Paris to Miami. He had plastic explosives drilled into his sneakers. The flight crew and passengers had been alerted to the smell of matches being lit and prevented him from successfully carrying out the attack. The 767 was safely diverted to Boston's Logan airport. Following that incident, the TSA began requiring all passengers to remove their shoes which were then put through the X-ray machines along with their carry-on luggage. Unfortunately for the traveling public, the X-ray machines would not detect plastic explosives, but the effect was what the TSA was most concerned with, how it looked to the traveling public, not if it was effective.

The complexity of Jamie's position as Secretary of Homeland Security was intertwined with the politics of the White House, the House, the Senate, the head of the TSA, and a multitude of lobbyists and outside non-governmental organizations. Such demanding political pressures often left her feeling inadequate, given that she had no previous experience qualifying her for this position. She had never traveled to the Middle East—not even to Israel. The cultures of that region were not only foreign to her, but completely impossible for her to comprehend.

"No sir, we don't have any additional information, but we are fairly certain that this was not Islamic terrorism," Jamie answered, trying to sound confident in her words without giving any detailed support to her statement.

The focus in the room returned to the President as he cleared his throat and began to bring the meeting to its conclusion. "I'm pleased with the initial reports and the progress that has been made. Let me reiterate my desire to be informed the moment anything is discovered about my wife. I feel it's imperative to move the physical evidence off-site and to keep it away from the press. If there is anything worth discovering with our inspections at Creech, we'll need time to coordinate a plan to proceed, and we don't need speculating purveyors of secrets polluting our strategies. If there is nothing else, you're all dismissed." The President rose and exited the Oval Office the same way he entered.

six

Grace dialed the phone again. She had not been able to reach Khalid for five days. Her concern was elevated because his friend, Imad, was supposed to have been in Vegas with Amy the night before the 747 crash. She hoped Khalid had heard from Imad and wished he had called her to let her know that Imad was safe.

Grace tried the number one more time. "Allo," was the response. "Grace, my darling, how are you?"

"Khalid, I was so worried about you. I've tried to get a hold of you for days. I'm sure you've heard about the 747 crash in Las Vegas. Have you heard from Imad? Did you know that Amy was on that plane? They still have not found her body."

"Slow down. You ask too many questions too fast," Khalid interrupted. "I did hear from Imad, a few days ago. He drove to Los Angeles to meet some friends who were driving to Mexico," Khalid informed her in a cold, matter-of-fact voice, failing to even mention Amy.

"Oh good," Grace breathed a sigh of relief. She wasn't sure if she could have handled any more bad news. Losing one of Khalid's best friends would have been too much for her to take.

"Grace, my darling, I have so many things to do this evening. I will call you tomorrow."

"Sure, Khalid," Grace replied, not wanting to be a bother. "Call me anytime tomorrow."

Grace mixed herself a screwdriver and retreated to the mind-numbing distraction of her master bedroom closet. "What a mess," she thought as she began removing a stack of cashmere sweaters to fold on her bed. She loved cashmere. Once Khalid became aware of her fondness for it, he presented her with a new cashmere sweater almost every time they met. As her hands touched each article of clothing, memories of romance flooded her mind. Each recollection was unique, and she cherished them all. She lifted up a dark purple sweater to her face and inhaled the lingering scents of Khalid's masculine cologne mixed with her perfume. Her mind took her on a walk up the Rue de Rennes on a sunny spring afternoon toward the exclusive designer shops in the Montparnasse district, which had become so familiar to her since falling in love with Khalid.

Soon tiring of chasing memories vicariously through her clothes, Grace wandered downstairs. Somewhat in a daze, she set her screwdriver on the kitchen counter with one hand and reached for a martini glass in the cupboard with the other. Her thoughts turned to vodka—to Grey Goose, in particular. She found her way to the living room sofa and began to cry. Life was becoming too much for her and she hoped the alcohol would soften the pain's intensity. Khalid being distant and Amy now gone were two realities whose intersection left Grace feeling alone and distraught. No longer would she share chocolate croissants with Amy before catching their flights from de Gaulle. She had never felt Khalid withdraw from her like this before, and she could sense the questions begin to multiply. She downed the martini, buried her face into the pillow, and sobbed.

From the other room, she could hear her cell phone ringing. "I must have left it in the closet," she thought, then reasoned that she didn't have time to reach it before it went to voice. She couldn't bear to get up from the sofa, even if it was Khalid calling her back. She finally forced herself to her feet and made her way back to her closet. The phone was on her dresser, she checked the log, it was Vera, but she had left no message. Rather than call her back, Grace dropped the phone into her shirt pocket and returned to her vodka and sofa. Vera could wait.

When the phone rang again, Grace reached into her pocket, pulled it out, and put it to her ear as if to answer, but she couldn't say anything.

"Grace, it's Vera, is everything okay?"

"Oh Vera," Grace sighed, her voice weak from crying, "Yes, I mean no, no, everything is not okay. I'm just so sad about Amy and the 747 crew."

"Grace, I know it's very difficult. I'm at the beach house and so grateful that Jeff's family had a 'no TV' policy for this place. I don't think I could listen to the news repeat this story over and over and over. I only allowed myself to read the news online after I finished dinner. I'm getting through this by taking Kelli for long walks. This is a very difficult thing to deal with, such a great loss—our crew, our 747, the passengers, the people in the Patriot. My god, the First Lady. This is almost too much tragedy to comprehend." Vera could tell Grace was still crying and wished she could say something that would console her.

"Vera, you're so lucky to have the beach house right now. I see our planes take-off and land from SeaTac and the sadness just washes over me. I tried to call Khalid, but he was busy, and when I told him about Amy, he didn't even seem to hear what I had said. I guess he was preoccupied with whatever he does, but I wanted to talk and he was too busy, damn him."

"Grace, I'm sure he was in the middle of some business deal when you called. What kind of business is he in again?" Vera asked.

"I have no idea what kind of business he does," Grace answered. "I never thought that was any of my concern, and he never mentioned being involved in any type of work or with any company. When I visit Paris, he's usually free most of the time I'm there. And that's all I care about."

"Well, Grace, I'm having a very difficult time dealing with this accident as well. I'm sure every employee is. For now, I've chosen to avoid hearing or reading too much. I knew the pilots—not well, but I've flown with both of them over the years. I also knew the lead flight attendant and Amy. The others I recall by their names, so I know I've flown with most of them at some point. It's like losing a huge part of my family and honestly, Grace, I try to put it out of my mind and keep it out. This is almost as hard for me as losing Jeff. It seems so multi-dimensional, and it's just so unbelievable. I keep trying to imagine what the President is going through. Imagine how awful to be in his position and endure the loss of his wife."

"My mother has invited me to the ranch for a few days," Grace said, "I couldn't even make a decision, but now I've decided to head down to Portland to spend some time with my parents and ride the horses in the hills. That's always been good therapy for me, plus I could use a good home-cooked meal or two—and probably a lot less alcohol."

seven

Details were slow to come out about the crash in Las Vegas. Eventually, it was discovered that 875 people had lost their lives. Over 800 more were injured. The Patriot Hotel & Casino was a total loss, but it was fully insured, which would allow reconstruction to begin almost immediately after the FBI had completed its investigation. A state funeral was held for Mica Sherman. Even though the public had not had sufficient time to get to know her well, the horrific way in which she died caused her essence to be etched into every citizen's memory. First Ladies had passed away before, but never one so tragically as Mrs. Sherman. The President, against the advice of his aides, offered the eulogy at her funeral. His love and devotion for Mica radiated eloquently through his words and his ability to keep his composure through the entire service conveyed a peaceful calm to the hearts of all Americans.

In the months following the funeral, the President never failed to inquire about the well-being of the many loved ones who had been left behind as a result of the disaster. With his dedication to Mica and to those who had lost their lives, he became the standard-bearer for love and devotion, which helped the nation to heal in the midst of such an awful tragedy.

Vera finally managed by mid-September to schedule the trip to Paris she had promised Grace. They had both been looking forward to this trip for a month. They had commuted from Seattle, but on different flights. When they saw each other in Detroit, Grace shouted, "Hey Vera, wait up," as she ran toward the opened elevator door and stepped inside. Vera swiped her company ID and entered the security code.

"How've you been, Vera?" Grace eagerly inquired. "I haven't seen you for a while."

"Well, I had several weeks of vacation, and I used a lot of it just being lazy," Vera laughed. "But, hey, I couldn't wait for this trip. You are still seeing Khalid, right, Grace?"

"Oh, definitely I am. I have plans to go to dinner with him and some of his friends while we're in Paris. Please, please come join us," Grace begged in an almost child-like whine.

"Oh, I'd love to meet this man," Vera smiled. "I won't make any guarantees, but if I can muster the energy, I'll gladly join you for dinner."

The flight to Paris seemed to take forever because the passengers were cranky and a bit unruly. Both Vera and Grace were happy to hear the landing gear and flaps begin to lower. Vera hadn't been to Paris since the second honeymoon trip she and Jeff had taken. As the crew bus drove past the quaint sidewalk cafés and tiny flower markets, Vera reminisced about the romantic time she and her husband had had. They stayed at the Eduard VI, a charming older hotel in the heart of the Montparnasse district and a perfect location for all the sightseeing they planned. They devoted an entire day to discovering the Louvre, where they fantasized about buying art for the dream home they hoped to build someday. The next day, they explored the Notre Dame Cathedral. Jeff insisted they climb the north tower and view Paris, as Quasimodo had done. He called her "Quasimodo" for the rest of the week—and any time after that if she so much as climbed a stepladder. One lazy afternoon, they took in the Eiffel Tower, tasted fabulous French wines, and indulged in some of the finest and richest foods Paris had to offer. That evening ended with an enchanting boat tour of the Seine River, where the nighttime magic of the city caused them to fall in love all over again. Vera found herself smiling on the outside. She still missed Jeff and all the joy he had brought into her life.

The crew bus came to a stop in front of their hotel. The crew filed out one by one, struggling with their tote-bags and purses. The flight attendants followed the pilots into the lobby, where Grace joined up Vera.

"Are you going to rest up before dinner?" Grace asked smiling. "I'm going to go shopping with Khalid in a couple hours so I can't rest, however, I'd love a quick latte before I head up to the room. There's a darling little coffee shop just around the corner that has the best pastries, care to join me?"

"Sure," Vera answered as she grabbed her room key off the granite countertop.

The narrow street next to the hotel was busy with small European cars, motorcycles, and pedestrians. The fall rain was surprisingly cold, and Vera wished she had brought a scarf. Luckily, the coffee shop was nearby and they quickly ducked inside. Grace ordered lattés and chocolate croissants at the counter, while Vera found a table for two near the window along the busy street.

"This is the meeting place," Grace informed Vera as she set their lattés on the table. "You'll make this your habitual morning spot whenever you fly to Paris, trust me. I've eaten chocolate croissants around the world, and these are the very best." They enjoyed the pastries and drank their lattes slowly. Both were excited to get to their rooms, but for different reasons.

Vera's room was quite small as most rooms tended to be in Europe. The layover hotel was a mid-grade hotel by European standards, which meant it had a private bathroom, albeit a very tiny one with a small shower in the corner. The room was wallpapered in a pink floral print that reminded her of her grandmother's house. She tested the bed with her hand then remembered it wasn't the beds in this hotel that were the problem, it was the heating and air conditioning. Still dressed in her uniform, she could feel a bit of a chill as she leaned back on the bed and kicked off her shoes. Before long she was into her suitcase looking for her slippers. Her intention was to relax until it was time to dress and meet up with Grace for dinner. She was looking forward to meeting this Prince Charming character that had become the focal point of Grace's life.

The loud distinctive European ring of her telephone woke Vera from a deep sleep. Before she could gather her senses a recorded voice in French and then English informed her that the call was her wake-up call. She hadn't remembered asking for a wake-up call and could only assume that Grace had something to do with the obnoxious noise. She felt as if she had been run over by one of the small delivery trucks she had seen earlier on the streets. She stared at the ceiling for a moment then slowly rolled over to face the window and was delighted to see the first lights of the city mixed with the pinkish hues of twilight bathing her view with astonishing beauty. "Ah Paris at dusk, is anything more beautiful?" She thought to herself.

Vera had no idea where Grace planned on taking her for dinner or even how long she would be out, so in the face of such uncertainty she opted for the little black dress that was her suitcase standard. She accented it with a single strand of black pearls she had purchased in Beijing for an occasion just like this, when she was unsure of how elegant her surroundings might be. She topped it off with a wide black velvet-and-faux-fur shawl, which she hoped would keep her warm enough. She filled a small beaded evening bag with the essentials—Washington State driver's license, passport, her airline ID card, and a tube of pink tinted lip gloss.

Grace was waiting in the lobby. "Vera, over here," she called out as the brass elevator doors opened. Grace was her usual animated self and began talking immediately, "Did I tell you that

Becky Hill is also coming? She's been dating one of Khalid's best friends for about six months now. He called her and told her to meet us in the lobby. The guys are sending a car to pick us up, and it should be here any minute. The doorman knows me very well and will let us know when the car arrives."

Vera heard what Grace said and nodded, but she was far more interested in how she was dressed, hoping that her little black dress would be appropriate for the evening. Grace was wearing a gorgeous deep purple beaded silk cocktail dress with matching shoes that looked custom made. She had a black mink jacket tossed alongside of her in the chair. Vera's eyebrows rose slightly as she realized she was not even remotely dressed in the same league as Grace. This was only one night out with friends, she told herself, trying to regain a modicum of self-confidence.

"Oh yes, Becky Hill, that will be lovely," Vera quietly replied regaining her composure as best she could.

"Becky will be down in a couple minutes, she slept in," Grace informed Vera. "Your little black dress is just perfect for tonight. I just love that shawl, too." Grace complimented Vera, yet thought she was a tad under dressed for Khalid's typical evening in Paris, but she was happy that Vera had decided to come along. She was even more excited to introduce Vera to Khalid. Becky joined them, dressed head to toe in a stunning teal-blue cashmere one piece outfit with a white mink jacket draped over her arm.

"Your outfit is just fabulous," Grace exclaimed, as they walked toward the revolving brass and beveled glass doors that opened to the street.

"Thank you, it's all new stuff, Ziad bought it all for me on my last trip. He hasn't even seen this outfit on me yet," Becky giggled.

A long black Mercedes limousine waited at the curb, Grace thought she recognized the driver, but before she could say anything, he lifted his gloved hand and offered it to the women.

"Mademoiselles," he opened the back door of the car, "I take you to your dinner." He continued in broken English in an accent that Vera couldn't quite place. She was normally pretty good with accents and attaching them to their corresponding countries of origin, she continued to listen closely for clues.

The ride to the restaurant took only a few minutes. The driver expertly weaved them through narrow streets and alleyways until he stopped in front of a very non-descript wooden building. A single doorman stood under a black canvas awning, wearing a brown and gold uniform. He stood as erect as a soldier and he reminded Vera of the guards that stood at Buckingham Palace in London, but without the big black furry hat. The driver quickly opened the back door motioning the women to step outside with a slight bow as he swept this arm toward the restaurant door.

"Ladies," he said with a smile.

The doorman stepped toward the women, "Reservations?" He asked in a strong thick French accent.

"Yes, we are meeting Khalid Al Hazmi," Grace informed him, as if every doorman in Paris would know Khalid by name.

"Very good, come this way," the doorman motioned with his hand as he held the heavy wooden door open.

The maître d welcomed them as they stepped inside the dimly lit restaurant. "You must be the woman Grace; Mr. Al Hazmi has described you perfectly to me," he said with a slight nod of his head, "please, come this way, the gentlemen are waiting for you in the private dining area."

He led them through the crowded restaurant and down into what Vera thought might be a wine cellar. The walls were of an ancient looking stone that appeared to be cut with very primitive tools. There were small alcoves set in the walls that were decorated with clay pots that reminded Vera of biblical times, similar to pots she was sure she had seen at The British Museum. The hallway opened up into a private dining area, at the far end sat Khalid and two other well-dressed gentlemen.

Khalid stood followed by the other men, who deferred their actions to him. He reached for Grace's hand and slowly kissed the back of it as he bowed toward her then rose and kissed her on each cheek. "My beautiful Grace," he whispered softly then turned to Becky, lifted her hand and kissed it, "wonderful to see you again, Becky Hill." Khalid always used both of Becky's names when he addressed her. Becky's boyfriend stood silently watching as Khalid then greeted Vera. "You must be the woman, Vera?" He said, as he lifted her hands and kissed them both. "Grace tells me wonderful things of you, Ms. Vera. My friends and I really love Americans. Of course, some of us have grown very fond of the Mexican people as well. You look very all-American apple pie, Ms. Vera." Khalid smiled, followed by his friends who both nodded and smiled in Vera's direction.

"Thank you," Vera found herself searching for the right words to say and trying to find some reassurance in the rather uncomfortable situation. She had not been on a date since Jeff passed away, and this was all of a sudden beginning to feel like a blind date. An anxious tension began to swell within her.

"This is my friend Waleed," announced Khalid, as Waleed reached for Vera's hand, but stopped just short of kissing it. "He is my most trusted and loyal comrade," he added.

"It's a pleasure to meet you," Vera replied. Waleed pulled out a chair for her to sit next to him as the others found their places around the large round wooden table.

In the center of the table was an array of small dishes offering up a wide variety of colors, textures and aromas. There were two types of bread in silver baskets. Next to Khalid stood a tall silver and crystal wine chiller and the table was set with crystal glasses, champagne, red wine and white wine goblets along with matching water glasses. The table setting was by far the most extraordinary Vera had ever seen. Grace and Becky seemed quite relaxed in the luxurious surroundings which caught Vera's attention and caused her to wonder about the personal price they had to pay for it all.

Once seated, Khalid clapped his hands together twice in rapid, yet quiet taps. The sommelier quickly stepped into the room awaiting Khalid's instructions. "The champagne, please," was his command. The sommelier pulled a bottle of 1995 Krug du Mesnil from the ice, wrapped the neck in a fine white linen and popped the cork as reverently as if he were in church. He gracefully filled each champagne flute with the sparkling golden elixir. Khalid waited for the sommelier to leave the room then lifted his champagne flute toward the center of the table. "Salute," he toasted. The others joined in; their champagne flutes lightly clicked together near the center of the table.

Khalid was the first to break the silence, "I hope you enjoy this, it is the most expensive bottle I could find here. I adore my Grace and all of her American friends, like you Becky Hill and to our newest friend, Vera." He lifted his glass again in a toast, "We shall have a wonderful evening together."

A waiter appeared in the room delivering small plates with three stuffed grape leaves on each, placing it in the center of each person's silver charger. The gentlemen passed around a tray of pickles, radishes, and baba ghanouj with pita bread. The waiter returned with bowls of vegetable sauces and large platters of vermicelli rice topped with slivered almonds. The champagne was replaced by a bottle of white wine, to be enjoyed with the next course. Vera learned that 'mezze' was the term for the small plates that were on the table when they arrived. When the meats were served the white wine was replaced by a delicious French Meritage. The final course was the most delicate and sweet baklava Vera had ever tasted, served with a flowery rose flavored tea.

Vera was so curious about these men. She had listened to their small talk about the food, the weather, and even the girls' latest fashion demands as the women whined about not ever having enough time to shop.

"What country are you gentlemen originally from?" Vera blurted out, looking at all three men around the table.

Silence.

Grace immediately looked at Vera with a shocked—almost horrified—expression, as if she had violated a well understood cultural taboo. Vera sensed her glare, but chose to ignore its message.

"So, do you know each other from college or are you somehow related?" Vera asked, trying a new approach in her investigation.

Khalid slipped a sugar cube into his mouth and sipped his tea silently as if he had failed to hear her questions. The other men did the same. Grace quickly realized that Vera had crossed a line that she herself had earlier learned should never be transgressed. Khalid and his friends were very generous and very wealthy, but they did not discuss their personal lives or any details of their homeland—particularly not their pasts.

"Becky, didn't you say you are going home for your mother's birthday later in the week?" Grace asked, changing the subject dramatically.

"Yes, I have to stay in Detroit the night we arrive. I have recurrent training the next day. I'll fly to Miami if the flight doesn't completely fill up with passengers. I will be home with my parents and my three sisters for the big party on the weekend. I don't fly again until the following Friday," Becky answered, offering more details than she usually would in hopes of leading Vera away from any more probing questions.

The men were stone silent, and Vera could feel the tension her questions had created. She looked down at her watch. "Oh my, I had no idea it was so late. I'm going to have to excuse myself and catch a cab back to the hotel. Gentlemen, it has been a pleasure to meet all of you." She reached out her hand to shake their hands as she quickly stood up to leave. Instead of shaking her hand, each of them kissed it.

Waleed volunteered, "Let me walk you to the door and make sure that you are safely into the car. We will not allow you to take a taxi, we have the limo waiting."

"I would appreciate that Waleed, thank you," Vera replied. She took his arm as he escorted her to the front door. The black limousine was parked directly in front of the restaurant, so with a quick kiss on the cheek from Waleed she bid him adieu and gracefully slid into the backseat for the short ride back to the hotel. She couldn't help thinking about the stone cold silence she had received in response to her questions. What kind of men were so private that even their country of origin had to remain a secret, she wondered as she entered the lobby and bee-lined it toward the elevators.

The next morning Vera darted across the narrow street and into the meeting place as the noise from the morning rush hour traffic filled the busy street. Becky and Grace had already arrived. Becky was seated at a table while Grace was ordering at the counter.

"I'm here now, Grace," Vera hollered and waved as she joined Becky at the table, knowing that Grace would order for her. "Good morning," Vera smiled toward Becky as she pulled up her chair to the wrought iron table.

Grace joined them carrying a tray filled with the usual lattes and chocolate croissants, "Good morning, Vera, you were very wise to leave when you did last night. We went to a nightclub after dinner and were out way too late. Look at poor Becky; she may not make it home without being sick, if there's any turbulence today."

Becky smiled, but the effort made her brow crease as if her skin hurt. "Just a slight hangover nothing serious," she added, as she reached to claim a croissant for herself. "Oh, and to think I have to sit through recurrent training tomorrow, I'm going to be so wiped out," she groaned as she sipped on her latte.

"Ugh, recurrent training is always so boring," Grace chimed in, "I just hate it. I think it gets more tedious and ten times more boring every year."

The three of them agreed that the yearly mandatory FAA training that every flight attendant had to attend was a complete waste of time, but it was something they all had to do and it was the only way for the FAA to get information to every flight attendant in the country regarding hijackings, crashes, evacuations, and any recent changes to the Federal Aviation Regulations. The training was standardized with very little deviation each year. They reviewed CPR, the Heimlich technique, basic first aid, ditching the aircraft in water, and various land evacuation procedures. They assessed the previous year's accidents and hijackings and reviewed the FAA standard procedures along with the current code words to be used in the event of a hijacking attempt. Vera had noticed in the year following the 9/11 attacks those hijackings were surprisingly never mentioned. The instructors ignored any attempt to ask questions about the ongoing investigations and the commission's findings. It was as if the company and government mentality was, 'ignore it and it might go away.' Vera was also very puzzled that the FAA never mentioned 9/11 in any of their many documents directed toward the flight crews. Worse yet, they had never received any details about how hijackers successfully entered the cockpits of those four flights.

"Vera, about last night," Grace interrupted Vera's thoughts. "I forgot to tell you, it must be some cultural thing, but Khalid and his friends do not like to be questioned about their private lives or pasts. Both Becky and I discovered that early on, they are very private people and those questions you asked last night were just, well, let's say, those questions were simply out of bounds. They come from a very different culture, one that is much more secretive about things than we Americans are."

"Do you even know where they are from?" Vera asked both women simultaneously. "I mean do you know what country they are from originally? Are they those Shiite Muslims that the FAA has warned us about for the past twenty years? Are they from Iran or some other fanatical Arab country that hates us for our freedoms?" Vera pleaded with both women for answers.

"No, they are not Islamic radicals from Iran or any other scary country like that," Grace protested. "They are wonderful nice gentlemen, Vera, they treat us like princesses. You saw that last night. Do you realize that one bottle of that champagne probably cost Khalid a thousand dollars? I have never heard them talk about religion; they love to gamble, and to drink very expensive alcohol. Is that what you think an Islamic fundamentalist does?" Grace asked with a giggle, not waiting for or even wanting an answer.

Vera sensed that she had hit a sensitive chord with Grace and Becky. It was apparent they were very protective of their men friends. "I was just curious," she defended herself. "You know how we are drilled by the FAA every year about Islamic terrorists from the Middle East, but they never really explain what one is, I guess that was on my mind since we were just talking about recurrent training."

"Sometimes we just have to let go of our prejudices and not think about work or terrorists or anything scary," Grace said. "They are terrific men and all of the flight attendants I have introduced them to usually start spending their Paris layovers in their company. Nobody has any fears like that. You must be watching too much television," Grace laughed, to ease the atmosphere she feared her reprimand had created.

Vera shrugged it off, knowing Grace well enough not to take offence at her comments. "Well, girls, I see the bus is parked in front of the hotel, bottoms up," she said, as she gathered her flight purse and reached inside for her company ID badge, clipping it on to her overcoat lapel. "Let's head on over there, this particular captain is a real stickler for on time departures and he is not a coffee drinker so he won't cut us any slack if we show up thirty seconds late with coffee cups in our hands."

The flight back to Detroit was uneventful and they were pleased to see the U.S. Customs hall wasn't very crowded for a Sunday. Vera, Grace, and Becky breezed right through the procedure. The dollar was so weak against the Euro that shopping in Europe was not common among flight attendants. U.S. Customs usually just waved them through when they arrived from Europe, which pleased Becky and Grace because they often had acquired thousands of dollars in clothing and jewelry while in Paris. Once they had cleared customs, Becky headed off to catch a hotel shuttle bus while Vera and Grace took a terminal bus to the domestic departure area for their flights to the West Coast. Stopping to check the departure monitor before leaving the international terminal, they discovered Grace's flight to Portland was at the gate next to Vera's flight to Seattle, both gates were directly above the in-flight service office, which gave them enough time to run down to the office to collect their company mail and turn in their in-flight paperwork.

Once seated in a passenger seat on her flight home, Vera thumbed through her company mail and a set of schedules for bidding trips for the following month. She fell asleep before the wheels were up and slept all the way to Seattle. The moment the wheels touched down, her thoughts turned to Kelli. They would both be so happy to see one another and spend the next ten days together.

eight

President Sherman stared out the window of the Oval Office. The gray clouds that had hung above Washington for the past several months had begun to release an early snow. The room was quiet. This was his single moment of peace before his first briefing of the day was to begin. His mind was filled with strategic plans and options that had been shared with him by various members of Congress to ignite an economy that had been nearly devastated by his predecessor's Administration. The underhanded and devious attempt to nationalize the healthcare system in America had created so much confusion and turmoil for large corporations and small businesses that hiring and job creation had never recovered. The mid-term elections had shifted control of the House to the Republicans. Their first target was to repeal the nearly 33,000-page bill that reached far beyond healthcare and impinged on citizens' freedoms. Unfortunately, the previous Administration's response to the Republicans was to act unilaterally by invoking executive orders. Sadly, nobody had the intestinal fortitude to stand up to these kinds of abusive power grabs, and the economy had continued to suffer as a result.

In April, President Sherman had eased the restrictions on drilling for oil in the Gulf of Mexico and around the shores of Florida and California. At the same time, he opened the Alaskan National Wildlife Refuge to oil drilling. Shortly after that, he opened more federal land to drilling and fracking by private companies. By October, the economy had begun to respond to his actions. In general, there was an improvement in consumer confidence. Even tourism had begun to improve, though Las Vegas continued to suffer as a result of the Patriot Hotel & Casino tragedy in July. President Sherman didn't outwardly show any effects from that day, but inwardly he endured his private agony. He traveled far less than he had originally planned and kept fully engaged in the nation's business from the White House.

A tap at his office door turned Joel's attention away from the falling snow and back to the business of the day. Jerald Reitz stood at the threshold. When he caught the President's eye, he exclaimed, "Mr. President, I am looking forward to our meeting this morning, sir."

"By all means, come in," replied the President. The National Security Advisor entered, soon followed by Department of Homeland Security Secretary, Jamie Napioli. They were accompanied by a few other analysts, who knew that being invited to a meeting with President Sherman meant you arrived a few minutes early—never late. President Sherman was a warm and congenial man who tolerated many things. Tardiness, however, was not one of them. The invitees found their way to the couches in the center of the room, and the President took his customary seat in his leather chair at one end.

"Jerry, please begin," said the President.

"Sir, I will make this as brief as possible. It seems everyone is looking forward to the upcoming Thanksgiving weekend. We have had a very quiet twenty-four hours in the United States, and the reports from our outposts worldwide have also been unusually quiet—nearly silent. Interpol has nothing of any consequence to report, and there has been no increase in chatter from our Middle East stations. I almost want to use the word 'peaceful,' but I know that would be a curse. Historically, we have always had heightened communications out of Iran and Saudi Arabia on or near our national holidays."

"And from your perspective, Jamie?" The President asked.

"I have nothing of consequence to report, sir. I, too, find it unusual that everything is so quiet right before Thanksgiving. As you know, it is the most traveled time of the year. Perhaps adding so many Muslims to our congressional staffs, along with the many I added at Homeland and the TSA, has helped prepare us to declare victory on the war on terror," she added confidently.

The President did everything in his power to maintain a straight face. Her level of competence was always in question, and now it seemed her lack of intelligence played a major factor in her performance. There still remained outstanding questions about the Las Vegas incident, and here she was prepared to declare victory. He wondered again if his decision to retain her as the head of DHS had been a huge mistake.

"I have plans to go to Camp David for the weekend, as you have been informed," Joel said, directing his statement at her. "I will expect to hear from you remotely. Jamie, are you planning to be in D.C.?"

"Uh, no sir. I'm actually planning to see some women friends of mine in Aspen, as a matter of fact. I plan to fly out shortly after this meeting. Of course I'll be available should anything come up."

"Let's hope you're right, Jamie. It would be nice to enjoy an uneventful holiday," the President replied.

The President checked on several intelligence issues with a CIA analyst from a previous meeting, weighed in on a few changes that needed to be made in an FBI protocol, and dismissed the meeting by shaking everyone's hand and wishing them the happiest of Thanksgivings.

The White House seemed especially quiet. Nearly every staffer had left to join family and friends for the weekend. The President roamed through the halls of the West Wing, wishing the best to those who remained. Then he decided to retire to the residence to spend some time in personal reflection. His heart grew heavier as his mind recalled the Thanksgiving dinners he had shared with Mica over the years, ever since they started dating during his senior year at Stanford. Once inside the residence, the President went to his private study, where he sank down into the soft leather couch and propped his feet up on the ottoman. He turned on the television and raced through the channels so fast that some of them barely had time to show up on the screen. It was clearly an exercise for his thumb, not his mind. "Maybe a good book or two for the weekend," he thought to himself as he clicked off the television and began looking through the shelves of books that lined one full wall. He knew he was avoiding his heart. He wished he could properly grieve his loss. He had been such a pillar of strength when the accident happened, consoling each and every one of the families who had lost a loved one on Mica's staff. They had appreciated his comforting words. But now, in retrospect, he realized that, almost five months later, he had not sufficiently gone through the stages of grief that were necessary for him to fully heal. A touch of anger had begun to surface as he blamed himself for allowing Mica to go to Las Vegas without him. At the time, it seemed like the right thing to do, but the "what ifs" started to play over and over again in his mind and tugged defiantly upon his heartstrings. He hated being alone, but for God's sake he was the President and he had to bear this pain in hidden isolation. This was not going to be an easy Thanksgiving weekend for him, even though his brother Steve and his wife Lucy were flying up from their home in Florida to join him at Camp David.

President Sherman opened his laptop. The homepage was scattered with news from nearly every major city in the United States and Europe. His eyes scanned quickly through the many headlines, but nothing earth-shattering caught his attention. He clicked on to his bookmarks and scrolled down to the Drudge Report. Apparently even Drudge had left early for the holiday;

his page looked exactly like it had the previous night. Perhaps, he thought, he should check out his Facebook account. His brother had told him that monitoring the patriots and the general public on social media such as Twitter and Facebook would be an excellent way to keep his finger on the pulse of America. Listening to his brother's advice, he had a Facebook account created for him on a top-secret, secure government server, so that even the best of hackers could never figure out who he was or where he was located.

His Facebook page only identified him with a Stanford "S" logo—featuring the famed Palo Alto evergreen tree. It was sufficient, he thought, since he didn't spend much time on this social medium. He had tried to friend both conservatives and liberals and to pay equal attention to their postings as well as their personal comments. He wasn't certain that his brother was correct in his assessment that Facebook was a productive use of his time, but at the moment he wasn't feeling motivated to do anything else. He got a kick out of the comments and cartoons people posted about him and tried very hard not to respond to some of the more inane and uninformed opinions circulating around his newsfeed menagerie.

nine

Seattle was offering up its typical Thanksgiving weather. A heavy windstorm was forecasted for the following day, and the outer bands of the system were already beginning to batter Alki beach. Whitecaps danced on the waters of the Puget Sound, and the wind brought a bitter chill to the bones of anyone caught in its path. Vera and Kelli had walked down the beach toward Starbucks for a late afternoon latte and a slice of pumpkin spice bread. Kelli, of course, was happy with the scents she picked up from the wind gusts along the way. Getting a morsel of Vera's pumpkin bread was an added bonus she knew was coming.

Kelli darted out ahead, pulling on the leash and dragging Vera as fast as she could walk. It was windstorms like these that had a tendency to blow down root-soaked trees throughout the entire Seattle area and caused power outages lasting for days. Vera knew these storms all too well and hoped that the winds the next day would not be as powerful as predicted. As she and Kelli entered the house, a strong gust nearly whipped the screen door from her hand. She pulled the heavy wooden door closed with both hands and locked it in place. Finding a lighter, she lit two large candles on the kitchen counter then turned up the thermostat to give the house a little extra warmth in case the power did go out.

She grabbed her laptop and curled up on the window seat at the far end of the kitchen. The lights of downtown Seattle were just beginning to illuminate her view of the city skyline. She clicked on the kitchen TV to briefly check the news. Big bold letters across the bottom of the screen read: BREAKING NEWS. The picture on the screen was a floor plan-type drawing of the Orlando International Airport. Vera recognized it by the unique design of the terminal. The drawing showed airplanes parked around the B terminal. One of the planes was depicted as a bright orange starburst, indicating some type of explosion. She moved closer to the television and listened intently to the announcer.

"An explosion has been reported at one of the gates in the B terminal. The ensuing fireball has affected several of the gates nearby. The Orlando Airport Fire Department is currently on the scene, and the airport has been closed to all air traffic. All arriving flights have been diverted to Tampa International. Early reports indicate that some type of explosion has occurred, possibly on board an aircraft parked at one of the gates. We have very little information at this time, but expect updates from our local affiliate WKMG-TV. We do know that this is the busiest travel day for most airports around the nation and Orlando has been exceptionally busy all week. Disney reported earlier that their resorts had been booked solid for the Thanksgiving Day weekend. We have no indication of casualties, but I can imagine, given the kind of damage that we can see in this very crowded terminal that there could possibly be significant loss of life."

Vera was staring at the screen in total disbelief. Her mind was having a difficult time wrapping itself around the fact that she was learning of yet another aircraft incident involving one of her company's jets. She was very familiar with the B terminal; it was the one her company used in Orlando. As the initial shock of hearing the news began to dissipate, questions flooded her mind. How could an aircraft explode at the gate? That had never happened before; planes just don't blow up for no reason while parked at a gate. She began to search her memory for answers.

She turned her attention once again to the announcer's voice. "Again for those of you just tuning in, there has been a massive explosion at the B terminal at Orlando International Airport. It is uncertain at this moment exactly what has happened. We are now getting word that it appears a 757 might have exploded while parked at the gate. The explosion created a massive fireball that erupted, we are told, from the jetway into the terminal corridor itself. Several aircraft are now fully engulfed in fire, as you can see on your screen. Airport officials and the TSA in Orlando are estimating a possible death toll as high as one hundred. There is just no way of knowing at this point. This incident occurred about thirty minutes ago at the B terminal in Orlando, Florida." The announcer's voice became louder and faster as he spoke into his microphone over the sounds of sirens and what sounded like small explosions in the background.

Vera had intended to open her laptop, check her email, and read a few news sites online, but this news was so upsetting she had forgotten about the computer completely. Kelli whimpered a concerned whine, which reminded Vera that it was her dinner time. "Okay girl, I'll get you your food." She put Kelli's dish down in the short hallway leading out to the garage then went back to the window seat to catch up on the latest word from Orlando.

The announcer continued, "The ticket agent who had been working that particular gate was thrown across the terminal hallway into the emergency exit doors and knocked unconscious momentarily. She escaped out those doors and is now reporting that it is believed that nearly all of the passengers had deplaned. She added that there was one passenger who needed wheelchair assistance and that the wheelchair had just arrived at the aircraft. She reports that, in addition to the wheelchair passenger, the crew—and perhaps several company employees who were traveling on passes—had not deplaned when the explosion occurred. The explosion was so huge that the percussion from the blast was felt several gates away. It is still uncertain how many aircraft may have been damaged, but we are hearing that at least three aircraft are currently burning."

The news was too difficult for Vera to watch. She switched off the TV and headed toward her bedroom. Kelli raced ahead of her as if she knew exactly where Vera was going. Once she got comfortable in her bed, she opened her laptop.

No sooner had her computer screen illuminated than her cell phone started ringing.

"Vera, it's Grace. Have you seen the breaking news—an explosion in Orlando?" Grace's voice was racing at maximum speed. "First we lose a 747 into the hotel where the First Lady is staying. Now this? Airplanes just don't explode at the gate. Do you think there was a fire in the APU that could have sparked the fueling truck? What the hell do you think could have possibly happened?" Grace was firing off questions too rapidly for Vera to offer an answer. There were no logical answers at this point, which magnified the pain and frustration Vera was feeling.

"Grace, I just don't have any answers. I'm trying to work through this myself. I had just stepped into the house and turned the TV on the moment this news broke. I do recall a Russian airplane exploded in 2010 right around New Year's Eve, but I seem to remember it happened on the tarmac, not at the actual gate area. I'll have to do a search for the details, but I have no idea what could have caused this explosion. I can only imagine the terminal was completely packed. I know the Orlando flights are all pretty full, especially this weekend. Let me call you back tomorrow. I am going to cancel my plans for Thanksgiving. There's a huge wind storm coming into Seattle and I doubt that I'll feel like eating and celebrating."

"We usually eat around three, but you can call me any time you find any answers," Grace told her.

"Will do, then," Vera confirmed. "I'll call you tomorrow. I wish I could say something that would ease the tension for both of us, but until we know more details, I'm afraid we'll both just have to suffer. Good night, Grace."

ten

President Sherman relaxed in his favorite overstuffed chair in the bedroom of the residence, caught between being lost in his thoughts and trying not to reflect too hard on his memories. He was just about to get up to find something to snack on in the kitchen, when Mike tapped at his door and informed him that he had a call waiting from Jerald Reitz.

"Thanks, Mike. I'll take it in here."

"Jerry, it must be important for you to call me on the cusp of a holiday. What's up?"

"Mr. President, it's important. I'm calling to inform you that an airplane has blown up at the terminal in Orlando and has taken out several other planes. There are numerous casualties and there's severe damage to the terminal. I'm just now receiving some initial information, but I would suggest you turn on the television, as the explosion has made its way to the news. Wait for me to fill you in on the details as I receive them."

President Sherman listened carefully to what he was being told, mixing that information with the knowledge that his brother Steve and his wife could quite possibly have been in that terminal or, even worse, on one of the airplanes. They were expected at the White House later that evening. The President motioned to Mike, who was standing in the hallway, to come in and turn on the television to a local Orlando station, while he collected his thoughts in an attempt to respond to his National Security Advisor.

"Jerry, you know my brother and his wife could very well be

involved in this tragedy. Have the Secret Service, with the help of the FBI, if necessary, begin an all-out search for them and let me know immediately when they are located. I have the television on now and will wait to hear from you. Say a prayer for me, Jerry. I couldn't bear another family disaster this close to losing Mica."

"I will, sir. I will pray with all the fervor of my being that they are safe, and I will happily report that news to you very soon."

"Thank you, Jerry," Joel said, feeling his strength somewhat diminished. He couldn't believe he was learning of another airplane accident involving a close family member. He hung up the phone and asked Mike to remain with him as they waited for information from the initial television reports to appear. When the news finally broke, the announcer's solemn voice filled the room. "There has been some type of explosion at the Orlando International Airport. Several passengers and employees are reported to be dead or injured. The numbers are unavailable at this time, but they seem to be rapidly climbing, even though this accident happened less than thirty minutes ago. There is a large fire burning in the B terminal area, and first responders are on the scene. Ambulances are being sent into the area from miles away to help with the injured. The airport has been closed and all flights coming into Orlando have been diverted to Tampa. If you are in the Orlando area and expecting family and friends for the holiday, you are asked to check with the airline they are scheduled to arrive on for further information. Again, all flights into Orlando have been diverted. If you were to pick up anyone arriving between 7:45 and 8:00, please call their cell phones if they do not show up at the baggage claim area. The airline involved is setting up a toll-free line for all inquiries, but that will take several hours. Stay tuned here for announcements and further updates."

"My brother, what time was his flight, Mike?" President Sherman asked.

"He was on the 8:45 flight out of Orlando, sir," Mike answered.

"Thank you, Mike, I appreciate your straight forward honesty and your pinpoint-sharp memory. Please try calling their cell phones throughout the evening, and let me know if you hear anything—if they answer or if someone else answers for them."

"I will, sir, and I will let myself out, Mr. President," Mike said, as he quietly exited the residence.

From the reports breaking on television the tragedy was growing in size. July 4th now Thanksgiving, the elements of coincidence were beginning to be overshadowed by the timing of such horrific events. In spite of his anxiousness for his own family, President Sherman began to focus on his duties to the country as his questions began to center on the possibility that both of these events were acts of terrorism against the country— or worse, against him personally.

eleven

Vera began searching online for possibilities that might have caused the Orlando airport explosion. She wished Jeff were still alive to help her. He was so good at researching, and especially when it came to ferreting out online information about airplanes and accidents. She recalled how he could spend hours digging into things. She had never paid much attention to what he was investigating, but she knew it must have been important to him, because he spent a lot of time on the computer whenever he was home. She remembered how excited he became one night when he literally leapt from his chair with his arms outstretched, loudly proclaiming, "I found it, I found the missing piece!" His sudden and loud burst of enthusiasm scared Kelli, who hid under the bed for almost an hour. Vera wished she had taken more of an interest in how he went about doing his online investigations.

The 757 was a very safe aircraft and one of her favorite jets to work. She had flown it for several years with only one major incident; one of the two engines had to be shut down. They made an uneventful, but unscheduled emergency landing. Vera continued to review in her mind all the company procedures for a typical arrival. She couldn't think of one thing that could possibly cause an explosion on board a plane while parked at the gate with the engines shut down. Reaching for the television remote, she turned on the news again, hoping to hear some details of what might have caused the accident. She continued to multitask, surfing through the internet for past aircraft incidents while listening for any new or detailed clues. The news was now full-time coverage from the Orlando airport and becoming repetitive. The usual airline experts were brought in to the newsrooms to discuss what might have gone wrong. One station interviewed two counter-terrorism experts who Vera thought she recalled from the early morning of 9/11. They were somehow quite certain that this explosion was the work of some Al Qaeda-related spin-off group, most likely from Syria or Iraq. Vera shook her head at the insanity of some terrorism expert making claims like that, when firefighters were still fighting the blaze and the NTSB hadn't even arrived on the scene. "These terrorism experts have no clue what happened," she thought to herself. It seemed to her that these guys were laying blame on this new terrorist faction without one scrap of evidence.

The voice on the television announced, "We are hearing from the local hospitals that there are more than one hundred people injured. Many are still being transported to medical facilities as far as fifty miles away. There are no official estimates regarding possible lives lost, but we are told that the number will climb. We are expecting a press conference sometime this evening, and we will have further details from officials on the scene at that time. Please stay tuned. We will be covering this story around the clock."

The incessant details that didn't make sense to her that were coming out of the mouths of the reporters added to her frustration. Her body was still suffering the effects of jet lag. Without even thinking, she turned off the television and reached for her recurrent training workbook—not to study, but to put her to sleep. Never had she experienced a more potent sleeping aid than this damn book. Once clutched in her hands she knew, she'd be asleep in minutes.

twelve

President Sherman heard the phone ringing and knew that Mike would be in momentarily. He had made some calls to the CIA to determine what, if anything, they knew about Orlando or if the intelligence had changed since his earlier briefing. Being hit by a terror attack was one thing; being caught totally off guard was unacceptable. He was waiting for an update and hoped this call was just that.

"It is Mr. Reitz again, sir."

"Excellent, thank you, Mike. Please put him through."

"Mr. President, we have located your brother and his wife. They were, in fact, both inside the B terminal when the explosions hit. They have been taken to the Sunrise Hospital in Orlando under priority care. Apparently they were both thrown into a row of chairs from the percussion of the first blast. They suffered cuts and bruises, but managed to safely escape out of the terminal before the additional explosions and heavier damage took place. Sir, they should both be just fine, but the doctors want to keep them overnight simply for observation. I have sent a security team to guard their rooms."

"Great news, Jerry. That's just fantastic news! Please see if you can arrange a call to them at your earliest convenience. Now, tell me more about what you think might have happened."

"The blast inside that terminal was very serious. We are receiving initial reports that it could have been terror-related. The FBI has managed to secure all videotapes from the parking garages to the front doors and from the agents' podium at the gate through the jetway. They should have a better idea and a possible clue as to who might be behind this and the details of what might have occurred before the plane exploded. We have not ruled anything out as of yet. It could have been a bomb inside the jetway or the terminal itself, although we can't imagine how a bomb could get into the secure side of the terminal."

"Thanks, Jerry," replied President Sherman. "I will look forward to your updates. I want to hear the moment you have found anything for certain. I don't care what time of day or night you phone, I want to know immediately. And Jerry, thanks for sending that security team to the hospital."

Mike McFee had an uncanny sense when it came to assisting President Sherman. Just as the president hung up the phone, Mike tapped on the door to the residence. "Your coffee, sir."

"Come in, Mike. Were you reading my mind again?" He asked, relieved that his family was okay.

"Mike, my brother and his wife were found safe in Orlando—maybe a little banged up, but safe and sound nevertheless. I'm waiting for Jerry to get a call through to them for me."

"I'm delighted to hear that, sir," Mike said with a smile.

"Mike, if it's not too much trouble, can you please contact my Chief of Staff. I'm going to need to cancel our dinner tomorrow at Camp David and make arrangements for videoconference meetings for those of us who now need to deal with this developing situation in Orlando. I will need to talk with him as soon as possible."

"Yes, sir," Mike replied as he stood at attention. "Consider it taken care of. I will have him on the line shortly."

thirteen

Grace tried calling Khalid's number in Paris one more time. He was usually quick to answer her calls, but this was the fourth time she had tried calling and still no response. "Where could he possibly be?" she wondered.

"Allo," Khalid's heavily-accented voice finally answered.

"I have been calling you for hours," Grace lit into him. "Where have you been? This is serious, Khalid. No, it is more than serious it is a matter of life and death, and when you see that I have tried to call you so many times, the least you could do is call me back."

Grace's rant was met with silence. Just as she was about to start in on him again, Khalid's calm businesslike voice spoke very clearly and with almost perfect enunciation, "I am very busy now. Perhaps I will call you some other time." And with that, her end of the connection went dead.

Grace was speechless. The only other time he had been too busy to talk was the last time there had been a tragic airplane accident. His cold matter-of-fact tone was both unwelcomed and uncalled for. Grace tried to imagine what on earth Khalid was doing that he would be so abrupt with her. Who was he with? What was he doing? As the words "too busy" echoed again and again in her head, a jealous rage began to build up inside of her. At first it centered on Khalid's time, but the more she nursed the feeling, the more her thoughts started to take on a feminine aura. She had been with Khalid in rather intimate moments when he failed to answer his phone when it rang. At the time, she found it rather thrilling to be the center of his focused attention. Into whose attention was he now focusing? Her fingers fought off the desire to redial his number.

She poured herself a glass of wine and called Vera instead. When Vera answered, Grace blurted out, "I'm having such a hard time. I just cannot believe what is happening to our company. How can these strange accidents happen? I tried to get in touch with Khalid, but when I called, he was short with me, saying that he was too busy to talk. He said that he would call me back some other time. And then he just hung up on me. I don't have any idea when he might call me back or even if he ever will." The alcohol was taking effect, and between the slurs and the sobs, Vera was having a difficult time understanding what Grace was telling her. But she felt it was best to just listen and let Grace go. "On top of everything else going on, I think Khalid might be cheating on me." And with that, she burst into uncontrollable sobs and dropped her phone into the couch.

"Grace? Grace?"

"Yes?" Finally came a reply.

"Grace, I know it's very difficult to handle another accident, if that's what this is. The news is still too sketchy and it is difficult to know what to believe. I understand it's frustrating. None of this makes any sense. Planes just don't blow up while parked at the gate, unless it's terrorism. And as for Khalid, I know so little about him. I don't know what to tell you, but I do know a woman's intuition in matters of the heart is usually correct."

fourteen

A slight glimmer of light seeped through the crack at the top of the curtain, casting a sliver of daylight in the otherwise dark room. Joel turned over onto his back and stared up at the ceiling, watching a ray of sunlight expand until it reached the opposite wall. It had been a long, restless night, and sleep had only managed to dart in and out of the President's consciousness. He couldn't remember dreaming, yet now he was awake to the nightmare that was Orlando. The thought that another holiday would be filled with sorrow for so many families was unbearable. He had not yet heard from his brother, but assumed that they would be able to connect shortly. His thoughts turned to addressing the nation with a speech he was not looking forward to delivering. He threw back the sheets and forced himself to face the day.

Mike had the President's morning coffee service waiting for him in his private office. President Sherman called his press secretary and asked him to make the needed arrangements for him to address the nation later that evening, he suggested early evening. He hated to interrupt everyone's busy Thanksgiving holiday plans during the day and he hoped he might have more details concerning the Orlando terminal by the time he gave his speech. Sadly, this was a speech he could write himself and made arrangements to do so.

"Mike, I haven't heard from, Steve. Has Jerry contacted you with an update for me? I assume Steve has been medicated and might still be sleeping, but I'd like to talk with him at the first opportunity."

"You are correct, Mr. President," Mike replied. The Secret Service is standing guard outside his room. Jerry informed me that he is receiving regular updates from the hospital staff and now that you are awake I am sure he will contact you directly and put you in touch with your brother."

"Thank you, Mike." Joel Sherman appreciated so many things about his friend and valet.

President Sherman finished the outline for his speech then went down to the Oval Office for his daily briefing and videoconference with Jamie. As he walked, he rehearsed in his mind what he knew about the Orlando explosion so far. Something had obviously triggered it; he feared there might be a terrorist connection. The thought that his own family members might have been targeted was terribly concerning to him.

The National Security Advisor met Joel just inside the Executive offices. "Thanks again for your excellent work last night, Jerry. What do you know since we talked last? I would love to hear your thoughts off the record. I already have a pretty good idea what Jamie and her people will report."

"Mr. President, we don't have all the analysis in just yet, but plastic explosives appear to have been involved, which indicates that it was a deliberate act. No word at all on responsibility, but all the signs are there and if they somehow knew that your brother would be in that terminal at that time, there is a real possibility that this attack was directed at you personally."

Joel nodded in agreement, indicating to Jerry that such a thought had already crossed his mind.

"Well, let's see what Jamie has to say. Maybe she'll surprise us," Jerry responded, wanting to smile, but holding it in, out of respect.

No new intelligence was brought forth in the briefing. The leads they were pursuing needed more careful analysis. Even Jamie agreed that the inconsistencies in their preliminary investigation had all the markings of a well-planned and well-executed terror attack. Of course she had no definitive idea who could possibly be responsible. The FBI had some indication that the plastic explosives used were not domestic in nature and that alone shifted focus to possible foreign terrorist groups.

"How could anyone get such a device past our security measures that are currently in place, Jamie?" The President asked. "Is there a security breach at Orlando that would allow explosives to be brought into the terminal? I want a complete investigation into the procedures at that airport and I want to know how this could happen before you tell me who made it happen. You do understand me, don't you, Jamie? This is just not acceptable. I want to know everything from the TSA agents' names to which companies are manufacturing the metal detectors and body scanners."

Ms. Napioli reassured the President that she would demand a thorough investigation into security procedures at Orlando and report back to him. She had access to all of the security tapes and she intended to review each one of them personally, if necessary.

The President muted the teleconference and gave his next directive to Jerry. "Run your own investigation using CIA operatives, and let's see what we can find. I just don't have as much confidence in DHS as I need."

"Yes sir," Jerry acknowledged the request. "I will get right on that."

"Alright, that will be all for now. Try to enjoy your Thanksgiving, but provide me with some answers. I am speaking to the nation tonight at 8:00 pm Eastern time, and I would like to be able to say substantially more than an official 'I'm sorry.'"

Once alone, the President walked over to his desk and pounded his fist on it, "Who do these people think they are, attacking me and my family? And to think they have the audacity to do it in my face on a holiday. Damn them! Damn them all!"

Just as he was composing himself, his secretary indicated that a call from his brother was waiting on line three and that he could take it in the Oval Office or she could transfer it up to the residence—whichever he preferred. "I'll take it here, thanks," he replied.

"Steve, how are you doing, buddy? Am I ever thankful that you're okay," Joel was happy to finally receive this phone call and to hear his brother's voice.

"Hello Joel, Happy Thanksgiving, sorry I blew up your plans for Camp David, no pun intended," Steve chuckled into the phone.

"Oh man, it's so good to hear you laugh, how's Lucy?"

"She's actually in better shape than I am. My big old fat blubber belly probably shielded her from most of the blast! She's a little sore with a few bruises, but I guess she won't be pestering me about my weight—for a few days, anyway."

"Tell me what happened. I have received reports, as you can imagine, but I would love to hear from you firsthand what your experience was and if you saw anything out of the ordinary."

"You ask that as if you think it was some kind of terrorism. Was it?" Steve asked.

"I don't have enough solid information about what exactly happened, Steve and anything you remember will help in our investigation. I'm sure the FBI will be questioning both of you as soon as you feel up to their intrusion."

"Well, we don't remember all that much," Steve began. "We were walking to our gate, which was next to the one that exploded, I think, although I really don't know that for certain. We saw a huge fireball. It looked like it was coming straight out of the jetway at us, and then boom, the windows in the terminal all blew out. That blast, as far as I can tell, sent us flying into a row of seats at the gate across the terminal. I don't remember anything else, but Lucy says she heard more explosions after the initial one that blew us over. I think I was knocked unconscious at that point. Next thing we knew, we were in an ambulance headed to the hospital. They sedated us pretty well, and I guess we slept until just a while ago. Does that help?"

"I will relay your information on, but as I said, I'm sure the FBI will be knocking on your door as soon as the nurses allow them to question you and will ferret out anything you can remember. I have a report from your doctor that says they will release you sometime later today, assuming no complications develop for either of you. One advantage of my job is that I can get better reports on you than you can," the President said with a laugh.

"Joel, how are you doing with all this? I know it must be a horrible reminder of what happened to Mica last summer. I just wish we were there with you. We were so looking forward to spending time together during this holiday." Steve knew how much Joel loved Mica and how very difficult her death had been for him.

"Well, fat boy, you have done all you could. You stayed alive and you protected Lucy, and personally that matters more to me than you can imagine. I'm addressing the nation tonight, and I have to tell you just talking to you, hearing your voice and your laugh are going to make that speech much easier than it might have been. So thank you. Give my best to Lucy, take good care of yourselves, get home, and get some rest. We'll arrange some time to be together soon. I have no doubt that I will be in Orlando in the next few days surveying the damage, and let me tell you Steve, it's a lot worse than you can imagine, unless you've seen the reports on television. When you get home I'll arrange for a secure phone line, and we can talk in more detail later. And you might want to reconsider that Secret Service protection you keep declining."

"Alright Joel, save me some turkey. I was really counting on that great cook you were telling me about at Camp David. You don't worry about us. We're fine. We'll be watching your speech tonight. Talk with you in a couple days."

The President ended the phone call feeling better, and was much more encouraged to compose his remarks for later that evening, but the nagging issue of terrorism—terrorism with no expressed purpose—only strengthened his resolve to find answers.

fifteen

The window seat that filled the large alcove in the kitchen beckoned to Vera. Many a day following Jeff's passing had been spent at that window looking out over the Puget Sound, counting the sailboats or just staring at the magnificent Seattle skyline. Something about that space could make time stand still and fill the loneliest of thoughts with hope. Vera brewed herself a large mug of herbal tea and situated herself along the window in her favorite position. The typical dark-gray clouds of November completely blocked the sunlight, accentuating the contrast of her view to an almost black and white scene reminiscent of an Ansell Adams photograph. The windstorm had not arrived—or at least had not been the disaster the television weatherman had predicted. Seagulls were circling high above and appeared to be enjoying the stronger-than-normal wind currents.

Vera reached for her laptop, which she had left charging on the floor next to the window seat. Part of her was still curious about Orlando, yet a larger part of her hoped that she could find something online to take her mind completely away from airlines, airplanes, and accidents. Her homepage was filled with news, which she managed to deftly avoid as she quickly navigated to her email. A careful perusal of her inbox showed the usual holiday shopping advertisements, an occasional winning sweepstakes notification, and an invitation to a retirement seminar that actually looked interesting. She refreshed her mail. To her delight, appeared the name Jim Bowman.

Jim had been a very close friend of Jeff's. They had flown

together in the National Guard for years and were both hired by the same airline company as pilots when their Guard commitments ended. Jeff had always looked up to Jim and was more than willing to accept his advice and counsel. There had not been many people in Jeff's life that had been such an influence. Vera had always appreciated Jim's calm demeanor when he made suggestions to Jeff. She was most grateful for his influence in persuading Jeff to upgrade to the 747. It meant he lost some seniority, but the change allowed him more time at home. When Jeff died, Jim graciously offered to help Vera with the overwhelming details that had a tendency to render a widow vulnerable and confused. He helped her with the funeral arrangements, explained to her the company pension and death benefits, and acted as a liaison with Jeff's insurance company. In the ensuing years, both Jim and his wife Mari had remained close to Vera, offering her help with any problems that arose.

Shortly after Jeff's death, Jim retired from the airline and began consulting on airport and airline security. She had overheard Jim and her husband talking about starting such a business together, but never thought either of them could give up their love of flying. She didn't know all the details about Jim's business, but she knew he had become an expert on the subject to the point of testifying before both a House and Senate subcommittee on airport security. Several times she had tried to ask him what he knew about the many holes in security that almost all airline personnel knew existed, but he'd always smile and say, "You have enough to worry about without knowing all I have learned about security." She couldn't tell if it was a polite way of telling her to mind her own business or if he was protecting her from the fear that was always just under the surface for every flight attendant. She recalled that a year earlier she and Jim had had an in-depth discussion about the infighting that existed between government agencies and how that affected the airlines.

Once Homeland Security was created and managed to insert its tentacles into the National Transportation Safety Board, more interagency confusion resulted; particularly in the event of an accident. When you overlaid the FBI and its resentment toward Homeland's control, it was not difficult to understand why the events at the Patriot Hotel & Casino and the death of the First Lady months earlier were still locked in an endless cycle of investigation. Jim had expressed to her his disappointment with the inadequate credentials of those that were hired into Homeland Security, particularly with the TSA agents and their supervisors. Now that two significant events had occurred in less than five months, many of the issues Jim had concerns about were becoming much clearer. She hoped his email was an invitation to talk more about these latest airline tragedies.

She clicked the email open and read:

Vera,

I've been so busy. Just a quick note to check in with you. This incident in Orlando has been devastating. No real information as to what happened or how. Very frustrating. I know how upsetting accidents are to all of us in the airline industry. If you think retirement changes that, I'm here to tell you that it doesn't. I'm glued to the television waiting for a logical explanation that my airline-pilot mind can accept. Nothing thus far unfortunately means anything, but it is still early and it was a huge explosion. We think of you often and hope we can get together over the holidays.

Love,

Jim and Mari

It was not particularly comforting to know that Jim was at a loss as to what had occurred in Orlando. She had hoped his email would shed some expert insight into the cause or at the very least some supposition as to what happened. She hit the reply button and typed:

Jim,

So good to hear from you. Yes, this is a horrible time for the company. I'm shocked that we have experienced another accident when our safety record had been so impeccable for so many years. I had to cancel my dinner plans today with a friend because I'm still too upset to leave the house.

I should have my flight hours finished up by the 21st of December. I'd love to get together with you two sometime between Christmas and New Year's Eve. Have a great Thanksgiving.

Love,

Vera and Kelli

She stretched out on the widow seat and propped her head up with a pillow. It was starting to get dark and she had yet to eat anything. Even Kelli had not complained about missing her regular eating intervals. It was a very odd Thanksgiving, and Vera was okay with it coming to an end.

She checked her Facebook page to pass the time. She had opened the account after Jeff died, at the encouragement of friends who wanted to keep in touch. The craze of social media never made much sense to Vera, and she used it only as a tool to check-in on friends and to laugh at some of the pictures people posted on her newsfeed. She was always amazed that every few weeks when she checked on her page that someone new had requested her friendship. She was already friends with the people in her life that mattered and chatting with strangers never appealed to her sense of excitement. She was well aware of the horror stories in the news about Facebook relationships that started from nothing and ended badly. She was too smart to be lured into that kind of a trap.

As her Facebook page filled the computer screen, sure enough there was a new friend request from 'Stan the Man'. Her immediate thought was that anyone who could not use their own photograph and their real name was not worthy of her time and could only mean trouble. The avatar, however, was the Stanford University logo, which caught her attention and she decided to look a little deeper into the profile. About all she could ascertain was that he was a male and had graduated from Stanford. "Pretty nebulous," she thought. Something drew her to accept the request. "After all," she rationalized, "how bad could a Stanford graduate be?" She clicked the "confirm" button and finished scrolling through her newsfeed and checking her private messages.

sixteen

President Sherman was standing in the Oval Office, trying not to pace, but anxiously awaiting Jerry Reitz's arrival. The President had summoned him to the White House on Saturday following Thanksgiving to discuss the new findings that had been conveyed through the FBI. One of the things Steve had mentioned about an empty wheel chair pulling up to the jetway just prior to the first explosion, caused them to question if a wheelchair could have been the delivery vehicle for the explosives. Analysis was still being done on the explosives to determine where it had come from and they were searching for metal fragments that matched the kind of materials used in the airports' courtesy wheelchairs. It was an intriguing theory—and one the President wanted to explore in more depth with Mr. Reitz.

"Jerry, welcome. Have you managed to eat any turkey the past few days with all this chaos going on?" The President asked.

"Well, you know me, Mr. President, I can sacrifice pretty much anything anytime, but holiday turkey always finds its way to my stomach. Thank you for asking," Jerry said, taking a seat and opening his binder to get down to business.

The President followed and sat on the adjoining sofa facing him. "Bottom line is this, Jerry. I don't think I am getting the information I need to make decisions in their purest form. Don't get me wrong, I don't think anyone is obstructing our investigation or purposely withholding critical data points, but something just doesn't feel right to me and I wanted to discuss it with you."

"I admit I have had those thoughts over the weekend and have wondered how best to present them to you," Jerry responded.

"Good, that's what I like about you, Jerry. We always seem to be on the same page. Personally, I think I am being blinded by two pernicious facets of our society: political correctness and liberal tolerance. Each of them manages to cloud the issues and collectively they combine to weaken the resolve of this country. I cannot abide that. My sworn duty is to protect, and if the information I receive or the advice I base by decisions on has been corrupted, then I am at a disadvantage I simply cannot afford."

"Mr. President, I think you have described the situation quite accurately, and I also have to believe that not only is the country's security at stake, but whatever is going on has you and your family directly in its crosshairs," Jerry said, checking for the President's reaction.

"Again we are on the same wave length, my friend. I haven't wanted to say anything for fear of being thought of as paranoid, but two accidents directly affecting me and my family is much more than coincidence, don't you think?"

"You could not be more correct, sir."

"Now is not the time to reorganize DHS or to neuter them in the midst of this investigation, so what would you suggest we do?"

"Well, Mr. President, my advice is something I think you will like. I believe you should engage Jim Bowman to help you get to the truth of what happened in Orlando. I know your history with him goes way back, and his firm is by far the most knowledgeable regarding airports and airport security in the country. His security clearance is 'Top Secret' and he has the ability to work under the radar while right under the nose of any government agency. Most importantly, I know you trust him."

"That is a terrific idea. I talk with Jim far more often than you realize. It has not all been about government business, but you are right, he is the perfect candidate to get information and to analyze it with the kind of intelligence and scrutiny we are looking for here. With your permission, I would like him to review the Las Vegas intelligence as well. Hopefully a new set of eyes will help us to see what we might have been missing."

"It would be an honor to share those files with him, Mr. President. I will begin making the necessary arrangements to get him on board and up to speed immediately."

The President leaned forward and patted him on the knee, reinforcing his commitment to Jerry's brilliant idea. The two rose together and shook hands. Their connection needed no more words. Clearly they were in the same boat and rowing hard in the same direction.

seventeen

As the days passed, Vera wondered how Grace was doing. It had been a while since they had spoken. Grace could be hard to understand at times—so full of anxiety and emotion then silent for days or weeks at a time. It was not an endearing trait, but Vera had become used to her erratic behavior and knew enough to call Grace in those silent periods in an effort to save her from herself.

"Hello, Vera," was the response, without as much as a ring on Vera's end.

"Grace, I'm just checking in with you to see how you are doing," Vera inquired.

A huge sigh could be heard through the phone. "I'm exhausted, Vera. There is nothing left of me, emotionally, mentally, physically, and any other adverb that comes to mind. I'm just drained."

"I can hear that in your voice. How can I help?" Vera inquired gently.

"You can shoot Khalid, put a sock in my mother's mouth, find me a new career, give me a massage, help me lose ten pounds, and convince me that life is worth living again," Grace replied without a moment of hesitation.

"Whoa, girl, that's one mighty tall order. Let's start with Khalid. I take it he is still not answering your calls?"

"Something like that. I have called him so many times that even my speed-dial thumb hurts. The few times he did pick up, he was still too busy to talk with me. I have been around this man for months. Up until recently he has completely adored me. But, all he says now is that he is too busy to talk, then hangs up. Vera, I swear he's having an affair. It's just not like him to behave this way, and if I find out he's doing someone else, after all this time I have spent with him, I will be furious."

"Maybe he's just really busy with something. I know you don't know what he does for a living, but it must be something important that requires his time," Vera offered, trying to instill a degree of hope in Grace's already-made-up mind.

"I just want to catch him. I want him to know that I know he's a damn liar and a worthless piece of crap. The only problem is, he's Mister Prince Charming on the days I'm with him, but most of the time I'm a ten-hour flight away and have no way of catching him in the act. It's not like I can sneak up on him. I can't even get into his building without him giving the doorman permission to let me inside. What am I going to do, Vera?" Grace implored.

"Well, I have an idea, but it's a little sneaky if you are up for doing something brave."

"Sneaky, you're damn rights I'm up for something sneaky. Tell me; tell me—anything to catch that bastard in the act."

"Jeff had a custom-made voice recorder that looks exactly like a Mont Blanc pen. It's voice-activated and, as I recall, he paid extra for additional recording time. It plugs right into a computer USB port for easy playback. You're welcome to borrow it if you'd like."

"Oh, that would be so perfect. I leave tomorrow morning for Paris."

Later that afternoon, Grace dropped by to pick up the recorder. They set it up and planted it around the house to test it to find the optimal distance Grace should set it up at Khalid's apartment. They tried talking loudly, whispering, and just having a normal conversation so they would know how sensitive the microphone was.

"I have half a mind to stick it between the mattress and the box springs," Grace exclaimed with more than a touch of sarcasm in her voice.

"Oh, I'm not sure that's the kind of information you really want to hear," replied Vera. "That's what imaginations are for, after you have all the facts. And speaking of facts, I'm working the Paris trip on the nineteenth of December, so I'll be with you when you pick up the pen and we can listen to the tape together. If it's the worst-case scenario, you won't be alone."

"Really, you are working that flight with me? I was going to ask you if you would, but I figured your schedule was already set and I know how you hate to fly after the twentieth of the month," replied Grace.

"I knew you were hurting, so I called and changed my schedule to be with you on that trip. There were two positions open on the crew orders, and seniority has its benefits if you live long enough to take advantage of them."

"You are such a dear, Vera, thank you. You have no idea how much that means to me."

Once they had recorded several different trial runs, they went upstairs to find Vera's laptop to play them back. Vera opened her computer and moved the mouse to bring it back to life. Her Facebook page was on and she immediately noticed a private message. Thinking it was important she clicked on the icon, only to find that it was a message from Stan the Man. She opened it and read, "Thanks, Vera, for accepting my friend request. I look forward to getting to know you better and learning how you think."

"Who's that, Vera, a new boyfriend?" Grace asked, not being the least bit bashful about reading Vera's message.

"Hardly," responded Vera. "I'm not really sure who it is. He friend-requested me a few days ago, and I accepted. This is the first communication I've seen from him, and I haven't said a word to him yet. I'm sure it's nothing. But I am curious as to how he knew I even existed."

"Well, maybe you commented on some thread of a friend of his and he liked your picture."

"Whatever," Vera shrugged and closed her computer.

eighteen

"Jim, Joel Sherman here."

"Mr. President, it's unlike you to call me directly," replied Jim Bowman. "I've grown so fond of that official voice saying, 'please hold for the President of the United States.'"

"Well, I know it's out of the ordinary, Jim, but this is an unusual situation. I'm going to have the Secret Service deliver a secure phone to you within the hour, and I'll call you to fill you in on the details after I hear it's been delivered. I just wanted to make certain you were home and planning on remaining there for a while."

"Oh, I'll be here, sir," Jim replied, trying not to sound overly curious.

Jim hung up the phone, wondering what the President could possibly want to discuss that was so important that it required a secure phone line. In the past their conversations had to do with candidates for appointments to ambassadorial posts and agency positions that had very little political consequence. The two had known each other for many years and had many friends in common. The President would often consult with Jim when he was thinking of making an appointment that involved someone they both knew. For several months after the President was sworn into office, he called Jim about once a week, after Mica died, maybe only once a month, and now it was just once in a while. Within the hour, Jim heard a knock at his front door. Two men dressed in black suits greeted him.

"Sir, I'm agent Randall and this is agent Andrews," the

taller agent said as they presented their identification badges and completely ignored Jim's extended hand. "Are you James Bowman?"

"Yes I am."

"May we see some identification, preferably a passport?"

Jim invited the two men into the house and offered them seats in the living room while he went to his office to collect his passport. He included his Washington State driver's license and handed them both to agent Randall. The agent scanned the passport barcode with a device he took from his jacket pocket, looked at the driver's license then handed them back to Jim.

"May we scan your fingerprints, sir?"

Jim willingly presented his hands palms down as agent Andrews rolled each finger and both thumbs across a tablet-style computer then waited for the results. In a moment he had what he was looking for and presented his hand to shake Jim's.

"Mr. Bowman, we apologize for the inconvenience and for the security, but we are on official business for the President of the United States, and we had to make certain that you are the man we have been asked to give this phone and information to."

Agent Randall opened a briefcase and showed Jim a peculiar-looking device and two thick packets of information. He reached for the device and showed Jim that it was indeed a telephone, and instructed him how to turn it on, make the only call the phone was capable of making— directly to the President—and how to keep it charged.

"The President will be calling you shortly, and he will explain to you what these packets contain. Here are the keys to the briefcase. We admonish you to keep the case locked at all times and remind you it has a built-in tracking device capable of sending its location from anywhere in the world to our office in D.C. Do you have any questions?"

"It all seems simple enough. I'm sure the President will fill me in when he calls," Jim said.

"Yes, sir, I'm certain he will. If that will be all, we will excuse ourselves and let ourselves out."

Jim walked them to the door anyway and opened it for them, all the while scratching his head and thinking what a strange job these two must have. He returned to the living room, unlocked the briefcase and started to examine the packets. He recognized them as intelligence briefing binders from work he had done for the Air Force, but he waited for his phone call with instructions before he investigated the information any further.

When the secure phone rang, Jim answered, "Mr. President?"

"Yes, Jim, I'm glad to hear you have the phone and there were no problems delivering it to you. Do you also have the briefing packets that should have been included in the brief case?"

"Yes sir, they are here," Jim answered.

"Good, these are the salient issues from the intelligence reports on the Las Vegas accident as well as the latest information concerning Orlando. I want you to review these with the eye of a pilot and let me know what you think. I don't feel as if I'm getting an honest assessment or all the information that's available from several people back here. Does that make sense to you, Jim?"

"I'm more than happy to take a look at the information and render my opinion, for what it is worth, but I sense there is something you aren't telling me, Mr. President," Jim pleaded.

"Look, here's the bottom line. My gut tells me these accidents were possibly hits against me. Almost like a shot across the bow, warning me to do or to not do something. I don't have specifics, but I'm beginning to feel like people are afraid of telling the truth about these incidents. I feel like I'm getting the runaround. Jerry Reitz is on board and he knows that you and I are talking. I trust him and I believe his intelligence is good, but it hasn't led to anything conclusive. As for the CIA, you never know what you're receiving from them. It may be spot on or it may send you off in the opposite direction. As for Jamie, I think I get told what her Muslim girlfriend wants me to hear. I don't trust her, I don't like her, and I am not in a political position at the moment to replace her. This is between you and me, but if you need help or answers, feel free to let me know, and I'll have Jerry contact you. I want you to look at this objectively, as I mentioned, but also through the prism of what I have just told you. Report back to me anytime you think it may be necessary, and don't let our friendship cloud your thinking or judgment in any way. Am I clear?"

"You are, sir. I will give you all I have," Jim answered.

"I knew you would. That's why it's in your hands now. Thank you, my friend, until we talk again."

"Of course, Mr. President, have a good day, sir."

Mari had gone out Christmas shopping, and that meant Jim would be undisturbed until she got home. For the next two hours, Jim thoroughly studied all the material from the briefing packets. It was obvious to him from the beginning, that both of these accidents were filled with strange anomalies. Most takeoff incidents occurred from failure to gain lift, and the pilots were full throttle back on the stick until the plane stalled. This Las Vegas flight seemed to Jim as if it were targeted with abject precision straight into the tower of the Patriot Hotel & Casino, but how? Jim mentally reviewed every ground accident in the history of aviation, but couldn't find one incident where a plane blew up while parked at a gate. This particular incident had all the hallmarks of a terrorist attack, but why would terrorists want to destroy the Orlando airport? There must be a reason, but whatever it might be; Jim was lacking enough evidence to come to a definite conclusion.

He could see that a thorough investigation into these recent accidents was going to take a lot of time and effort. This was the kind of work Jim loved and he had contacts all over the country that could help him formulate answers to these difficult questions.

nineteen

Vera was looking forward to joining Grace on her Paris trip. It had been a week since Grace had planted the recorder pen, and Vera was curious to find out what, if any, information had been captured on the tape. Khalid was such a mystery, and any news about him was sure to help her form a more accurate opinion. Grace walked along side of Vera, "I'm so excited to get back to Paris. I'll explain to Khalid that I have a backache and need to soak in his Jacuzzi. I'll pick up the recorder and make up some phony excuse to come back to my hotel room before we go to dinner. I can hardly wait to find out what has been going on in my absence."

The flight landed at de Gaulle on time, but Vera felt more exhausted than usual. As the last passenger deplaned, she slowly pulled her luggage and tote bag from its stowage space and adjusted her heavy purse on her shoulder. Grace sidled up beside her in the aisle and they walked off the plane together.

"I'm having dinner late tonight with Khalid—someplace wonderful, I hope. Would you care to join us?" Grace asked quietly. "I'm sure Khalid would be delighted to see you again."

"Oh Grace, I'm so beat, I think I'll just stay in tonight," Vera explained, "but thank you for offering, and give my best to Khalid. I know you haven't seen him for a week and you probably want to spend some quality one-on-one time together."

Within minutes they had their room keys and were headed for the fifth floor. "Let's meet at the coffee shop about an hour before pick up tomorrow morning. I will have listened to the tape by then and will fill you in on all the details."

"Sounds good, Grace. Have fun tonight," Vera responded, almost flippantly as she stepped into her room.

Vera slept straight through until the next morning. Her alarm clock rang, indicating she had less than an hour to meet Grace. She showered quickly, dressed in her uniform, and pulled her hair into a French braid, a style she was unaccustomed to wearing, but thought it appropriate for the flight home. She checked her watch as she fastened it to her wrist and saw she was running late. Grace was never late for anything.

Vera pushed the large brass handle on the glass door to the coffee shop and stepped inside. She carefully looked around to locate Grace and was surprised not to see her. Vera decided to text her cell phone: "I am at the place, where are you?" She waited for the chime on her phone to indicate Grace's reply. It never came. Now, she was beginning to worry. She sent off another text message, just in case Grace had overslept: "Grace, are you OK?" The crew bus pulled up in front of the hotel, ready to load in less than twenty minutes. She darted back across the street and back into the hotel lobby.

"Has anyone seen or heard from Grace?" Vera asked the entire crew as she approached the group.

Everyone shook their head emphatically no.

"Grace had better show up soon. We're about to board the bus," the captain announced as he began to roll his suitcase and flight bag toward the door.

Vera went to the front desk and asked the concierge to immediately telephone room 521. He did as he was asked. Vera could hear the loud European style ring buzzing. No answer.

"Thank you. May I have a key to room 521, please? One of our crew members is not here, and it's time for us to leave," Vera explained.

"Do you need a doctor, Madame?"

"Oh, I'm sure everything is fine," Vera reassured him with a smile, "I'll call you if we need a doctor or anything else. She's probably just getting a late start this morning."

The concierge handed Vera a key to Grace's room. Vera grabbed the last flight attendant by the shoulder as she was heading toward the bus, "Tell the captain I'm going to Grace's room to check on her and to not leave for the airport without us. We'll probably be down in a minute or two."

The flight attendant nodded and said, "I will let the captain know. You still have about eight minutes before the bus is scheduled to leave. Even if Captain Franklin is a stickler for leaving on time, he'll wait for you."

Vera appeared calm and in control on the outside, but she had a foreboding feeling in her soul that was growing with each passing minute. She was well over the fact that Grace was just late, even still, she held out a sliver of hope she would find her asleep—a problem Vera could easily deal with even if she had to dress Grace on the bus. She knocked loudly on Grace's door. No answer or sounds came from the room. She banged on the door louder this time, calling Grace's name then she slipped the key into the lock and opened the door. As Vera's eyes quickly scanned the room, she could see Grace's flight purse sitting on the table next to the small television set. Her uniform jacket was draped over the back of the desk chair. "Grace, Grace," her voice rose louder until it echoed through the hallway of the hotel. Her eyes darted towards the light emanating from the small bathroom. Protruding from the doorway was a leg. "Oh Grace, Oh my dear girl," she exclaimed, rushing toward her.

Grace was lying on the floor, fully dressed still wearing a silk cocktail dress from the night before. Her head was angled up against the bathtub. There was no sign of blood that Vera could see as she kneeled next to her and cradled Grace's head in her arms. Her skin was pasty white, her body was cold and her eyes were open still. "Oh my God, Grace, what has happened to you? What have they done to you?" Instinctively, she reached up under Graces' jawbone, hoping to find a weak pulse. There was none. Pure adrenalin surged through Vera as she stood up and quickly reached for the phone. "Hello, this is Vera Hanson. A co-worker in room 521 is dead. Send someone immediately to the room please. Call whatever authorities are necessary. And please send someone to the crew bus waiting in front of the hotel. Speak only to the captain. Tell him there is an emergency and he is needed in room 521 immediately."

"Yes, yes, I will take care of this, Madame," responded a shaken voice on the other end of the line.

Vera's hands were trembling as she set the receiver back on top of the phone. She turned to face the open door to the hallway, and stood there in silence. Captain Franklin soon appeared, filling up the doorframe.

"Vera, what happened?" he asked, stepping toward her, noticing she was visibly shaken.

"I have no idea. Grace was supposed to meet me across the street for coffee an hour before pick up. She was late, and she's never late. When I didn't see her in the lobby for pick up, I asked the concierge for a key. I found her," pointing towards the bathroom. Captain Franklin kneeled down and felt Grace's neck for a pulse. He looked up at Vera and shook his head slowly no.

A soft knock on the door was heard as the hotel manager let himself into the room. "I have called the police and they will be here in a few moments. We must not touch anything," the young man said. The Captain and Vera slowly stepped out of the bathroom.

"I have to make this flight. My crew member, Vera, will stay here and wait for the police to arrive. She will answer all their questions," the Captain told the manager. Turning to Vera, he added, "You will need to stay in Paris for as long as necessary. I will call crew scheduling and the station manager about re-crewing the flight and take care of all those responsibilities for you. You are going to need to talk with the police and I don't know how long that will take. I will let the station manager know of your situation and if you can give me your cell phone number I'll have him contact you about your hotel arrangements and your return flight. I know this is a horrible time with Christmas being in a few days, but Vera, you are the best we have and as awful as this is, I know you can do this for Grace and for the company. Don't forget to collect Grace's airline ID, passport and wings. Remember we don't want them falling into the wrong hands. I wish I could stay and do this for you, but I can't," Captain Franklin said, hoping that his words were somewhat encouraging.

Vera quickly jotted her cell number on a small tablet from the desk and handed it to the Captain. He thanked her and embraced her tightly. Vera wanted to break down and sob, but she knew she had to maintain her composure. As soon as the Captain left, Vera reached into Grace's purse and found her airline identification card and passport. She also found the tape recorder pen that Grace had borrowed, meaning she had seen Khalid. She unfastened the wings from Grace's uniform and quickly dropped them all into her own purse. Within moments, three Paris policemen arrived. "Where is the body?" They asked in broken English.

"In the bathroom, there," Vera pointed toward Grace's lifeless body.

The policemen peered into the small tiled bathroom. One of officers walked inside to check the body, another stood at the doorway, and the third remained with Vera.

"We will need to call for a coroner to declare this a death," the officer next to Vera explained. "Now what can you tell us about this unfortunate circumstance?"

"Her name is Grace Lewis. She was on my crew flying from

Paris to Detroit today. She was late for our crew pick up. I asked the front desk for a key and found her here. I checked for a pulse and noticed that her body was cold. That's when I had the hotel call for you." Vera could hear the words she was telling the officer, but it was as if someone else was speaking them. She felt shaky and light-headed. The officer noticed the color had drained from her face and pulled the desk chair toward her. "Please, Madame, sit here." He smiled gently as he held the chair with one hand and guided Vera into it with the other. The police officer sat down on the bed right in front of her and spoke in a soft voice trying to speak his best English, "May I ask you some questions?"

"Yes, I am sorry, this is just such a shock," Vera tried to explain.

"That is quite understandable," the officer continued, "can you tell me what you know about this woman? If you could write down her name, age, address, and a phone number for your airline company that we can call, that would be very helpful."

Vera did as she was asked and handed the information back to the policeman. After a brief moment of reflection, she blurted out, "How did she die?"

Calmly, the officer replied, "Oh Madame, it is much too early to know the answer to that difficult question. We will keep close to you and inform you when we know a better answer." The coroner and a crew with a stretcher entered the room. The officer spoke to the gentleman that Vera assumed was the coroner in their native French. The two men with the stretcher stood at attention in the hallway, waiting for their signal to remove the body.

"We would like to have you accompany us to our station nearby to help with our report, if you can bring your identification, it will only take a few minutes of your time," the officer sitting next to Vera explained. "We do not suspect you of any crime, we just need to finish the paperwork and include your information.

I hope you understand. I know this is a difficult experience for you."

"Yes, I can do that," Vera agreed as she steadied her purse strap on her shoulder and waited to be escorted by the officers.

At the police station she offered her Washington State driver's license, her U.S. passport, along with her airline ID which were all copied and immediately returned to her. The younger of the two officers explained that the coroner should be doing his examination of the body shortly and that would provide some answers. He offered her a business card with the phone number to the information officer, should she wish to ask any questions. He also handed her his business card with his cell phone number hand written on the back side. "This is my cell phone number. Should you remember any details that you feel we should know, please feel free to contact me." He smiled warmly, which helped Vera feel more at ease. She had already decided not to say anything about Khalid unless the report coming back indicated some kind of foul play. If that were the case, she suspected, they would be coming back to her with more questions.

"I will do that, sir," Vera agreed, taking the card and sliding it into an inside compartment of her purse, next to her airline ID.

"We can take you back to the hotel now, if you would like," the officer told her, as he held out his arm and pointed toward the door.

The stark reality of Grace's death weighed heavily upon her entire being. She suddenly felt trapped in this foreign country and imprisoned by her thoughts and fears.

twenty

The hotel manager greeted Vera in the lobby and escorted her to his private office. "Madame, I have received a call from the police department, they feel a need to have you here in Paris should they find the cause of Miss Grace's death. I have arranged for you to have a very private executive penthouse suite while you are here." He handed Vera a small gold-embossed envelope containing keys to the room. "We are very sorry for this most unfortunate incident, and I know you must be very upset. Your friend Grace was the hotel staff's favorite crew member. We looked forward to her stays with us and always appreciated how very kind and generous she was with all of the employees. The news of her death has sent the entire staff into a deep sadness. That is why we want you to stay in this very nice room. It is one of our very finest, most beautiful rooms, with a lovely view."

Vera felt a lump forming in her throat and her eyes began to fill with tears as she accepted the manager's kind words about her friend. "Thank you, sir, I appreciate your kindness," was all she was able to mutter before her voice grew weak and the tears began to flow freely down both cheeks.

The hotel manager quickly jumped to his feet to assist Vera with the door. He waved his hand to the bellman to bring Vera's luggage. "Please assist Ms. Hanson to her room, and make certain that everything is just perfect for her."

The bellman took the envelope from Vera's hand and motioned for her to follow him. When they arrived at her room, the bellman opened the double doors and stretched his arms wide to present Vera the finest the hotel had to offer. Vera stood stunned by the size and magnificence of the suite as she followed the bellman inside. Her eyes were drawn toward the living room decorated with gorgeous cobalt blue silk wallpaper, the walls accented with stunning classical artwork surrounded by beautiful ornate gold frames. The furniture was an elegant carved mahogany which added to the luxurious splendor of the room. Vera was speechless. The bellman pulled open the heavy brocade drapes to reveal a sweeping panoramic view of Paris. Below was Opera Square and just beyond was the neighboring Opera Garnier. The hotel had sent a large fruit basket complete with a bottle of wine. The bathroom was filled with a beautiful bouquet of red and white roses mixed with baby's breath and ferns. On the nightstand next to the bed was a box of chocolates with a single red rosebud in a dainty cut-crystal bud vase. The king-size bed was turned down, revealing white Egyptian cotton sheets surrounded by a gorgeous dark blue raw silk duvet.

Vera smiled and thanked the bellman, offering him all the Euros she had in her pocket. He politely refused any form of gratuity. She nodded slightly in his direction and he bid her adieu.

The silence that filled the suite began to magnify her sense of loss. She sat on the beautiful brocade sofa and stared out over the city skyline, sorrow followed by anger, chased by fear, and then abandoned to loneliness left Vera confused and distraught. She tried to focus her thinking away from the memory of Grace's lifeless body on the floor. She shuttered and closed her eyes, hoping to drive the image from her mind. She buried her head in her hands and pressed tightly against the bridge of her nose hoping to push the picture into oblivion. Sadness overwhelmed her and she knew she needed to cry in an attempt to wash it all away. She flung herself on the bed and sobbed, letting her body heave until she was exhausted and fell asleep.

Several hours later she decided to venture out of her room in hopes of finding something to assuage the feeling of hunger that had overtaken her sorrow. She had not heard back from the police and hoped that was a good sign. She bundled up as best she could, knowing how damp and cold the morning hours had been. The quaint Parisian shop windows were beautifully decorated. The multi-colored Christmas lights that reflected off the wet cobblestones reminded her of a huge kaleidoscope. She was weak, but it felt good to be outside in the fresh air. She inhaled deeply as she stood at a corner trying to decide which direction she should take. Of course it really didn't matter, as long as she could find her way back to the hotel. She kept her eyes open for an inviting little wine bar or cafe along the way that might offer an open-faced sandwich or a tasty hors d'oeuvre.

She stood looking through the window of a chocolatier's shop eyeing the delectable sweets when she had an uncomfortable feeling that someone was watching her. She quickly turned around, but only the Parisians in the streets attending to their business or walking to their destinations came into view. There was nobody out of the ordinary. She was about to step into the little shop when something or someone—darting into a narrow ally—caught her eye. It was a flash of black—nothing definitive, yet it sent a shiver of fear through her entire body. Why would someone be following me, she wondered? An image of Grace's lifeless body returned to her mind. At the same time, almost-unconscious words she uttered when she found Grace—"what have they done to you"—returned to her memory. For the first time, she felt she was in danger. She darted into the chocolate shop and tried to look as inconspicuous as she could in her dark red raincoat.

"May I help you, Madame?" A young girl asked from behind the counter.

"No merci, Je suis waiting por mon amiee," she replied, trying to blend in as best she could with her limited French vocabulary, but nervously keeping an eye on the window in case the person in black passed by or, worse, came into the shop.

After several minutes of waiting, she purchased a small box of chocolates from the counter, handed the young girl a Euro bill from her wallet and didn't wait for the change. "Merci Madam," said the young, girl waving some money in Vera's direction, but it was too late. Vera had already dashed across the street and was making her way back to the hotel. Her pace was now brisk. The quaint little shops she passed held no interest for her. From time to time she would glance back over her shoulder and scan both sides of the street to see if anyone was following her. When she could see the black wrought-iron Juliet balconies of the hotel, the fear inside her began to subside, but she did not slow her pace. She checked over her shoulder one more time. To her horror, she saw a man, maybe only a hundred feet behind her, on the same side of the street dressed entirely in black.

Instinctively she froze then quickly turned as if to look into the window of a nearby shop. She could see in her peripheral vision that the man had also stopped and was looking into a shop window by where he stood. A myriad of questions surrounding this man's identity and purpose pummeled her thoughts. Who could he be? Was he one of Khalid's friends? Had he been sent to kill her? She turned and walked as fast as she could towards the hotel, crossing the street more than once hoping to attract some attention and thinking that might add to her security. As she flew through the revolving door of the hotel, she collapsed in the first chair she saw in the lobby. The manager, who was just leaving for the day, witnessed Vera's unusual entrance and came over to her and asked, "Is everything alright, Madame?"

Feeling somewhat safe now and thinking that perhaps she had embellished her fear to its paranoid peak, she sighed again then answered, "I have been out walking and I think I may be just a little hungry that's all."

"Oh Madame, that I can do something about. Our lobby café has some of the finest food in all of Paris. Come with me," he said, escorting her by the arm to the café.

"Jean-Pierre, this is Madame Hanson," he said to the maître d. "She is staying in our penthouse suite; please see to it that all her needs are taken care of while she dines with you."

Vera whispered, "Merci, merci," to the hotel manager and followed the maître d to a table not far from the bar. He started to pull back a chair for her, but she immediately pointed to another, one from which she could see everyone who entered the café. The fear in her had subsided, but her cautious nature demanded her vigilance.

A waiter presented her with a menu, none of which she could adequately read in French. Her appetite had returned, and with it a painful reminder that she had been neglecting it all day. She ordered a glass of merlot and a plate of assorted hors d'oeuvres, but kept her eyes on the café entrance as she sipped her wine and waited for her entree to be delivered.

Just as the waiter presented her meal, a lone man dressed entirely in black entered the café and stood waiting to be seated. All of the fear she had felt outside suddenly came rushing back. Was this the same man who had been following her? Vera stared at him, but hadn't had a good enough look at him to tell if this was he. The maître d began to escort the gentleman to a table on the other side of the room. Halfway through the café, the man stopped, pointed, and whispered something. They both turned in Vera's direction and walked to a booth directly behind her, where the man asked to be seated.

Her heart began to pound and fear overtook her. She stood up from her booth, approached the maître d and insisted that her meal be sent to her room along with the rest of her bottle of merlot. Vera's heart was still racing as she unlocked the door to her room. Who was that man? Was he the same man from the street? How did he know who she was? Could he have murdered Grace? Her hands were still shaking when the doorbell to her suite rang. "Madame, room service." She understood the words clearly, nevertheless, she checked through the viewer before she unlocked the door.

twenty-one

"It won't be long until the Redskin's game will be on, sir. Would you like some lunch in here or will you come down to the kitchen?" Mike asked, as he stood at the open door to the President's study.

"That's a tough choice, Michael my man. Where did I have lunch last Sunday when the Skins lost?" The President joked.

"I believe in the kitchen, sir. You were taunting the staff, who were all Giant's fans and wagering days off before Christmas if the Giants won, which explains why you have only a skeleton staff until after Thursday, sir," Mike answered, happy to see the President's spirits so high.

President Sherman laughed. "Now remember, Mike, they were going to get those days off anyway. It would be rude of me to remain in the White House over Christmas and keep a full staff here just for my benefit, when they should be spending time with their families. That's our little secret, right? As for lunch, hmm, the Redskins need to win this last game of the season against the Cowboys to make the playoffs, so I'd better have you bring me a turkey sandwich up here. And of course, you are more than welcome to join me. The Cowboys need all the fans they can get to win this one."

"But I'm an Eagles fan, sir."

"Eagles Smeagles, they've been out of the playoff picture since October. Come join me this afternoon and I won't make you wear a maroon sweatshirt," the President said, laughing.

"Very well, Mr. President."

"Or a feather," the President shouted, but Mike was too far down the hall and didn't hear him.

Joel became an avid football fan once his college playing days were over. When he moved to Washington, D.C., and became involved in politics, he felt it best to sacrifice his public attendance at games and rarely attended one in person at Fed Ex Field. When he became President, that rule was even more strictly enforced. However, when he was home alone on weekends and not involved in pressing matters of state, he would indulge his former passion and watch a game or two on television.

He glanced down at his watch and took note that the game would begin in about thirty minutes, just enough time to see what was happening on Facebook. Since the President used Facebook only to glean information, rather than to disseminate it, rarely did he ever have notifications to check. He scanned his news feed and saw a status update from Vera Hanson which read, "Stuck in Paris for Christmas."

"How tough could that be?" The President thought to himself. He remembered a time when he and Mica had vacationed in Paris at Christmastime. It was heavenly—the lights, the sounds, the food, the wine. "How bad could Christmas in Paris be?" He bravely typed on her thread.

Vera was surprised to see a comment from her new friend Stan the Man. She debated if she should even answer or just let the comment slide—hoping some of her real friends would comment, she could easily ignore him. She waited a few minutes, but her curiosity overrode her common sense and she typed back, "Oh, if you only knew."

Joel smiled to himself, because he did know. He knew Vera was in Paris and he knew why she couldn't leave, but he wasn't about to tell her. "It must be about dinnertime there. Enjoy the wine and the music," he quickly replied.

Vera chuckled to herself, yeah I have my dinner next to me

and I'm afraid to leave my room, as for the music, I'm not exactly in the mood to sing. She typed back, "Well I can't go into it, but I'm kind of like a prisoner here, so mood music and wine are out of the question."

"Maybe tomorrow you'll feel better and you can take in the Louvre, have lunch at the Eiffel Tower, or hang out in a boulangerie sipping coffee and eating pastries," the President typed back, hoping he had spelled everything correctly.

The cynicism wasn't lost on Vera and she replied, "Mr. Stan the Man, I must go. I'm trying to make contact with friends in the States to take care of my dog and some other things while I'm stuck here for who knows how long. It was nice chatting with you." And then without thinking she added, "Perhaps we can chat again."

Immediately, Joel typed back, "Yes that would be nice, I'd like that." Just as he hit the return key, Mike appeared with the sandwiches, wearing an Eagles sweatshirt and a smile. He turned on the large flat-screen television just as the game was about to kickoff.

twenty-two

Around mid-morning, Vera decided to enjoy a luxurious bath and had just about filled the spacious marble tub when she heard the doorbell to her suite ring. She peeked through the privacy hole in the door. She hadn't ordered room service. She couldn't imagine who would be there; she knew that if the hotel management had something for her they would have called first. She saw a young woman dressed in a black and gold uniform just about to reach out for the doorbell again. Before she could, Vera opened the door a crack, leaving the security chain in place, and in her best French greeted the woman with, "Bonjour."

"Ah, bonjour Madame, j'ai des fleurs por vous," she replied, pointing to what looked like a large box of flowers. Vera knew just enough French to recognize the word flowers; of course the picture on the box may have helped. She unlocked the chain and motioned for the girl to enter. She was presented with a dozen red long stemmed roses. She searched for a card wondering who could have sent them. Down towards the bottom of the box was a card that had obviously come loose from the bouquet. She picked it up and read, "Paris should be fun." There was no name on either side. Vera looked at the girl with a puzzled look on her face. "From whom?" She asked.

"Je ne sais pas," replied the girl shrugging her shoulders.

It was apparent between Vera's poor French and the young woman's inability to speak English that they were not going to solve the mystery. Vera tipped the girl and with a slight curtsey and a "merci, Madame," the girl was on her way. Vera stood holding the box of roses in her arms admiring their beauty, but totally confounded as to who could have sent them. She replaced the flowers in the vase that had been in her suite when she checked in and arranged the roses so they displayed beautifully. She set them on the desk next to her laptop and was thrilled even though their origin was unknown.

Vera spent what little was left of the morning sending emails to friends explaining her unusual circumstances, without going into detail about Grace's death. She made a special request of her neighbor Jenny to pick up Kelli at the kennel on Wednesday, the day before Christmas, and asked if she would keep her until she returned home. It was hard to feel like a prisoner in these luxurious surroundings, but it was her inability to make any plans or to keep a schedule that was causing her the greatest amount of consternation. She decided to try to make the most of her situation. Vera called down to the concierge desk and asked about the possibility of visiting the Louvre on such short notice.

"Ordinarily, Madame, visiting the Louvre requires a few days of preparation, but it so happens that if you can be ready to leave the hotel in thirty minutes, we have a VIP pass that is available to you as our special guest. Our limousine leaves promptly at one o'clock. Shall I count on your presence, Ms. Hanson?"

"Oh yes, I will be there at one, merci beaucoup," Vera replied.

She didn't have much of a wardrobe with her, since she was expecting only a one-day layover in Paris. She checked out the window and could see that the weather was similar to the day before—cold, damp, and a little on the windy side. The only change of clothes she had was a pair of dark slacks, a cashmere sweater and her red uniform raincoat. "Good enough," she thought and dressed quickly. The concierge was happy to greet her and handed her the special pass in a gold envelope, along with an umbrella emblazoned with the hotel logo.

As she waited inside the lobby for the limousine, she thought she saw the same man dressed in black standing across the street staring at the hotel. She wasn't quite as gripped with fear as she had been the day before, but seeing him again caused her to question, at first her own sanity and then her safety. She ducked out of view, standing behind a pillar in the lobby, but in a position that allowed her to see him clearly. She wanted to try to memorize his features to make certain she could identify him in case they were to meet up again. She peered from behind her post and was surprised to see him taking pictures of the hotel— or perhaps he was he taking pictures of her. Fortunately, the limousine pulled up at that moment. The doorman opened the door to the backseat and beckoned for Vera to enter. As she was about to step inside, her eyes met directly with those of the man in black. He had crossed the street and was staring at her. His eyes were dark, as was his complexion. He had an unforgettable, not-quite-straight part in his wavy black hair. Vera wanted to look away, but her stubbornness and loyalty to Grace forced her to stare. The memory was now permanently etched; she would never forget his face. As the door to the limousine closed behind her, Vera sank back into the comfort of the Corinthian leather seats, wondering what the hell this man wanted.

Later that evening, Vera posted a photograph on Facebook of the Mona Lisa with the caption: Still stuck in Paris, but Lisa and I are having a blast. Several of her friends who were aware of her predicament commented on her thread and tried to help her feel better about being stuck in Paris by offering up suggestions of things she should do or places she should visit. Her neighbor Jenny had received her email and had private-messaged her that she would be delighted to pick up Kelli and keep her until Vera got home.

Back in Washington, the House and the Senate were putting the finishing touches on a lame duck session and hoping to wrap things up before Christmas, thereby putting an end to the 113th

Congress. Not much had changed in the general election of 2014. A few Senate seats changed hands as a result of retiring Senators, and the President's party picked up four seats in the House, increasing its margin to a total of 27 seats. The President spent most of his time on the phone trying to persuade recalcitrant Senators of the importance of the defense authorization act of 2014. It was the last major piece of legislation that needed to be passed before Congress could adjourn. By late Monday afternoon, he had the last vote secured, and with any luck, the following day he could sign the bill into law and everyone could go home for the holidays. Washington D.C., at Christmas was like a college town. Everyone disappeared to various parts of the country, and only the locals remained to attend to the day-to-day business of running the city. In the political class, if you were left alone in Washington for the holidays, you were by definition lonely. President Sherman definitely fit that description. Life wasn't the same without Mica. He had access to the world's most sophisticated private jet, he could go anywhere in the world he wanted for the holidays, but without her, his world seemed empty and the holidays seemed wearisome. It was much easier for him when there was work to be done and presidential duties to perform. At those times, when the pressure of his position subsided, the stillness of his reality would settle in his heart and begin to drag him through all the stops on the road to despair.

After dinner he worked on his Christmas message to the nation, something his predecessor had neglected, which left most of the country feeling overlooked and unimportant. This was President Sherman's first opportunity to share a message of hope and peace to the country. He wanted to establish the correct tone and then build upon it to affirm to the nation that his life was built upon Christian ideals and that his Administration would govern based on principles of truth and honesty. Such a message would be cathartic for him, and he hoped it would serve the same purpose for the nation.

Before he turned his computer off for the night, he clicked over to Facebook to see what Vera was doing. He didn't expect to find her online, since it was early morning in Paris, but if she had posted anything on her wall, he could catch up with her that way. He smiled when he saw her comment about the Louvre and how she and Lisa had hit the town. He clicked on the comment button and wrote, "Nice to see you out and about, it looks like Paris is no longer winning."

To his surprise, a 'like' instantly appeared on his comment. Vera quickly responded by typing: "I'm a tough bird, not even a Parisian jail can clip my wings."

Joel smiled, thinking how much like Mica Vera's comment was. He followed up with, "Any word on your sentence?"

"Nope, but I sure would love to get home to my doggie before Christmas."

"I'll have to see what I can do about that. Dogs should have their mom's home for Christmas."

Vera laughed and then typed, "LOL, what can you possibly do?"

Joel knew he had to be careful, nevertheless he typed, "Well I get along well with dogs and French cops. Maybe I can give them both a biscuit and they'll set you free. BTW, what kind of dog do you have?"

"A golden named Kelli, sweetest dog in the world, who by now is probably thinking I have abandoned her."

"I'm turning in for the night. I'll send biscuits to the cops tomorrow. Let me know if it springs you."

"LOL, alright I will, goodnight, Stan the Man."

"Goodnight, Ms. Hanson."

twenty-three

Vera had a rather restless night and had not fallen asleep until the early hours of the morning. Just before noon the phone rang, waking her up. Thinking it was the hotel management and assuming whatever they wanted could wait, she rolled over and hoped that the distinctive European ring would soon stop. The ring continued until out of exasperation she reached for the phone and said, "Hello."

"Madame Hanson, this is Inspector Killy at the police station. How are you this fine morning?"

"Tired and wishing I were home in my own bed," responded a not-quite-awake Vera.

"Well, that will not be possible for some time, Madame. You see, the autopsy report has been returned on your friend Grace Lewis, and it is clear that, due to the massive blunt-force trauma she sustained, she was murdered," the inspector emotionlessly explained.

His words shocked Vera, but her heart instinctively knew what she was hearing was indeed true. From the moment she held Grace's lifeless body in her arms, Vera knew that she had been murdered.

"It is also clear to us that the murder happened elsewhere, because the coroner has marked the time of death around midnight and Grace's room was not entered until almost three that morning. Her body had been staged to look like a fall, but we know differently. Can you tell us where Grace was that night or whom she was with that evening?" The inspector asked.

Vera's fears now needed to be verbalized. "I don't know where she was, but I know she was with Khalid, whose last name I do not recall. She had been seeing him for the past several months when she came to Paris."

"Yes, we are aware of Khalid and have been keeping an eye on him for some time now. He can be a very dangerous man, Madame. I would advise you to keep your distance," warned Inspector Killy. "This will require some serious investigation, and therefore you will have to remain in France for the foreseeable future. We will need your help and assistance as we investigate this murder. You are free to come and go as you please, but you cannot leave Paris just yet."

"Okay," she said. She waited for the inspector to hang up the phone and then slammed down the receiver with all the force she could muster. The situation was becoming intolerable: She was devastated by Grace's death, frustrated by the unknown, and angry at being trapped by the Paris police. She threw on some clothes and headed down to the hotel's café, hoping to rectify the only thing she had some control over—her hunger.

She was able to fill her stomach, but it didn't dissipate any of the anger she was feeling toward everything in her life. She gasped as she saw the man in black sitting in a chair right by the elevator. Her initial response was fleeting and she blurted out, "Get a new outfit, you look drab in black." As she rode up the elevator, Vera couldn't believe what she had said to the man, who may have been sent to kill her. Her anger had overtaken her fear, and nothing seemed to matter anymore.

Vera was even mad at Stan the Man, and when she returned to her room, she felt it necessary to give him a piece of her mind. She opened her Facebook and sent him a private message, "Your dog biscuit trick on the police was a major choke. According to them, I'm going to be here awhile. Who knows, I may even be here to celebrate Bastille Day with them in July." She didn't bother to wait for a reply.

President Sherman delivered his Christmas message to the nation that afternoon. The initial response was overwhelmingly favorable. In less than a year, he was developing a connection to the people and an ability to communicate much like Ronald Reagan had. The nation trusted him and looked to him for leadership. When his speech was concluded, he retired to the study and began reviewing the Christmas messages from world leaders. The message from the President of France caught his attention and reminded him of the plight of that poor woman stuck in Paris. He stopped his reading and checked in with Facebook. After reading her private message, he phoned the Secretary of State.

Vera spent another restless night and again was awakened by her phone ringing, only this time it was hotel management. "Madame Hanson, I have such wonderful news for you. The police called this morning and you have been released to go home. Your airline has made arrangements for you to fly to Seattle this afternoon. I'm very happy for you, Madame. We shall miss you."

Vera shrieked with excitement. She would be home for Christmas after all. She emailed Jenny the great news and then sent Stan a message, "Woof, woof going home in a few hours. It will indeed be a Merry Christmas."

twenty-four

When the plane finally touched down at Sea-Tac, no one was happier than Vera. Her ordeal was finally over! She could spend what was left of Christmas with Kelli in peace and quiet at home. She called her Jenny to announce she was back and to ask if she could come by to pick up Kelli. The dog was so excited to see her that she literally pushed Jenny out of the doorway when she heard Vera's voice and wouldn't leave her side for the rest of the evening. After dinner, the two women sat around the fire, each with a glass of wine, while Vera told Jenny all about Grace, the murder, the man in black, the hotel suite, and the mysterious box of red roses. She chose to keep the information about Khalid to a minimum because his mysterious nature stirred an anxiety within her that she was not prepared to confront.

It was nice to be home and back in her normal routine with Kelli. The weather was unseasonably warm and dry for Seattle, which made the walk along Alki beach unusually pleasant for a late-December morning. The seagulls circled high above Kelli, diving and soaring ahead of her as she ran along the beach. The familiar sounds of the ferryboats and large ships blowing their horns near the docks grounded Vera. Their ritual walk to Starbucks reinforced her feeling of security, and the barista's greeting her by name as she entered the establishment only added to Vera's sense of well-being.

"Merry Christmas," Vera responded to the young woman behind the counter.

When her coffee was ready, she turned to find her favorite

chair by the fireplace and noticed someone already sitting there. "Could it be?" She questioned. "No, that's not possible." Nevertheless, she stepped closer to get a better look. She couldn't see his face, but she was almost positive it was the man who had followed her through Paris. She turned quickly, then dashed out the door and unhooked Kelli from her post. Vera couldn't help notice her hands shaking; she felt her heart begin to beat faster and her mind convinced her that he was indeed that man. She wanted to get away from him as fast as she could, but she wasn't sure if it was safe to go home. Obviously he knew where she lived. Perhaps she would be safe at Jenny's house. She shortened Kelli's leash and darted into the street.

Terror was returning, she was no longer thinking clearly, she couldn't decide which way to turn. When she looked to her right, she could see a large black SUV barreling toward her. She froze and held Kelli close to her. The vehicle had enough time to see them and move out of the way, but instead it seemed to aim directly toward them and accelerated. Vera was sure both she and Kelli were about to be hit and let out a horrifying scream. Then, at the very last moment, the black vehicle swerved and missed Vera. She heard a loud thud as it passed and a sharp yelp come from Kelli. She knelt down beside the dog to feel for broken bones. Vera felt a rush of emotions fill her as she burst into tears. Within minutes the police had arrived and were asking her questions. She told the officers that she lived a few blocks down the street and asked if they could help her get Kelli home. One officer gently lifted the dog into the back of the patrol car and then invited Vera to sit in the passenger seat. When they arrived at her house, Vera realized she hadn't brought her purse with her. She asked the officer if he could stay with the dog while she ran into the house to get her purse and to open the garage door. He was more than happy to oblige. As Vera's hand reached to open the backdoor, she noticed the window was broken. The panic inside her ratcheted up as her heart began to pound again. The door had been left unlocked, she couldn't understand who would be at her backdoor and why would someone break the window? She quickly grabbed her purse and opened the garage door. Greeting the officer, she yelled out, "You're going to have to come inside for a minute, I'm afraid someone has broken my back window, and they could still be inside the house."

The officer immediately rushed in through the open garage door. "Can you show me what happened?" He reached for his radio, informed his partner of Vera's address and requested his presence immediately, thinking he might need backup. He inspected the broken window and scanned the kitchen area, checking for anything unusual.

"Do you think there might be someone here?" Vera whispered loudly as she took note of her television set still sitting on the counter. "Nothing looks like it's been touched here. This just doesn't make any sense, officer. The backdoor was unlocked. I never lock it when we run over to Starbucks. Why would someone break into a house when they could have simply opened the door?"

"Not sure, ma'am, as soon as my partner gets here, we'll go through room by room to make certain no intruders are here. Then you can take a look to see if you notice anything missing," the officer informed her.

Vera was worried more about Kelli than what might have happened inside the house. "I'm going to call my neighbor and have her come over. She'll be here in a moment. If anyone was in my driveway, she might have noticed." Vera called Jenny and told her what had occurred.

Jenny pulled up in front of Vera's house and rushed over to give her a hug.

"Jenny, I've got to get out of here. I have got to get Kelli to the vet. Someone almost killed us crossing the street and hit Kelli.

I know this sounds crazy, but I think the man in black was in my favorite chair at Starbuck's this morning. Someone is after me and I think they're trying to kill me." Vera was filling in her friend as the second police officer came through the garage door.

The officers searched through the house and couldn't find anything broken or anyone hiding in any of the rooms. They requested Vera take a closer look later and advised her to call them if she found anything of value missing.

She took her friend into the garage so the officers couldn't hear, "Jenny, when I get back from the vet's office, I'm heading to the beach house. I don't want anyone to know, not even the Seattle police. Please stay here with them and answer all their questions, then pack me a couple of suitcases full of clothes. I have no idea how long I'll be gone, but I'm not coming back until I'm safe and have gotten to the bottom of this. If you need to contact me, use Facebook or text my cell phone."

Vera started the car, threw it in reverse, and backed onto the lawn around the patrol car to get to the street, while Jenny went inside to deal with the officers. The police were not happy to learn that Vera had left and was no longer available to answer their questions about either incident. They dusted for fingerprints and left Jenny with a copy of the incident reports.

Jenny had just finished packing two suitcases when she heard Vera's car pull into the garage. She ran downstairs, "How's Kelli? Is anything broken?"

"Thank goodness she'll be okay," Vera replied. "They took X-rays and there were no broken bones, but she has some deep contusions. The vet said she would be sore, so no exercise at all for her until she feels better. He gave her some pain medication, but all in all she is very fortunate to be alive. I guess I am as well. I see you have my suitcases packed, is there anything left in my closet?"

Jenny laughed, "Well, I had no idea how long you'd be at the beach, so I packed everything you might need for a long stay."

"I certainly appreciate all you've done for me this morning, Jenny. You're such a good friend. If you'll please lock up the house for me, I want to get Kelli down to the beach before dark."

twenty-five

The drive to the beach house was always enjoyable for Vera. Once she was past the traffic in and around Tacoma, the roads became less crowded and the view of the Puget Sound became more prevalent. The closer she came to the ocean, the more its peacefulness began to calm her frazzled nerves. As she pulled up to the house, she could feel a sense of serenity wash over her.

Kelli seemed to enjoy the ride as well. Even though she was safely ensconced on a memory foam dog bed in the back of the SUV, she seemed to know where they were going. Vera helped her out of the back and into the house. Whatever pain Kelli had been feeling was eased by the medication and the sheer joy of being at the beach.

Vera lit a fire in the river rock fireplace in the family room and brought the dog bed in for Kelli. The rhythmic sounds of the waves on the shoreline played their music which resonated inside her. It felt good to breathe the salt air and to feel a sense of peace finally returning to her world. As night fell, Vera didn't want Kelli to have to climb the stairs to the master bedroom, so she decided to make a bed for herself on the couch. She opened the linen closet at the end of the hall and saw the blankets she wanted on the top shelf. She jumped up and grabbed at the bottom blanket, when she did, a large manila envelope protruded from the bottom of the pile. Suddenly, her attention shifted from blankets to what was inside the envelope. She reached up and pulled it down. It was thick in the middle with Jeff's handwriting on the front; written neatly on a label that read: 'New York Photos.'

She had never seen this envelope before and couldn't imagine why Jeff would have hidden it under a stack of blankets. As she started to back away from the closet, the bedding tumbled out onto the floor nearly hitting her as it fell. She paid it no heed, being far more intrigued by what was in the envelope. She sat down at the kitchen table and poured the contents out. There were mostly pictures that looked like some kind of demolition. On the backsides were words written in Spanish. She examined each photo and determined that they were pictures of the 9/11 devastation. There were nearly a hundred photographs in crystal clear detail showing angles and places never shown by the media. She looked at the papers that accompanied the photographs and couldn't quite make out what they meant. There were chemical formulas that referred back to the numbers on the photographs. She set them aside and tried to figure out exactly what it was she was looking at and why Jeff would have had them hidden.

What was Jeff into? She wondered. She knew he didn't speak fluent Spanish, but she did remember that shortly before his accident, he had gone to Argentina for a few weeks. His explanation was that he was investigating some kind of conspiracy, and a gentleman there had some evidence he was willing to share. Vera had never paid much attention to the conspiracies Jeff was always researching. They didn't interest her in the least, and he was polite enough not to discuss them with her. Occasionally, he would mention some obscure fact about something, but she just ignored him and he was happy to have the freedom to pursue his own interests. Was he into that 9/11 'truther' nonsense? There were a lot of things that didn't make sense to her about 9/11, particularly in light of her airline training. They were all too painful to deal with and she had chosen to not broach the subject of what really did happen that day. Jeff had never mentioned anything about researching 9/11. Now, right before her eyes, she had evidence that he was deep into that investigation and it frightened her, though she wasn't sure why. Did Jeff have information that no one else had? Could that be what the man in black was looking for? She put the photographs and papers back into the envelope, then tucked it into her tote bag. Vera returned to gather up the blankets in the hallway. It was time for bed and a good night's sleep would be welcomed.

She woke to Kelli softly licking her hand. "You must be feeling better this morning, girl. Do you want to go outside?" Kelli walked over to the backdoor, slightly favoring her sore leg. "Well, it doesn't look like you'll be chasing the seagulls today, which will make them happy." Vera opened the door for the dog who immediately disappeared over a sand dune. She hadn't slept well. It might have been the couch, but more than likely her restlessness was due to the discovery of Jeff's photographs of the terror attacks.

It seemed like Kelli had been gone longer than usual. Vera searched out the large picture window and couldn't see the dog, but she did notice a man standing on the beach with some type of dish-shaped device pointing in her direction. She hurried upstairs to the bedroom and focused the large antique brass telescope toward the man. Sure enough, he was pointing a parabolic dish, designed to listen from a distance, directly at her house. The peacefulness of the ocean had been breached, she knew she had to run, but to where? She hurried downstairs, opened the backdoor and called out to the Kelli. Hearing her name, she came hobbling. Vera poured some dog food into a dish, grabbed the water bowl, and whispered to Kelli, "Wanna go for a ride?" Immediately, Kelli stood at the garage door. Vera let her into the garage, helped her into the back of the Mercedes, and then returned to the kitchen to grab her purse and tote bag. Fortunately, her suitcases were still in the vehicle. She opened the garage door and quickly backed into the street. Where to go, she thought, but before she had time to make a decision, a black SUV appeared in her rear-view mirror.

"Damn."

She stepped on the accelerator and tried to outrun the SUV, but it was gaining on her. She signaled left, but turned right. That didn't matter; it was right behind her. She knew of an alley up ahead she could turn into. The streets were narrow and the side streets were not paved. She turned quickly onto one of the dirt roads and accelerated to create as much dust as possible, then took a sharp right into the alley and stopped. Kelli began to bark knowing something was wrong. "It's okay girl, we'll be alright," Vera called back to her.

The black SUV missed the alley turn and Vera could see it pass by slowly. She honked her horn drawing its attention to her, knowing it would back up and come after her. What the unknown driver didn't know was that the yard she was stopped in front of could be driven over and she could double back onto the street. She made her move and could see the SUV turn into the alley. She managed to get back onto the main street. She turned up a street near her house that looped onto an old logging road then back down onto the highway. She took the corners as fast as she could, all the while trying to comfort Kelli with her words, knowing her food and water were now all over the back of the vehicle. Once on the highway, she headed north towards Seattle as fast as she could. Her only thought now was to call Jim Bowman. She trusted him. She desperately needed help, and he was the only one she could think of that could offer any.

She dialed his number from her cell phone, constantly searching the rear-view mirror for any sign of her pursuer. The phone rang and rang then went to voice.

"Damn, Jim, I need you," she said under her breath.

A few minutes later, she tried again. "Hello," answered Mari's sweet voice on the other end.

"Mari, this is Vera. I'm in danger and I need Jim's help. Is he there?"

"Yes, he's right here, let me get him for you. We were just on the back deck shoveling off the snow."

"Vera, what's the matter? How are you in danger? What can I do?" Jim's calming voice spoke into the phone.

"I'm so glad you're there. You're the only one I could think of to call. I can't explain it all over the phone. It's a long, complicated story that began in Paris about a week ago. I'm being followed—actually, I'm being chased, but I've lost them for the time being. Is there any way I can come and stay with you for a while up at your cabin?"

"Of course you can come here, Vera. You know the way, right?"

"Yes, I can punch it into the GPS, but I think I remember how to get there."

"No, don't do that. After we hang up I want you to turn off the GPS and turn off your cell phone and take the battery out. If they're following you, they can track you by either the phone or the GPS unit. Do you understand?"

"Yes, I think so, Jim, but who are these people? They tried to kill me yesterday and hit Kelli instead. Oh, I have Kelli with me. Is it alright to bring her along?"

"Of course it is. We'll be waiting for you."

"Okay, I'm doing what you told me—hanging up and turning off all my electronic devices."

twenty-six

Jim was waiting in the driveway when Vera arrived. He directed her to back her vehicle in underneath the carport so that if it snowed she could pull straight out in four-wheel drive. "Just a little precaution we take around here in the winter. Glad to see you made it here safe and sound. Where's Kelli?"

"She's in the back and not feeling too well. I told you she was hit by a car yesterday and then with all the excitement trying to leave the beach house, I'm sure she still has her head down and is afraid to look up. Can you help me lift her out of the back?"

Jim opened the tailgate and reached out to scratch Kelli behind the ears. "It's good to see you, girl." Kelli wagged her tail, recognizing Jim's voice. "Is she able to walk on her own or should I carry her into the house?" He asked.

"If you just help her down, I think she can walk okay. She probably needs to go potty anyway."

Jim set Kelli down, and then gave Vera a hug. "I'm very glad you're here. We have a lot to talk about you and me. Perhaps it should have happened earlier—maybe years earlier. Here, let me help you with your bags." He reached into the back seat and grabbed both of Vera's suitcases, then motioned her toward the house.

Mari was waiting for them in the doorway. "I'm so happy to have you come see us, Vera, and you too, Kelli. Jim filled me in on some of your adventures." She raised her eyebrow and added, "We'll take good care of you both." She opened her arms and embraced Vera warmly.

Kelli immediately staked out a spot near the fire and laid down while Jim and Vera got comfortable in the living room. Mari headed off to the kitchen to start a fresh pot of coffee. "Now Vera," Jim began, "what's been going on with you and why is your life in danger?"

Vera had a feeling that Jim knew more than he was letting on. They had been friends for such a long time that it was impossible to play coy when something really mattered. She knew Jim cared about her and was protective of her like a big brother.

Mari brought the coffee in on a tray with a selection of homemade Christmas cookies then sat down beside Jim. Vera proceeded to tell them all about what had happened to her in Paris, beginning with the first trip, when she met Khalid and his friends. She went into great detail about her questioning by the police and made several references to the man who kept following her during her extended stay. By the time she had finished with that part of the account, she was about out of breath. Jim encouraged her to relax, but to continue with her story. He was taking mental notes of everything she said. His eyes never left her face the entire time she was telling of her ordeal. Vera took a sip of coffee and continued with the events of the previous morning, how the man from Paris was at her neighborhood Starbucks, how they had been nearly mowed down in the street, the broken window and then all of the events that occurred earlier that morning at the beach house. When she was finished, she asked Jim, "What do you think it all means? Oh, and one more thing," she added, almost as an afterthought, reaching for her tote bag. "I found this envelope hidden under some blankets at the beach house. Do you think there is somehow a connection?"

Jim took the envelope from Vera's trembling hand and spread the contents out on the coffee table. He began to carefully examine the photographs and was especially intrigued by the writing on the back.

"I think it's 9/11 stuff," Vera said.

He nodded in agreement, but didn't take his eyes of the pictures. He held them up to the light and began comparing some of them side by side.

"Did you know Jeff was into this stuff? I mean was he one of those truthers who believed that 9/11 was done by our government or some crazy cabal that wanted to usurp power?" Vera started to feel as if she were talking to herself; she couldn't understand why Jim was more interested in these photographs than he was in the danger that was threatening her life. After what seemed like a very long time, Vera finally blurted out, "What's going on, Jim? Is there something in these photographs that's worth killing me and Kelli over?"

The suddenness and the intensity of her question shocked Jim. He put the photographs down and looked directly at Vera. "Yes, I believe there might be a connection. I was aware that Jeff was heavily involved in doing research on 9/11. Many of us pilots have tried to answer questions that the government investigation simply ignored or failed to provide answers to. Jeff was more involved than most and made a special trip to Argentina; where he apparently got a hold of these photos. These photographs came from a FEMA videographer Jeff knew who had moved to Argentina. This photographer had been called to report to New York City moments after the first plane hit the North Tower. He was one of the only photographers who was on the scene immediately. He stayed for a month or so, filming the initial search and rescue as well as the first few weeks of debris removal." Jim went on to explain, "Jeff had learned some very disturbing details about the terror attack—specifically, the missing gold from the vaults and the mysterious collapse of Building 7. It looks as though Jeff built a solid relationship with the photographer and that he had given Jeff some of the most important photographs with the details that eventually landed him in hot water with the federal government. He was framed for the murder of his wife only three months after the 9/11 attacks. Two months after he returned home to Colorado, his wife committed suicide. The government must have feared what he had seen and photographed details they didn't want the world to see, so they framed him for her murder. He was jailed and held for another four months, even after the court had thrown out his case for lack of evidence. He soon realized that there was a reason for the false accusations and that his own government was after him to silence him. He went to Argentina on a vacation, only to discover that his worst fears had become his real-life nightmare. The Feds had broken into his home numerous times, searching for tapes he had of the ground zero site. It seems he had taken videos of details that might incriminate someone—perhaps our own government. He had kept several tapes with over 22 hours of film that he realized were being sought by the Feds. What you see on the back are the photographer's notes in Spanish, along with Jeff's calculations based on the research he was doing. It's clearly unfinished work, but if certain people knew Jeff had this information and was doing this type of research, there is a likely possibility that Jeff's death was a murder, and that is why he hid these photographs—to protect you."

Vera sat stunned as she listened to the details of Jim's story. There was a part of her that always questioned the official account of Jeff's death. It never quite felt right, but there was no proof and she could see no benefit in pursuing it any further. He was dead, and nothing was going to bring him back to her. Jeff's dying by accident was more comfortable for her to consider than the alternative. Finally, Vera spoke, "So, Jim, if what you say is true and maybe Jeff was murdered, could this information be why they want to kill me?"

"I don't know, Vera, I just don't know. I do know that these photographs could be a threat to many people. Maybe their intent was only to scare you, but somehow you've gotten too close to something and it's threatening to them," Jim admonished.

"Who is 'them,' Jim? Who are these people? What is it they want from me?" Vera implored.

"How willing are you to help me find out?" Jim asked.

Vera looked puzzled by the question; what could Jim mean by willing to help and what kind of risk would it require? She didn't have an answer to his question. She wanted to think about what had happened, what Jim had told her, and how she felt about conspiracy theories that might have mortal consequences. "I'm going to need to think about this for a while, Jim. What I'd really like is to take a hot shower, change my clothes, and maybe even take a short nap."

Mari, who had been listening quietly, taking in all the details of the conversation, showed Vera to the guest bathroom down the hall. Jim continued his examination of the photographs and documents on the coffee table.

Vera felt much better once the road dust was gone and she had had a few hours of rest. "Okay, Mr. Jim, I want to talk more about all this. I've had a little chance to think about what you said. For thirteen plus years, I've stuck to the government's story to avoid being labeled a kook, a fanatic or a truther. But, as a flight attendant with my years of seniority, experience, and training, there were several things that just didn't add up with the government's story, from day one. I've shoved those inconsistencies out of the realm of consideration because the alternative—thinking that the American people were lied to and that I was lied to as an airline professional—was just too uncomfortable for me to explore."

Jim didn't jump to any conclusions about what Vera was telling him. These were the same feelings he had had as both a military and a commercial pilot for years. He had eventually decided to investigate the many anomalies in the 9/11 Commission Report after his retirement. He leaned back into the couch and asked, "I'm curious Vera, what didn't add up? What details of 9/11 have you had trouble explaining?"

"Well, for starters, not one of the nearly thirty flight attendants on board those four airplanes followed any of the FAA hijacking procedures that had been drilled into them from the beginning of their careers. Why the hell not? Not one of them mentioned the code word to indicate a hijacking in progress. I can understand if it didn't happen on one plane, but not on all four, not going to happen. What really got me were the places and people they called during the hijacking. They were downright crazy! Reservations, maintenance, their parents and spouses, none of them followed protocol by giving the details they should have given. And even more insane, they supposedly used their cell phones. Everyone knows cell phones don't work at cruise altitude, especially in 2001. We have all tried them, in the bathroom, in our jacket pockets, under a blanket. To this day, they still don't work. So, how did people make cell phone calls from those planes? And lastly, not one pilot squawked 7500, the universal hijack code. You know how easy it is to do. We have probably both been on flights when it was accidently hit, and all hell broke loose. The pilots were all ex-military. Those guys would have done whatever it took to let air traffic control or the companies know they were being hijacked. Yet not one of the eight pilots did. Why not? Now there is other stuff, but those were my first red flags."

"Yup, there is other stuff alright," Jim nodded in agreement.

"You asked me if I wanted to help you. What does that mean, help? I'm not too keen on being murdered like Grace was. If there is a possibility that Jeff was murdered over this stuff, I'm willing to set my fears aside for the time being and do what I can to help you get to the truth. I will commit to that."

Jim reached over and patted Vera on the knee. "Here's the deal, Vera. Joel Sherman and I are good friends and have been for many years."

Vera's eyes widened, "Joel Sherman, as in President of the United States, Joel Sherman, with the house, the jet, and the helicopter, Joel Sherman?"

Jim smiled, "Not to mention the Secret Service, Camp David, and the most aggressive call screeners this side of the Pope."

"How do you know him?"

"We were in the National Guard together, in fact, Jeff knew him quite well too. I'm surprised he didn't mention that to you when Joel won his Congressional seat in Washington State."

"Maybe he did, but that was a long time ago, and Joel Sherman would have been in a different district than we were at the time. I don't know, but anyway go on," Vera implored.

"President Sherman has been consulting with me about airline and aviation security information over the years. Anyway, a few days ago, he called me and sent me a secure phone that I can reach him on directly without having to go through his call screeners. After I received this special cell phone, we talked for about an hour. He's concerned about the last two plane incidents involving our airline."

Vera interrupted, "Were they accidents, Jim? There seems to be something very suspicious about them, isn't there?"

"Yes," replied Jim. "I knew both captains of those planes very well and have been doing some research into what could have happened ever since the Las Vegas crash. But here's the thing, Vera. There's something going on. It's a feeling shared by me and several others, including the President: Something else is about to happen and we want to be able to stop it before it occurs."

"Why do you need my help?" Vera asked.

"In the back of my mind, I have sensed there was a connection to what happened on 9/11 to what is going on with these recent incidents. The pictures you provided me from Jeff only reinforced that feeling. I want to get to the bottom of all this and your experience as a career flight attendant, your keen intellect, and your love for Jeff provide all the ingredients to help me with what I am about to do."

"Just what exactly is that?" She asked, looking at both them.

"I promised the President that I would gather information from all my contacts across the country and help him to put the pieces of this puzzle together. I plan on leaving in the next couple of days for Salt Lake City. I want you to accompany me on this investigation. It will probably be best if you take a leave of absence from the company for a while. I want your undivided attention and assistance and don't want you to have to think about bidding your next month's flying," Jim explained.

"Leave of absence, how long do you think this investigation will take us?"

"I'm not sure. It's going to take some time and travel. I'm going to guess it will take us at least one full month. You should ask for two—maybe three—months off. Besides, you can probably use some extra relaxation time after all you've been through. We'll go where the investigation takes us and provide President Sherman with all the information we can find."

"I would love to take a leave of absence, in fact, I'm thinking about retiring altogether in light of what has happened this last year. But, what will I do with Kelli?"

"She's more than welcome to stay here with me," Mari piped in. "We've had dogs all our lives and look at her; she certainly has had no trouble making herself right at home."

"Well, that's for sure," quipped Vera. "She's eating, drinking, and sleeping. What more is there to a dog's life?"

"Plus, she'll be good company for me while Jim is away. I hate it when he goes on these undefined jaunts and I never know when he's coming back."

"I'll tell you what, Vera, you sleep on this tonight, and we'll talk more about it tomorrow. I'm excited to have you join me.

Together we can accomplish much more than I could alone. In fact, President Sherman had suggested I find someone I could combine efforts with to accompany me. I hadn't thought of asking you because of your job, but this is perfect timing. Maybe things happen for a reason."

Vera's fears had been replaced with a sense of anticipation and a new found feeling of resolve. She was beginning to feel a burden lifting by admitting to her own apprehension about researching the details surrounding the 9/11 terror attacks. She was starting to feel a deepened desire to discover the truth.

twenty-seven

"Have you been to Salt Lake City?" Jim asked as they were on final approach.

"I've landed here a few times, once when we blew an engine out of Seattle heading to Houston. It was early in my career."

Jim called Jonas Stevens to inform him that they had arrived and told him they would send a text when the bags came off the carousel. "This guy Jonas we're meeting with today is a very interesting fellow. I'm sure you'll like him. He taught at one of the universities here as a physics professor. He had done a lot of research into cold fusion prior to 9/11. Then, when that tragedy stuck, he became very involved in research surrounding the collapse of the towers. I want to talk to him about what he thinks happened in these last two incidents. Perhaps between our airline knowledge and his scientific expertise, we can come to some valuable conclusions."

A large white Suburban pulled up to the curb outside the baggage claim area. The driver waved as he and Jim made eye contact. The rear door popped open and Jonas ran to the back to meet them.

Jim quickly introduced Vera to Jonas as they loaded their luggage into the back of the vehicle. A few moments later, they were exiting from the freeway and within a few short blocks were pulling into the small parking lot of a local café. Jonas explained, "This is one of my favorite hide-a-ways and a great place to eat, we'll have plenty of privacy here."

Jim continued to explain to Vera how Jonas had, as a

physics professor, published peer-reviewed research papers on the collapse of the World Trade Center towers—and how those papers ignited a firestorm of attacks by both the mainstream media and the blogosphere.

Once seated in a corner booth, Jonas reached into his brown leather briefcase and pulled out two large manila envelopes setting one in front of each of them. "I have included my original paper for your review. I also added a chronological timeline as to what happened to me once the mainstream media got a hold of my research paper. That in itself makes for some real interesting reading," he smiled a boyish grin in Vera's direction. "I watched in horror, as we all did, on that September morning, but I saw things that didn't make sense to my logical, mathematical, and scientific mind. I saw the symmetrical collapse of buildings that had originally been designed and built to withstand the impact of multiple airplanes of similar size. The planes that struck the Twin Towers actually weakened one side or in the case of the South Tower, it actually weakened a corner of the building, yet both structures collapsed symmetrically in less than ten seconds. Whatever caused that collapse created a very fine dust that has been tested and proven to contain traces of thermite and nano-thermite explosives, indicating that the towers were taken down by a controlled demolition—and not by office fires caused by jet fuel. You'll find all of the research data that I collected and studied in the paper provided. It's obvious that the official story is anything but the truth. I, like many other scholars, architects and engineers, would like to see a real investigation done by those of us who don't have a political agenda and are not in any way connected to the military-industrial complex or the New World Order. And we would like to be able to do it without the fear of losing our employment. The powers that be have made it so that if you question their official explanation, your job, your credibility, and sometimes your life are threatened. They are not kidding either. My first research paper was published in 2006, and surprisingly enough, it got some attention from the mainstream cable news media. Of course, they did a clever job of ignoring my discovery of nano-thermite. The fact that explosive residue was found in the pulverized dust of the towers is proof that there had been either a well-planned demolition set up or that some type of explosives were set throughout the towers. Either way, the process of rigging those two buildings to symmetrically collapse at the speed that they did, would have taken weeks to prepare. Instead of discussing my findings, I was ridiculed, mocked, and made fun of by every network. Newscasters mocked anyone who questioned or brought forth similar discoveries. Someone knows the truth and many of us know that the American people and the world are still being lied to. The event we witnessed that morning could not have been orchestrated by an Arab living in Afghanistan. The buildings would have had to have had no security for weeks to allow as many men as it would have taken to place detonations and to make the required cuts in the steel beams. It would have taken several days or even weeks to set that up. A demolition crew would not have gone unnoticed. How NIST could report what they did in the commission report is mind boggling to anyone with half a brain."

"NIST?" Vera asked, confused by the acronym.

"Oh," laughed Jonas, "it stands for National Institute of Standards and Technology."

There was a long pause while Vera tried to digest the information Jonas had shared. She was trying to keep an open mind, but these kinds of facts were exactly what she was afraid of discovering.

Jim cleared his throat and spoke before anyone could add anything else. "We're actually on another mission now, Jonas, although I'm sure both Vera and I will enjoy reading all your research papers and the other documents on the 9/11 event. We need to tackle our primary agenda. We are doing a study, shall I call it, about airport and airplane security, to see if the changes made to security after 9/11 were effective." Jim tried to explain their current mission as best he could without mentioning the presidential request. "I did want Vera to meet you and to understand that many expert scholars such as yourself, have tackled the 9/11 event and found that the government version of the story is scientifically impossible to believe. Her late husband, Jeff, was a member of the Pilots for 9/11 Truth group. He dedicated many hours of research to the event from a pilot's perspective."

They enjoyed their meal while listening to Jonas talk about local tourist information and last winter's record snowfall. Vera was slowly absorbing the reality of the information she had just heard coming from this professor's mouth. The image of her government, her country, and the entire 9/11 event were collapsing as fast as those Twin Towers. Her logical mind and memory worked overtime replaying the scenes from that September morning.

The government wanted to kill their own photographer who had given Jeff hundreds of photographs. Vera couldn't help but wonder if the government knew that Jeff had met with this man in Argentina. Could it be possible that Jeff had more photos or videos stashed away in the house or the beach house? Could that be what the break-in was all about? Could that be why the SUV was headed straight for her but missed and clipped Kelli instead?

Jim nudged Vera's elbow, breaking her spell, "Ready to get checked into the hotel? Jonas probably has to get back to his work." Turning to Jonas, he thanked him and told him that he would be in touch by email with the questions they wanted him to answer.

"I'm more than happy to help you two. Your hotel is only a few minutes from here," Jonas offered as he wrapped his wool scarf around his neck.

The short ride to the downtown Salt Lake City hotel was breathtakingly beautiful. Vera sat quietly in the backseat enjoying the afternoon hues that danced off the snowcapped mountains surrounding the city. They checked in at the front desk, then rode the elevator to the tenth floor.

"Vera, what do you say we meet in the Lobby Lounge at five o'clock, we can have a glass of wine and some dinner while we discuss the information Jonas gave us," Jim suggested.

"Sounds like a plan, Jim. I'll be devouring his research paper until then," Vera confirmed as she stepped into her room. Once inside, she quickly spread the contents of the packet out across the bed, organizing them as best she could. She started reading the scientific documents, but soon became lost in the detailed descriptions. She flipped to the back pages, hoping for an overview that she might be able to understand. She reviewed a stack of detailed photographs—some showing the impact areas and others with the towers burning and spewing out thick black smoke. She remembered watching the television that morning and the shock she felt seeing that aircraft crashing into the south tower. Through her many years of annual recurrent training, she had studied nearly every airplane crash that had occurred over the past twenty-five-plus years. She recalled how shocked she was as she watched what appeared to be a 767 magically disappear into the South Tower, much like a hot knife through butter. Her mind momentarily recalled how she thought what she was watching on CNN was some kind of trick photography. She knew what she had just seen on the television screen was impossible. The nose of the aircraft was made of a very fragile composite plastic, and the wings were far too fragile to slice right into a steel building like they did. She had seen firsthand; nose cones so badly damaged from a bird strike or a hailstorm that it seemed impossible for an aluminum-and-composite airplane to completely disappear into a building, without the wings or tail section splitting off. She began to feel her own latent fears rise to the surface as she recalled those initial questions she had about the hijacking event. The FAA had never informed flight crews about any terrorist by the name of Osama bin Laden or any group by the name of Al Qaeda, and certainly never warned that a terrorist group was planning to use commercial jets as weapons. She remembered sitting at her kitchen table that morning watching the live news reporting from the Pentagon and the confusion about which airline and what type of aircraft had hit the building. One eyewitness being interviewed described a plane that looked like a large humpback whale. Vera recalled her shock at not seeing any remnants of any type of commercial aircraft anywhere near the Pentagon—no tail section, no landing gear, no tires nor any of the typical parts of an aircraft that always survived impact.

A strange feeling began to well up inside her, the scientific documents from Jonas were only adding to her fears; they indicated the fires that started high up in the towers by the aircraft jet fuel were not hot enough to melt steel and cause a skyscraper to collapse. The cement floors and the furniture and the people trapped inside had all been turned into a fine dust, pulverized by some incredible force that was not something jet fuel or office fires alone could have provided. She remembered seeing the streets of Manhattan littered with papers. There were thousands of papers raining down from the towers, not on fire, just white sheets of paper floating down everywhere. After the collapse, she recalled how the people who had escaped the buildings were completely covered with a very fine grey dust and yet they shuffled through ankle deep papers. She remembered seeing an interview with a New York City firefighter, telling of hearing multiple explosions in the towers saying, "There were multiple explosions. We heard boom, boom, boom, right before the towers collapsed."

Vera needed to stop thinking about that day and decided to check the news headlines on her laptop. She scanned through her favorite news sites, nothing of serious importance caused her to do more than scroll through the headlines. She clicked her Facebook icon, some of her Facebook friends were better news reporters than many of the professionals on television. Main stream media had proven to be so biased and had been caught manufacturing stories so many times that they had lost their credibility and more and more people were now turning to the alternative news sites on the internet.

A private message icon lit up on her page. It was from the Stanford Tree guy. It read, "Hi there Vera. I haven't heard from you in a while. I hope you are not planning another trip to Paris."

"Hi there, Stanly Manly," she replied back, wondering what this guy really wanted. "I actually arrived home Christmas Day, and things have been crazy ever since. I was just about to head out to meet a friend for dinner. Have a great evening."

Vera arrived early to the Lobby Lounge and chose a small marble-topped table near the window. She was immediately greeted by a handsome gentleman, who promptly presented her with a menu. She ordered two glasses of merlot and chose an assortment of cheeses with an artichoke dip. Jim appeared in the entrance and quickly navigated his way through the tables to join her.

"You're early," he smiled as he pulled the tufted leather chair closer to the table. "Thank you for ordering. I have been on the phone most of the afternoon and I'm drained and a bit stressed."

"I hear you," Vera chimed in. "I've been reading through that packet from Jonas, and I have more questions and deeper emotions than either my mind or my heart can handle. Jim, I'm in shock over what I'm reading about the Twin Towers and what could be the real scientific story of their collapse. Jet-fuel fires didn't—couldn't—cause that, so how are we expected to believe the official story? The dust samples showed chemical traces of nano-thermite explosives. What happened that day?" Vera's voice began to shake as her words picked up a faster pace with each question.

"Listen, Vera, as I'd mentioned to you at my cabin, many of us in the industry knew from day one that something wasn't right with the story. We knew that kerosene jet-fuel couldn't make a building explode the way the towers did, and we also knew that a 767 could not..." Jim paused, "...would not, fly straight into a building and simply disappear. The tail section, the engines, the landing gear, something would have been found on the outside of the buildings. Professional airline pilots have studied the official flight paths released by the FAA. The altitude and the speed that the FAA claimed some of the planes took that day were impossible. As I might have mentioned to you, to fly either aircraft at the speed and altitude reported, the wings would have sheared off and the planes would have literally fallen apart. I just can't believe the government data that was provided."

Vera took a slow sip of her wine, holding the glass above the table top as she spoke. "There were many details that bothered me from day one, but I honestly could never face doing any type of investigation because my world was safe. I believed the government and our military were in place to keep me—to keep us all—safe. When they started talking about some terrorist group that we had never been warned about, I remember thinking: Why didn't the FAA tell us crew members about this group and their plan? If they would have just sent out one FAA directive to the flight attendants and pilots, we would have stopped this at the boarding door. Surely, they must have had at least one name of those nineteen hijackers. Why didn't they let us know? This tragedy could have been easily prevented."

Jim understood what Vera was feeling. He knew that this truth was hard for most Americans to swallow, especially those whose lives and careers centered on the world of aviation. His military experience combined with his airline career made dealing with the possibilities of the 9/11 event even more difficult. In the airline, there had always been an assurance that in the event of a hijacking within US territory, military jets would be scrambled immediately. Air Traffic Control would go to work instantly alongside of all the government agencies, the Navy, Air Force, NORAD, the FAA, the NSA, the CIA, Special Ops forces, and the FBI would all be there to rescue the passengers and crew and to keep us safe. He took a sip of wine and said, "To believe the official government story of 9/11, we were asked to believe that somehow a ragtag group of middle easterners from at least five different countries managed to control our satellites and more. Then they somehow gained complete control over our military, every alphabet agency that we trusted to keep us safe, Air Traffic control computer systems, and even airport security at three major U.S. airports. We were told and expected to believe that somehow this complicated terror attack was managed and coordinated from Afghanistan of all places. We were expected to believe that aircraft that were designed to fly at 460 miles per hour actually flew nearly 700 miles per hour that day without damaging the integrity of the aircraft—pure bullshit. Vera, what you are about to learn tomorrow night when we visit my old friend Maxwell J. Hager in Minneapolis, will open your eyes in a big way to what really happened that day. While we are here in Salt Lake City, you will probably do yourself a favor to prepare mentally for an overwhelming amount of information. A great deal of it will truly be hard to digest. Max was the editor of a magazine for many years. He put together several books and has done investigative research on nearly every aspect of 9/11. Max doesn't yet know all the details about how it was done, but he does have all of the salient questions and most of their answers."

"What time does our flight leave tomorrow?" She asked.

"We leave about ten o'clock. I'll check with the airline to make sure the flight is on-time and let you know."

"Terrific," Vera chimed in.

As they approached their rooms after dinner, Jim said, "I have a book I want to give you, it will be very enlightening, it will help refresh your memory of what the media and the government told us all on 9/11 from the moment it happened."

Vera waited in the hallway at Jim's door while he retrieved the book. "Here you go, dive into this. I suggest you start reading at chapter seventeen. It's a complete timeline of everything that occurred, the boarding of the planes, the Air traffic controllers, the flight attendants phone calls, and basically what time everything happened." He chuckled, "I guarantee you'll be shocked by and disappointed in all those agencies we used to think we're going to be there for us."

Vera looked down at the dark red cover: Terror Timeline. "Thanks, I'll start reading it tonight."

twenty-eight

The cab driver pulled up to the curb for departing passengers. He was about to get out to help Jim and Vera with their luggage when Jim looked at his watch and said, "Driver, we have some time. Would you mind pulling around again and dropping us off inside the parking garage?"

Vera glanced at Jim with a puzzled look as the driver calmly replied, "Sure man, whatever you want."

"What are we doing Jim? It's a much farther walk from there and it's cold," Vera questioned.

"Yeah, I know it is, but remember when we arrived yesterday, we commented on all those blue wheelchairs at the entrance that were free for the taking?" Jim asked.

"Well, yes, but what does that have to do with the parking garage?"

"If you don't mind, I would like to check something out."

Vera shrugged her shoulders as if to say, "whatever" as the cab driver drove around the perimeter of the airport and pulled back into the parking garage.

"Over there," pointed Jim, "over by that wheelchair in the corner. Please let us out there."

The driver did as he was told. He helped them with their luggage and Jim paid the fare along with a very handsome tip.

"Did you want to push me into the airport so I could pretend to be crippled? Is that what this is all about?" Vera asked, as she shook her head in disbelief.

Jim laughed, "I hadn't thought of that, but if you want me

to push you, I would be more than happy to do so. These are courtesy wheelchairs, property of the airport that anyone can use. Look, there are two more of them over there."

"And your point is?"

"My point is this: My guess is that some airport employee comes around every so often and collects these chairs and puts them back inside the terminal. Now, why couldn't anyone, oh, let's just say anyone like a terrorist for example, take one of these chairs home. I mean, if we had a van right now, we could load this wheelchair into it and who would ever know?"

"Why would we—or better yet, a terrorist—want one of these cheap, lousy wheelchairs?" Vera wondered out loud.

"Humor me, Vera. Perhaps when he had it at home, he could stuff these hollow aluminum tubes with plastic explosives. Can you imagine how much damage one of these could do if it were filled with several pounds of explosives?"

"Orlando!"

"Bingo, you catch on fast," smiled Jim. "So, my dear, why don't you climb aboard? We'll check the luggage and then I'll wheel you through security, and we'll see how much scrutiny this wheelchair gets from the TSA."

"Oh, this mission is starting to become fun," Vera said, giggling.

Jim pushed Vera past the long security line. When they approached the actual screening area, Jim helped her limp through the magnetometer and then went through himself. Both of them kept their eyes riveted on the wheelchair. A TSA agent quickly lifted up the black vinyl seat, robotically checked underneath it, then wheeled the chair around security and brought it to Vera, who thanked him graciously and sat back down in the chair. Jim collected their carry-on items and wheeled her toward their gate.

When they were safely out of earshot of the TSA agents, Jim whispered, "That is one hell of a security flaw. We were merely the traveling public; imagine what little attention the TSA would have given a skycap who brings thirty or more wheelchairs through each shift. They probably wouldn't have even looked under the seat. Now how difficult do you think it would be to rig a remote control device to a wheelchair filled with plastic explosives?"

They dumped the wheelchair at an empty boarding gate then talked about the implications of their find and how it might have related to the Orlando bombing. As they proceeded, they also noticed several Muslim women working at the shops on the secure side of the terminal. They were obvious by their Islamic head coverings, their airport ID cards hung on lanyards around their necks. That ID gave them complete access to the tarmac and to the aircraft parked at the gates.

"Doesn't it seem logical to you, Jim that if our government was so certain that nineteen radical Arab Muslim hijackers took down those airplanes on 9/11, they would be a little more circumspect in their hiring practices? I mean, with this security hole we've just exposed, how hard would it be for a radicalized Muslim airport employee—or anyone—to do what we have just proven is possible or worse? Did you notice how many Muslim women are working in this terminal?"

"I know exactly what you mean, when I was still flying for the company, I was practically strip-searched by a young TSA agent named Mohammad, while I was wearing my captain's uniform. There's a lot that just doesn't make any logical sense—not the least of which was the previous Administration's hiring Arab-Muslims into some of the top positions at Homeland Security. It's almost as if they know these people are not a serious threat and so no scrutiny is applied. Either that or it's a case of political correctness run amok."

They were still discussing various security breaches when the first class section was called to board. Jim was assigned 2B and

Vera was two rows behind him and across the aisle in 4C. Vera noticed a clean-cut gentleman already seated in 4D. She carefully situated herself into her seat without disturbing him. Her intent was to keep reading the book Jim had given her, so she removed it from her tote bag and placed it neatly in her lap. The man next to her looked over at the book, then looked at Vera and said, "Nine eleven, huh? It's been more than thirteen years, why are you interested in that old stuff?"

Vera didn't want to get into a protracted discussion about anything, especially 9/11, with a complete stranger. Part of that reoccurring 'truther' fear was making a comeback and she decided to answer him with the simple rejoinder, "Oh, this stuff puts me right to sleep, and it's a two hour flight." That should give him the message loud and clear, she thought.

The man was silent as Vera secretly claimed victory. "I was in the Pentagon that day when it was struck," the man blurted out.

"You were what?" Vera asked, wanting to make certain she had heard him correctly.

"Yeah, I was in the building when it hit and I was out there on the lawn afterwards," he replied, shaking his head in a slight bobbing motion.

"Who are you, if you don't mind me asking?"

"Oh, pardon me, ma'am," he said, extending his hand, "I'm Gary Gill, United States Air Force retired."

"Vera, Vera Hanson, why were you in the Pentagon on 9/11?"

"Oh, that's a long story. I spent thirty years in the Air Force. I was a weatherman with Special Ops. Now, I wasn't your partly-cloudy-with-a-chance-of-rain-on-Friday kind of weatherman. I was assigned to SEAL teams, Rangers, and the blackest of the black operation guys. My job was to measure air pressure, wind vectors, wind velocity, and situational information to give a three-dimensional picture, capable of giving the okay to send down missiles, JDAMs—or just to help a sniper line up a target.

I've worked with all of them, and I've been everywhere—and I do mean everywhere. Anyway, I was in the Pentagon between assignments that day, but three days later I was on a Blackhawk in Afghanistan."

"So, you obviously weren't injured then when the plane hit the building?" Vera asked calmly.

"No, ma'am, I was on the other side of the Pentagon when it was stuck, but I raced around to where it was hit and tried to help the injured as best I could," he replied.

"Did you help remove bodies from the plane and things like that?" Vera asked.

"I attended to the dead and injured and did indeed remove bodies from the building. Sadly, that's something I've done all my life with my job in the service," Gary said, almost reverently.

"Well, I've been a flight attendant for more years than I care to admit. I've studied every kind of plane crash and hijacking since the days of D.B. Cooper, so I hope you don't mind me asking you questions about this plane crash. In all these years, never once has that crash or any of the 9/11 plane crashes been discussed in our annual FAA recurrent training."

"Plane? I never said anything about an airplane," Gary responded almost indignantly.

"What do you mean? American Flight 77, Boeing 757 with nearly 60 passengers and crew didn't hit the Pentagon on 9/11?" Vera asked, confused.

"No, ma'am, it did not. I can guarantee you that a 757 did not hit the Pentagon on that day. I was there. There was no 757. There were, however, multiple pre-set explosives throughout the building."

Vera was silent; she hadn't read much about what had happened at the Pentagon that day, only about the World Trade Center. When she finally spoke, she said, "Not a plane? I heard the television commentators report that it was first a US Airways

737, then that it was an American Airlines 757 that hit."

"You watched it on television?" He asked. "Then may I ask you, did you see any signs or evidence of an airplane crash in front of the Pentagon?"

"I told you I'm flight attendant; I've seen pictures of almost every plane crash that ever happened, but no, I didn't see any aircraft parts or any trace of a plane crash outside the Pentagon that morning. I always thought that was strange, but I'd never given it much thought until recently. The oddest part of that day to me was that the Pentagon was struck. I had always thought that it was considered to be the most secure, well protected, and the most heavily guarded building in the entire world. It made no sense at all to me that some foreigners could have figured out, not only how to evade our military jets and the system in place to protect us, but also manage to somehow get through the heavy security and protection in place around the Pentagon."

"Ma'am, I can assure you of one thing, what happened that day was not at all what any of us were told by the news reporters or the government," he replied smiling.

Gary's information was beginning to overwhelm her. She found herself reflecting back to those first television broadcasts of the Pentagon. There were so many details that were suspicious to her at the time. She remembered the President's speech later that night and then again at the State of the Union, a few months later when he said, "You are either with us or you are with the terrorists." And then later he said, "Let us not believe in wild conspiracy theories." She recalled thinking what a strange thing for the President to say. Why would he even mention conspiracies at a time like that? This was an act of war, all the government needed to do was to figure out what country was behind the attack and take it up with them. She remembered how the airline handed out American flag stickers to everyone as they returned to work after flights resumed their normal schedules. Everyone put American flag stickers on their luggage, and they were even found stuck to the aluminum galley carriers on many aircraft. Jeff had collected dozens of them and had decorated his metal toolbox in the garage.

Gary broke the long silence with something that was equally shocking to Vera when he said, "I'll share with you another little-known fact about this supposed war on terror. As I mentioned, I was in Afghanistan three days after 9/11. Well, we had been on the ground less than a week when we had Osama bin Laden in our gun sights—a dead to rights shot—and we could not get permission to fire."

"What? What are you telling me?" Vera demanded.

"Oh, it didn't happen only once. We had him in the crosshairs again at Tora Bora; you know when they told you people back home that he magically slipped out of our grasp and fled into Pakistan. Well, that was total bullshit. We had him again right in the crosshairs and were ordered to stand down. Apparently, the military machine that runs this country had other plans. I guess they needed Osama bin Laden to be alive—to continue to be used as a real big threat to America. So they had to do what they could to keep him alive. That's the only explanation I can offer you."

"Who gave such an order? How high up was it, a general? The White House?"

"Ma'am, I'm retired, but on this one matter, I'm afraid I'm not at liberty to answer any questions about from how high up those orders came. But, if you were to learn they came from someone higher up than a General, you could probably figure it out. You see, it was vital to the expansion of their orchestrated wars to have an elusive boogeyman; one that American's believed was smart enough to plan those attacks and someone clever enough to organize them smack into the middle of several pre-planned military war games. I mean, for hell's sake, the largest annual war game exercise, Vigilant Guardian, was ongoing that morning." His voice slowed as he continued, "Yes, we were all expected to follow our leaders and blindly believe their claims. They expected us to believe that some guy living in a cave half way around the world was clever enough to organize this extremely complicated attack on America, just like we were supposed to believe that he was smart enough to evade our special forces in Tora Bora." Gary began to sound sarcastic as he continued, "There's so much more involved in those two wars—the American people have no idea. If the day ever comes that they figure out who was really behind the attacks on 9/11 and the ensuing war on terror, well, let's just say they won't be very happy. I guess it's probably best for some people that the American public doesn't know the truth." He paused again, his head pushed back into the headrest. "The American people have been lied to on so many fronts. If those parents, who've lost kids fighting in Iraq and Afghanistan, knew the truth about what their kids were really fighting for—the heroin, the gas pipelines, the destruction of entire civilizations— they'd be ready to turn on their own government. The truth about these wars and how they really started, along with who has been making billions off of them, could start a revolution."

The aircraft landed about twenty minutes later than scheduled into the Twin Cities. Vera thanked Gary for the enlightening conversation, thanked him for his service, then wrote her personal information on a card and gave it to him. "Let's keep in touch. I think we might have a lot of information to share in the near future."

Gary agreed and handed Vera his card. "I hope I didn't scare you too badly, ma'am. I have a tendency to do that when I get going." Gary laughed as Vera shook his hand again then quickly caught up with Jim in the jetway.

Jim called Maxwell as they walked through the terminal toward the baggage claim, "Max, we're going to check in at the

Marriot for tonight. Can you pick us up in the morning around nine o'clock?"

When he finished the call, Vera told Jim about her seat mate, "He was inside the Pentagon that day, Jim. Can you believe that? And do you know what he told me?" Vera was excited to give Jim all the details.

"Let me guess," Jim answered somewhat abruptly, "He told you that it wasn't a 757 that hit the Pentagon, and it wasn't a 737 that hit it either, in fact, it wasn't even a commercial aircraft." Jim smiled, waiting for Vera to reply.

"You already knew that?" She hit his shoulder teasing.

"Did he tell you how that thing that hit the Pentagon was reported by ATC to have made a 270 degree corkscrew turn at nearly Mach 1 before it crashed into the building barely above ground level, right into the Office of Naval Intelligence? Now, I'm the best damn pilot I know, Vera, and I couldn't fly an F-16 like that to save my ass. So how in the hell could someone just out of a rudimentary flight school have so skillfully flown a cumbersome 757 to hit the exact target that would destroy all the evidence to the missing trillions of dollars the Secretary of Defense had announced the day before?"

"Well, no, he didn't mention all that. You obviously know a lot more about this part of the story than either he or I do. It really did strike directly into the very office that was doing an investigation into those missing trillions? How or why would terrorists want to destroy an investigation? Moreover, how would a terrorist from the Middle East even know which office was doing such an investigation? How would it benefit a terrorist organization if they actually stopped such an investigation?" Vera stopped walking, her jaw dropped as she realized that a strike on that office would only benefit those responsible for the missing money.

"I'm sure Maxwell will be able to fill us in on what actually occurred at the Pentagon that day," Jim replied, pulling her elbow to continue walking.

"When we get into the cab, I'll tell you what he told me with regards to Osama bin Laden. I know you don't know this story," Vera said, with a smile.

"Can't wait."

After dinner, Vera got ready for bed and propped her pillows up behind her so she could read the timeline book in the most comfortable position possible. Her conversation on the flight with Gary kept replaying in her mind. Chances were she wasn't going to find anything he had told her this book. The more she read, the clearer some aspects became. She read with great interest how NEADS was convinced that Flight 11, which was the first plane to crash into the North Tower at 8:46, was still in the air at 9:24 when they finally scrambled jets to intercept it, thinking it was heading towards Washington. How could that be, she wondered, wouldn't their radar lose track of Flight 11 the minute it crashed into the tower? Something was definitely amiss with the radar. The only thing Vera could conclude was that either Flight 11 did not crash into the North Tower, as reported or there was some kind of a phantom signal on the NEADS radar. Neither one of which was a comforting or confidence provoking thought, but then this whole day had proven that things truly were not as they seemed.

twenty-nine

Jim pointed out the hotel lobby window, "I think that's Max, there in the green Range Rover." The Range Rover looped around the parking lot one complete turn, then pulled up underneath the portico. Out stepped a large barrel-chested brute of a man wearing a Panama hat with a purple-and-gold Viking's sweatshirt.

Jim stepped forward with his hand out, but ended up embracing him. "Maxwell J. Hager, how the hell are you, buddy? Damn, it's good to see you alive and well and fat as ever."

Max let out a loud hearty laugh, "I couldn't be better Jimbo. Who's the little filly you got with you? I thought you were traveling alone. Does Mari know about her?" Max questioned, raising a jaundiced eye.

"Max, allow me to introduce you to Vera Hanson, a senior flight attendant who is starting to become a pretty good researcher and she's a nearly lifelong friend of mine and Mari's. We're doing some in-depth investigating on the recent accidents in Las Vegas and Orlando. I had some more questions for you about the 9/11 event and I have something new to show you."

"Well, I'm mighty proud to meet you, little lady," Max said, while extending his large weathered hand to Vera.

"What does the 'J' stand for in your name?" She politely asked.

"Oh that," Max laughed again, "Jim's the only one that ever calls me by my full name. He reminds me of my mother when he does, but the J stands for Jeffrey, Maxwell Jeffrey Hager, at your service, ma'am."

"Vera's husband was an incredible 9/11 investigator, you might have seen some of his articles on the truth movement web pages. His name was Jeffrey Hanson," Jim informed Max.

"Hot damn, your husband was Jeff Hanson? Damn rights I knew that boy, he got some of the pictures from Argentina I couldn't get. I was sure sorry to hear about his accident, but I've always wondered if it wasn't something more. The truth movement really suffered a damaging blow when we lost him. Anyway, we're going to get along just fine, ma'am."

Max's words only served to reconfirm the conclusion that Vera had been coming to regarding Jeff's death. "I'm looking forward to hearing all you have to say Mr. Hager; in fact I can't wait, but let's get in the car before I freeze to death."

Vera hopped into the front seat and Jim climbed in behind Max. "Hey, what's up with the ponytail?" Jim asked, noticing Max's long gray ponytail protruding from the back of his hat.

Max reached back and lifted up the ponytail, "Its fake, see," he laughed. "I had to ditch that military style hair-do. I stood out too much and couldn't blend in with the younger crowd. Besides, this look fits my anarchist attitude. If I could, I'd grow my own. I actually have a wardrobe of wigs and hats I wear whenever I leave the house."

"Now about that 9/11 event," Max blurted out. "That day really did wake me up to what the hell is going on and has been going on in this world for quite some time. That was, among other things, the biggest bank robbery and gold heist in history. Yep, that was quite the interesting event. My involvement in trying to expose the truth drew a lot of attention from the feds. Now they fly drones over my house a couple times a day. Don't scare me, though. I just keep posting information on that website of mine, pisses them off every time I do. I'm aware of them and I'm staying one step ahead of them— usually. A person has to be smart these days; the government wants total control of all the information that's why the internet scares them so much. People like me, we get a hold of one of their created messes, like 9/11, and we tear it apart stem to stern. We exposed it for what it was, bank heist, stock swindle, insurance fraud, gold theft, cover-ups, murder, and more." He paused for a moment to take a breath, "Hey, you two ready for some breakfast?"

Jim answered for them both, "Fantastic idea, lead on."

Max pulled into a parking space in clear view of a security camera, which he pointed out. "You see that camera? It's aiming straight at us, so they'll know we're together. The bastards keep bugging my house, so I won't take you two there. It's much safer here in the Mall of America. They won't try anything stupid here with so many shoppers around. I hope that don't scare you guys. Ever since I posted that last piece I did on the 9/11 event, they seem to want to silence me one way or the other. They have their shills assigned to my blog and man, they are some nasty mothers." Max let out a hearty laugh, "That's how I know I'm on the right track and digging right into the truth—when they sic those trolls and shills on my blog to try to discredit me and anyone else I associate with."

The mall wasn't particularly crowded when it opened at nine-thirty, which made their visit to Starbucks in the food court rather pleasant. "Just love these little coffee cakes here at Mr. Shultz's place. They help me to maintain my youthful figure," Max said with a grin, rubbing his large stomach.

"Let's head over there to that table across the way." Max pointed to a lone table at the far end of the food court. "I like to sit where I have a full view of anyone who might come our way. That way, I can answer your questions and keep one eye on that main hallway. If I stand up in the middle of a sentence, mine or one of yours, just stand up and follow me a few steps, then both of you break away quickly. Off to the right, there's an emergency exit just past that candy shop. Go out that door and keep going—

don't stop and don't worry about me. I'll get to the Rover and meet you in front of that big Nordstrom store you saw when we arrived. Just wait for me there inside the double glass doors. I'll drive past once, circle the parking lot, then come by again and stop right in front. When I circle around, get outside and get in the car as fast as you can. I won't come by for you until I'm positive the coast is clear, but you never know with these freaks."

Vera held her latte in both hands as she listened to Max's instructions; while she studied Jim's face for his reaction. Jim didn't seem to be surprised or overly concerned with what Max had told them. She wondered what type of information Max had about 9/11 that made him feel so paranoid. Vera tried to look relaxed on the outside as she felt her nerves sharpen and a touch of fear start to run through her veins.

Max pulled a thick white envelope from his large leather satchel. "Here, Vera, put this in your purse. If you two need to evacuate for any reason, you'll have pretty much everything you need to know about 9/11 right there. There's a great book in there called, Who Should Go Down in History, written by a good friend of mine, Chuck Maultsby. It's a must read. You'll find several videos on discs; they'll give you every bit of information you ever wanted to know about who did what, how they did what they did, and how they managed to not get caught. Now listen, have you guys ever read about something called Brady bonds?"

"No, I can't say that I have," Jim admitted. Vera just shook her head no.

"This is some pretty heavy stuff," Max told them. "It's pretty complicated, so let me try to put it in a nutshell for you. For more in-depth details, you can read the book in the packet called, Nine Eleven GOLD, you'll find it right near the top of the stack."

"So, what is a Brady bond and how does it relate to 9/11?" Vera asked.

"Well, let me try to give you the Cliffs Notes version," Max explained. "According to some leaked documents out of the Office of Naval Intelligence in the Pentagon, about ten years before 9/11, one of our ex-presidents pulled off a very, shall I say, shady deal. Not a small deal either, you see, only about $240 billion—that's billion with a 'B'. Several household names were involved in this plot. I'm talking right at the top of both political parties—not small fries. You will recognize many of the people involved. Some of them are considered to be financial or counter-terrorism experts or some such load of crap, but I digress. Some stolen gold was used to manipulate the economy of the old Soviet Union in order to collapse their system. These fraudulent bonds were called Brady bonds and they were set to expire on September 12, 2001, yep, that would be the day after the infamous 9/11 event. It seems one of our past presidents stole a great deal of physical gold from a few countries you two may have some knowledge of, Russia or the old Soviet Union, the Philippines, and Czechoslovakia. That stolen gold had to be introduced back into a heavily monitored gold market. It was a very complicated procedure involving these bonds and several banks known as bullion banks. Some of the biggest names in the banking industry and investment firms in the United States, not to mention several top politicians and some intelligence organizations, were up well past their eyeballs in this scheme. You'll find all the documents and proof to help you understand this part of the multifaceted event they called a terror attack on America. On a side note, those bonds were physically being held either on the exact floor of the North Tower which was struck or in Building 7. Either way, those bonds were destroyed. Bottom line, those Brady bonds were never a problem after 9/11, but you can be guaranteed that a whole lot of money was pocketed by a whole lot of people on top of the pig pile."

Jim and Vera sat silently enthralled in the story and the details Max was sharing with them. Max continued, "Lots of crazy stuff went on behind the scenes that day, not many Americans know about. There was a massive amount of insurance fraud. I met a guy that worked for Baltimore Life who was astute enough to recognize something fishy going on when several of those big financial institutions that were located in the World Trade Towers, started taking out large life insurance policies on their employees. This started occurring about six months prior to the attack. He quickly put two and two together and contacted the Houston office of the FBI. Instead of looking into the possible insurance fraud, he had alerted them to, they started harassing him. He was threatened shortly after 9/11 in a way he felt was an attempt on his life. He fled to Mexico where he's still living, last I heard. The planes or missiles or pre-set explosives, were remotely controlled to hit exact coordinates. The financial institutions, yeah, those same ones that had taken out all the life insurance policies on their employees were also the handlers of all the U.S. government bonds and treasury transactions. Apparently, these financial institutions are also customarily participants in the military war games that are played annually and conveniently were rescheduled to occur that morning. So far, none of us can pinpoint exactly who it was that rescheduled those war games for September 11th. There were millions of dollars' worth of put options placed on both airlines involved in the attacks. Nobody knows who placed those orders, but they were extraordinarily outside the normal transaction range for a typical trading day. There were several FBI investigations ongoing involving international gold movement from one party to another. Many of the major bullion banks were being closely scrutinized, as were several very big names in the banking and investment world. It seems there was a whole lot of price fixing going on with gold and it just so happened that all the documents of those investigations were held on the 23rd floor of the North Tower and most likely some were in Building 7. Most of those investigations were scheduled for court the first week of October, 2001. The big money boys were running out of time. Those fraudulent gold bonds were coming due the next day. Drug money, illegal arms deals, price fixing, you name it, it was all being done by people whose names you'll no doubt recognize when you hear them."

Max took several big gulps of coffee then continued. "Interesting to note, Building 7 that fell nearly eight hours after the towers collapsed, happened to house the largest offices of the Central Intelligence Agency outside of Langley, Virginia. That building also was home of the SEC offices that contained all of the investigation documents on the ENRON, Global Crossing, and World Com scandals. There are way too many people who still, to this day, don't even know that Building 7—having not been hit by an airplane or any significant debris from the falling towers— came down at free-fall speed at five-twenty that afternoon. It looked to most eyewitnesses and television viewers like a controlled demolition. Hell, there were even a few TV talking heads on camera with Building 7 standing in the background, telling their viewers that it had collapsed, twenty minutes before it actually did. You see, when you sit down and devote as many hours as I have to a real investigation, it allows you to see strange anomalies that stack up so high and so fast that you finally start to see the forest through the trees. It's what I refer to as 'the awakening,'" he laughed. "Yeah, that's when you find yourself looking into all the details surrounding 9/11 and the only things you see are truth and you start an awakening process. It's pretty damn painful for most people. I have to admit, even though my scientific mind questioned those buildings being brought down by airplanes and the resulting kerosene fires, I found myself believing what I was seeing and being told on the television that morning. Luckily, my best friend from college had been a New York firefighter, and he shared his doubts with me about what really went on that day. He and many others reported multiple explosions inside the towers—many of them were on the lobby level. Hell, the minute those words came out of his mouth, it was like a firecracker went off in my head. All of a sudden, the spell that the controlled media had me under was broken and I started to think critically. I was up all night for weeks studying every detail I could find on the internet, reviewing the initial reports, reading articles that interviewed the first responders, and eye witnesses. I was obsessed with learning the truth, yet at the same time a big part of me inside—I don't know, like my heart—that didn't want to know what I feared I would find. I knew if I discovered that it wasn't in fact, nineteen radical Muslims who barely knew how to fly a Cessna, at the helm of those jets, I would have to face a reality that would change my life forever. I was going to have to face the fact, that in order for this event to have been pulled off, our government, our intelligence agencies, and maybe a foreign government or two had to be involved." Max paused suddenly, his mind reliving those first painful moments of realization. "I spent two years fighting for this country in Viet Nam, I sure as hell didn't put my life on the line over in that armpit of a place for a government that would kill its own people just to start another quagmire of a war to keep the damn military-industrial complex alive and well. Unfortunately, when you get to the bottom of this rabbit hole, that's pretty much what you discover. Only the most evil and corrupt humans, if you can call them that, could conjure up and pull off a day like nine eleven. If you dig just below the surface, not even all that deep, you find most of the players from the old Iran-Contra scandal. Coincidence? I don't think so. I don't want to overwhelm you with too much information, but I want you to know, I've researched this event and those behind it and I've discovered an overwhelming amount of involvement by many very wealthy people who all connect. I've worked with some of the most intelligent minds in the country to put all this information together. None of us have made any money from this research; we just wanted to get to the truth. Many people instinctively knew from day one that something was very wrong with the official story the media was playing over and over on our TV sets. The CEO of the financial conglomerate that took a direct hit didn't go to his office in the North Tower that morning. He ended up conveniently in a television studio two or three hours later, telling the world it was a terrorist attack and lo and behold the commentator is telling us this man is now a counter-terrorist expert. Oh, surprisingly, a couple years later, this same CEO was appointed to be the governor of Iraq. He then, hired the former New York Police Chief that managed to find a pristine passport belonging to one of the alleged hijacker's, laying in the street. A few years later, that police chief was hired to train Iraq's new police force, but I seem to recall he was later busted for either drug running or fraud, maybe both. I think he served about eight years in prison for whatever it was he was involved in, the guy was just real dirty. And then we had another guy—I forget his name, Jerry Hauser or something like that—sitting there on CBS with Dan Rather; within a half hour of the first plane strike. He telling us that someone in Afghanistan named Osama bin Laden was behind the attacks. A closer look at this guy; is about as enlightening as a rattlesnake biting your ass. He coincidently worked for the company that ran security for the World Trade Center. That company is so connected to the CIA, they might as well change their logo. Someone in that security company had ordered the bomb-sniffing dogs to stop their patrolling a week or two before the event and a complete power down of the building, the entire weekend before all hell broke loose that Tuesday morning. He was also working with the Department of Health and Human Services and claimed to be an expert in bioterrorism. Wouldn't you know he also ended up being connected to the anthrax that showed up a couple of weeks later? He had told the White House to start taking the antidote for anthrax, called

Cipro, on day one or maybe it was the week prior to the attacks. Oh, best part of that anthrax scare, the first guy they claimed was responsible, actually sat on the board of directors for SAIC— Scientific Applications International Corporation. In addition the heads of the CIA, Department of Defense, TRW, and the New York Office of Emergency Management sat on that board. There are so damn many connections to the CIA, the government, our military and all the companies that supply our military in times of war, it will blow your mind. I always wondered what was meant when people said 'military-industrial-complex'—I think I have a little better understanding of it now. It's one hell of an evil machine and it's controlled by people we were raised to believe we could trust, honor and respect. No, this entire event was just way too complicated and way too connected to the U.S. government and lots of big name-banks to be cooked up, managed, controlled, and pulled off so flawlessly by some Arab halfway around the world. He'd have to have been the smartest and one of the most well connected individuals on the entire planet. You just have to follow the money—as they said in the movie, All the President's Men—and it will lead you to the guilty parties." He ended his statement with a laugh, but his eyes remained fixed on the corridor.

"Well, I wasn't sure if you wanted to talk about the 9/11 event when you called, you said you had something else in mind. I apologize for bloviating on like an old fool, but you know how passionate I am to all of this. Now how can I help you Jim?" Max asked.

"Vera and I are particularly interested in the 747 crash in Las Vegas that killed the First Lady and the explosion in the Orlando terminal. On the way over here, we discovered a huge security breach with airport wheelchairs. We conducted a little experiment and found that you can sneak anything through security in one of those. This is not public information, but the last thing the President's brother remembers before the explosion in Orlando was a wheelchair heading into the jetway of the plane that exploded. End of the day, we don't think either event was an accident. We want your help determining just what did happened," Jim explained.

"On first blush, I tend to agree with you, but then I'm a certified conspiracy nut," Max chuckled. "Let me go home and make a few phone calls to some of my favorite 9/11 researchers and see if I can find out if these were another false flag like 9/11 or real terrorist attacks. It will take several hours for them to all get back to me either by phone or email. How about we meet back at your hotel for dinner tonight?"

Jim and Vera agreed on the plan and liberally thanked Max for the morning lecture series. On the way back to the hotel, Jim tried to get Max to promise to bring one of his ponytail wigs. He wanted to send a picture to Mari to see if she would be down with him growing one. Vera turned toward Jim and rolled her eyes, "I'm not so sure that's such a good idea, Jim," she said. "Why don't you save that for Halloween some year?"

thirty

Air Force One touched down at Andrews Air Force Base at exactly four-thirty p.m. The President had spent the morning with community leaders in Dallas, showing his support for their widespread initiatives on job growth. Texas was a bastion of free enterprise. Its governor and legislature had nullified many of the onerous federal laws and regulations that had nearly forced small business out of existence. President Sherman had replaced the former Attorney General with one who had no desire to sue individual states for non-compliance of such governmental interference. His appearance in Dallas had been all about making a statement that Texas was a sovereign state which had the right to govern and regulate its affairs under the tenth amendment. His breakfast speech to the Chamber of Commerce, clearly stated that federal government interference would no longer be tolerated and that states should compete with one another to attract business and growth. Both he and his speech were well received. He attended a lunch reception and fundraiser, which always seemed to be a part of any travel itinerary. Having only run for office as a Congressman from a rural district in Washington State, fundraising on a national scale was new to him and not very appealing. The President actually hated the pompous choreographed receptions he had to attend and there were many reasons for his detest, not the least of which was his having to attend them without a First Lady. The few events that Mica had attended with him were so much more enjoyable. The two of them had always worked well together as a team and could easily play off each other against some of the more obnoxious donors. He tried several times inviting single female members of Congress from his party to attend these events with him, but that only made matters worse because of the rumors the press circulated following the fundraisers. He could barely stand to read the papers the next day. Presently, he just sucked it up and did the best he could under the unpleasant circumstances.

The short ride from Andrews to the White House lawn was always Joel's favorite part of any trip. He loved seeing the city in all its splendor day or night, but his favorite part was landing on the lawn and saluting the Marine guards who stood at attention as he exited the helicopter. Having served his country in uniform, he knew what these men's world was like, and he truly appreciated their service. When the cameras weren't rolling, he often engaged them in conversation to get to know them on a personal level. Those short conversations meant a lot to the President, but they meant even more to the guards.

When the President arrived at the residence, Mike was there to greet him in his study, holding a tray with a bowl of his favorite ice cream and a fist full of red licorice. It had become a tradition with these two and a carryover from years earlier when Joel arrived home late in the evening. Now, it was just anytime he came home on Air Force One. "How was your trip to Dallas, sir?"

"I love Texas, Mike. I wish we could move the executive branch to the Lone Star State. They understand what this country is all about and are proud to put it on display."

"If you recall, sir, I was originally from Texas. I lived there until I was ten. Texas blood never expires. Will there be anything else, Mr. President?"

"I'm good, Mike. Oh, so why aren't you a Cowboy fan?"

"I never cared for Tom Landry's hat, sir."

"That will indeed be all, Mike," the President said, laughing.

Joel hadn't heard anything from Jim since he and Vera had left Seattle. He wondered how Vera was doing and if she had been able to sink her teeth into their security research project. It was enjoyable for him to connect with her on Facebook without her knowing who he was. Of course, for security reasons that was necessary and it added a certain amount of intrigue to their budding friendship. He knew that no long lasting relationship, however, could be built on deceit. Joel flipped open his laptop and looked for Vera. He checked to see if she had recently posted on any Facebook thread and when he noticed she had, he sent her a private message. "Hello, Ms. Hanson, where are you flying to these days, hopefully not Paris?" He waited for a few minutes and was delighted when her response came back.

"I'm in Minneapolis this afternoon, relaxing and about to step out for dinner with some close friends."

"Minneapolis? That doesn't sound like the kind of schedule you would keep. I thought you were an international kind of gal," Joel quickly responded.

"I'm actually on a leave of absence from flying and doing some research with a friend of mine. So you're right, Minneapolis isn't a place I'd normally schedule to fly to, in order to earn a living, lol."

Joel thought he would test her a little by asking, "Oh, what kind of research are you doing?"

He waited for a response. Perhaps she was thinking or maybe she just didn't want to tell him about her personal business. Either way, Joel was impressed with the type of discretion she employed.

When her response finally came, it read, "We are researching some aviation history and how it relates to current aviation events."

"Damn," Joel thought, "this woman could be an ambassador." He prodded her a little further. "I'm kind of a flight history buff myself. Is it anything I might be interested in knowing?" He asked.

Her response was immediate. "Why, yes, it might be something you would enjoy. If we ever write a book, I'll make sure you get the first copy."

The President could see he wasn't going to get anywhere with this woman. She was indeed someone who could be trusted and he liked that, so he closed with, "I will let you prepare for dinner. Message me if anything exciting in aviation history blows up in your face."

"Ahh, yeah, I shall," she responded.

Vera was enjoying her cyber conversations with Stan the Man. She was very happy he had never asked to call her on the phone and he was always a gentleman. He didn't monopolize her time and his questions were always about her which made her feel good. When she thought about it, she had never really asked him too many questions. When she did, she certainly didn't get an in-depth answer. She wasn't quite sure how she felt about that, but it didn't matter, who could she possibly meet on Facebook of any consequence?

thirty-one

Max sauntered into the hotel restaurant exactly at six o'clock, wearing a black shirt tucked all the way into his jeans—but only on one side. His Panama hat didn't look like it had moved from his head. But it must have, because this evening his ponytail was a fashionable dark blonde. For all his disheveled appearance, he prided himself on being punctual. He looked around for Jim and Vera, and when he didn't see them, he found his way to a table in the corner and positioned himself with his back to the wall. This seating ritual was an old Mafia trick he had been practicing for the past decade and one that he claimed had kept a bullet out of his back.

Fortunately, his wait ended about the same moment he became comfortable in his chair. Jim saw Max immediately and escorted Vera to the table.

"Love you as a blond—it does wonders for your eyes," Vera commented with just a hint of sarcasm, "may we join you?"

"By all means folks, glad to see you could finally make it tonight," Max replied, playing her game. "Let's order dinner and enjoy our meal, then afterwards we can get down to business with a pot of coffee and a subtle hint to the waitress to kindly leave us alone. Does that sound like a plan?"

Vera liked that idea very much. She knew they were going to receive another heavy dose of information tonight, so a slight delay was welcomed. Jim just looked at Max's ponytail again and laughed, "You're the boss, buddy. I'd follow that ponytail anywhere."

Once dinner had concluded, Max had the waitress clear the table completely and bring a large pot of coffee. "Now then, let's blow the lid off this fairytale," Max said, dumping an envelope full of pictures onto the table. "I think you both know the story about Kurt, the FEMA photographer in Argentina who your husband met, correct?"

Both Vera and Jim nodded in the affirmative.

"Now Vera, do you have the pictures with you that Jeff brought back?" Max asked.

Vera reached into her purse, pulled out her envelope and placed it on the table.

"Good, I'm glad you have these. I want to compare them to the ones I have and see if I can reinforce what I believe occurred that day down in the basement of Building 4. I hope you had a chance to read through some of the material I left with you this morning about the gold. If you have, this will all make a lot more sense to you."

Vera and Jim both silently nodded.

Max continued, "The Bank of Nova Scotia had a huge vault in the basement of Building 4. Inside that vault was upward of two hundred billion dollars' worth of gold." Max thumbed through his pictures pulling out the exact one and then sorted through Vera's photographs until he found something even more fascinating. "Now look at these," he pushed the two pictures in front of Jim and Vera. "In this picture you can see a completely empty vault and in Vera's you can see the same vault covered with a fine dust or powder on the empty shelves with the name KURT written in the dust. Here's another one, with the door to the vault clearly open and falling off one of its hinges. Now what does that tell you?"

Jim studied the pictures carefully and said, "All the gold bullion had been removed from the vault at the time these pictures were taken."

"But," piped up Vera, "it had to have been removed prior to the towers coming down or there would be spaces on the shelves where the gold had been stacked."

"Correct little lady, you are exactly right and these pictures of Jeff's make that point even more clearly. When the search and rescue teams reached this vault, there were two trucks filled with gold trapped in the debris from the collapse of the building. The mayor claimed they recovered two hundred million dollars' worth of gold and the media claimed it was a full recovery. Look at this, here is an actual photograph of one of the two trucks from Vera's stack, notice how the front end of that truck is crushed and it looks like the front tire is flat. So what we have here, ladies and gentlemen, is a damn gold heist taking place just prior to those buildings collapsing."

"No wonder they're hunting Kurt down. This is proof that someone knew these buildings were not only going to be hit by airplanes, but that they were going to implode. They knew the precious metals were in this vault. Max, you're right, this event really was one hell of a gold heist," Jim remarked staring at the photographs.

Vera's heart sunk. The implications now were all too clear. If someone was trying to get to Kurt to kill him and if they knew Jeff had copies of Kurt's photographs, they would have killed Jeff as well. She gasped a deep breath of air. Jim knew exactly what she had just realized. He motioned to Max with one hand to hold up a minute and tried to comfort Vera with the other.

"I'll be okay, Jim. This isn't a total surprise, now it's just all too real," Vera replied, in the bravest voice she could muster.

After a few minutes, Jim motioned to Max to continue.

"Not only that, but this stuff was all insured and the insurance was paid out on the lost fortune that was really stolen. Who knows where it went or how it got there. This, along with the put options on the two airlines—worth hundreds of millions—and the illegal transactions that were rushing through the computer systems as the attack was ongoing—there is no way to know what the total price tag could be," Max explained.

Jim suggested they retreat to his room for further conversation. After paying the bill and generously tipping the waitress, for her excellent lack of service, they headed upstairs.

Once inside Jim's room, Max began again, "We as a nation are headed for real trouble." He cleared his throat, "I'm not sure how much of this I can dump on you. First, about the most recent airline disasters, they're being researched by some of the same people that helped to bring out the truth about 9/11. I should have more information in the coming days. Second, there's something else going on. I told you I have boots on the ground in Vegas, and I do mean on the ground. These guys are retired intelligence and black ops fellas who split away from the alphabet agencies not long after 9/11. I like to refer to them as the good guys in white hats." He let out a chuckle. "You see, sometime after the Kennedy assassination, something happened to our government. There was a fracture of sorts. That's the best way I can explain what was happening. Things really started going in the wrong direction at a rapid pace about the time of the first World Trade Center bombing in '93, followed by the Oklahoma City bombing in '95. Both were inside jobs that started the ball rolling. Shortly after the Oklahoma City bombing, the 1996 Antiterrorism Act was passed. That was the first assault on our Constitution. Then came the US Patriot Act, followed by the National Defense Authorization Act, the NDAA for short. Each time an event happens, we lose more and more of our rights and freedoms as Americans. I'm sure you two have seen drastic changes in airport security and how they handle or should I say mishandle the traveling public and crew members. Those Homeland Security freaks with their TSA thugs stop traffic for no reason on our highways now, just to show control and instill fear. These power-hungry jerks are turning our country into a police state not much different than Hitler's Germany. But, I digress. Something is up. We have intelligence and lots of it, indicating that something monumental is cooking. Our group is good, and they know how to do things undetected, no matter how nasty those government freaks try to be. I can almost feel it in my soul. The 747 crash in Vegas that killed the First Lady shook me up—really got my antennae up, so to speak. Those photos I gave you and the information I'll be sending you in the next few days, means that you two are in danger. Those photos of the empty vault and the trucks leaving with the gold are proof that they don't want anyone to have. If word gets out that someone had prior knowledge of this event, the entire banking industry, the Federal Reserve, and hell's bells, even the White House and all of D.C., will come unraveled. People around the world will become outraged and demand the perpetrators pay for their crimes. You two had better start being more alert than you've ever been in your lives. These people have eyes and ears everywhere. You're dealing with more than one agency that has the ability to monitor phone calls, internet activity, and much more. One more false flag terror event and we'll find ourselves living under martial law. I'll be in touch in the next day or two, might take me three at the outside."

As Max headed toward the door, he turned and smiled. "Here's a little something I memorized from a YouTube video, one of my favorites. It's James Corbett's, 9/11 in a Nutshell." He turned and stood with his back straight against the door like a little boy ready to recite a Christmas poem.

"You know, they are asking you to believe that on September 11, 2001, nineteen Arab men armed with box cutters, managed by a guy living in a cave fortress, half way around the world on kidney dialysis, using a satellite phone and a laptop, directed the most sophisticated operation on the most heavily defended airspace in the world, overpowering the passengers and military trained pilots in the cockpit of four commercial aircraft before flying those planes wildly off course for an hour, without being molested by a single interceptor fighter plane. These nineteen hijackers were supposed to be devoutly religious fundamentalists who like to drink alcohol, snort cocaine and live with pink haired strippers, managed to knock down three buildings with 2 planes in New York. While in D.C., a pilot who couldn't handle a single engine Cessna was able to fly a 757 in an eight-thousand-foot descent in a 270-degree corkscrew turn coming in exactly level with the ground, hitting the Pentagon exactly at the budget analyst office where the Department of Defense staffers were investigating the mystery of the 2.3 trillion dollars the defense secretary had just announced missing in a press conference the day before. Luckily for the public, the news anchors knew who did it within minutes, the pundits knew within hours, and the administration knew within days, while the evidence literally fell from sky and into the lap of the FBI when a hijacker's passport was found intact, blocks away from the World Trade Center. For some reason, a group of crazy conspiracy theorists demanded an investigation of the greatest attack on American soil in history. That investigation was delayed, underfunded, and set up to fail; a conflict of interest and a cover up from start to finish. It was based on testimony extracted by torture, records of which were destroyed, and which failed to mention building seven, able danger, PTech, Sibel Edmonds, Osama bin Laden, the CIA, and the ongoing drills of hijacked planes that were being simulated at the precise time the events were actually happening. It was lied to by the Pentagon, the CIA, and the Administration. The President and Vice President testified in secret, off the record, not under oath, and behind closed doors. It did not bother to look at who funded the attacks because they claimed that was of little practical significance. Still the 9/11 commission did a brilliant job of answering all the questions the public had, except the questions of the victims' families. No one involved as much as lost their job and the commission determined that it was a 'failure of imagination' because no one in our government could imagine terrorists flying planes into buildings, except the Pentagon, FEMA, NORAD and the NRO. The DIA destroyed 2.5 terabytes on Able Danger because it probably wasn't important. The SEC destroyed their investigations into ongoing insider trading before the attacks, NIST has classified the data they used for a model of the WTC Building 7 collapse and the FBI has argued that all of their investigation of 9/11 should be kept secret from the public. Osama bin Laden lived in a cave fortress in the hills of Afghanistan then he was hiding out in Tora Bora, but somehow he got away. Then he lived in Abbottabad for years taunting the most comprehensive intelligence dragnet, employing the most sophisticated technology in the history of the world for a decade, releasing videos with complete impunity and getting younger and younger as he did. So, before finally being found in a daring SEAL team raid, which wasn't recorded on video in which he didn't resist or use his wife as a human shield and in which this crack team of special forces panicked and killed this unarmed man, supposedly the best source of intelligence about the most dastardly terrorist on the entire planet. Then they dumped his body into the ocean before telling anyone about it then, a couple dozen of those team members died in a helicopter crash in Afghanistan. That is the story of 9/11 brought to you by the media. If you have any questions about this story you are a bat shit crazy, paranoid, tin foil hat wearing, dog abusing, baby hater and will be reviled by everyone. If you love your country and or freedom and happiness and rainbows, rock-n-roll, puppy dogs, apple pie, and your grandma, you will never ever express doubts about any part of this story to anyone, ever! The government's motto is 'Ignorance is Strength.'"

Max took a bow. Before he turned to walk out the door said,

"You two just think about that, it's from one of the best videos I've ever seen. I've used it many times to help people wake up to the truth. People usually feel like they have been hoodwinked by the press and our government after watching this video. Like I said, the media and the government are two arms of the same beast—or should I say two tentacles of the same octopus."

Jim and Vera sat silently staring at the door as it closed. After a few minutes, Vera said, "I'm wishing I had a martini and I don't even like to drink martinis. I honestly don't know what to say. Those pictures along with all the information Max gave us, clearly indicates that the events of 9/11 had very little or nothing to do with nineteen Arabs that were horrible pilots. It truly is impossible to believe the government story now." She chuckled, thinking of Max's little recitation and then she said, "How stupid does it make you feel to think they want us to believe such a nonsensical story?" Vera stood up and headed for the door, "I guess I have my homework to do. What's the schedule for tomorrow, boss?" she asked.

"We'll stay here in Minneapolis for a day or two. I want to be able to contact Max again when he has more information and it's much easier to do that in person. So, for the next couple of days, I want you to digest all this information. Max has spent years compiling what he shared with us today; no doubt it will take time to understand it all. Just the fact that there's a force out there evil enough to kill thousands of people, makes the truth unbearable. It steals our innocence and causes us to look at everything with a jaundiced eye. We were brought up in a generation that was led to believe that the media was there to keep the politicians honest and to inform us of the truth. What we have now—and have had for several years—is a media that's complacent or has the same agenda as this evil force."

Vera was intending to head back to her room, but as she turned to walk down the hall, the elevator seemed to suck her inside; she could hear the martini calling. She found a dark booth in the corner of the bar and sat with her back to the wall facing the entrance. Was she getting paranoid now after learning this shocking new information?

"Whatcha thinking about?" A tall young man asked, breaking her spell by tossing a coaster in front of her.

"Oh, I need," she paused, "I would like, no, I really need a very dry martini, Grey Goose, if you have it—shaken not stirred. I plan on meeting James Bond later," she said with a smile.

"One Grey Goose all shook up, yes ma'am."

Just then, Vera noticed Jim stroll into the bar, heading in her direction.

"You weren't kidding about that martini, were you?" He laughed, "To be honest with you, the idea struck a responsive chord in me too. I know what you must be feeling about now. I'm sure all of this would have been a little more palatable if Jeff had shared all of his information with you, but I knew him well and I can tell you, he's smiling down on you right now. He knew what a confusing and conflicting journey this truth trip would be for all who were brave enough to endure it to the end. It's a hell of a lot easier and much safer to stay in the make-believe world, where we all once resided. What you'll find on this journey is not nice—it's downright evil. And you can bet your bottom dollar, it didn't stop at 9/11. I'm not one hundred percent certain of the information Max is going to bring us, but I have a pretty darn good idea and it's not something we ever thought we would have to worry or even think about as Americans."

The waiter returned with Vera's drink and placed the Martini glass in front of her. He took one look at Jim and remarked, "Mr. Bond, I presume?"

Jim smiled and replied, "Yes, Bond, James Bond. I'll have what she is having, only make mine a double."

The bartender gave him a quick nod as he shook the stainless steel cocktail shaker and poured Vera's martini, then quickly reached for the chilled bottle of Grey Goose for Jim.

When Jim's drink was poured, he lifted his glass to make a toast, "To research and recovery!" Their glasses clanked together, "May your research be fruitful and truth-filled and your recovery both swift and strong."

thirty-two

The next morning when the phone rang, Vera reached for the receiver, knowing that it could only be Jim. "Hello," she said, trying to sound cheery and wide-awake.

"Sounds like I woke you. Are you up for breakfast in fifteen minutes?" Jim asked, trying to be generous with time.

"I'm going to need thirty, Jim. I'll meet you in the coffee shop. Go ahead and order me a glass of orange juice."

"Got it, see you in thirty," Jim confirmed.

Vera joined Jim and immediately started in, "I'm still troubled by the phone calls that came from those four airplanes. Reportedly, the calls came from both cell phones and in-seat airphones."

Jim looked past his coffee cup and asked, "Okay, you're point?"

"I have several, so bear with me, please. We've talked about cell phones working at altitude and the impossibility of that scenario being real. Yet, many of the people on the receiving end of those calls swear that they were cell phone calls they received from their loved ones."

Jim started taking notes on his napkin and nodded to Vera to continue.

"Six of these calls were from flight attendants made to phone numbers they might not ordinarily have had access to, but worse to family or friends, which was strictly against procedures and FAA protocols. Now, I can understand that happening in one case, maybe two, but at least one flight attendant made a personal call on every one of those flights. I can't buy that. Are you with me so far?" she asked.

"I'm here to listen and rely on your expertise, so please continue."

"When I read the transcripts of all those calls, there were several glaring irregularities that stood out. For example, why would someone in this case, an adult passenger, call his mother and use both his first and last name to identify himself? Why would a flight attendant say that they 'think or we might' be being hijacked? If they were being hijacked, there would be no doubt. How could one say that mace was used in the forward cabin and yet no coughing or choking was heard in coach? Jim, you know what would happen if mace was released in a pressurized cabin, the whole damn plane would be hacking in seconds, including the hijackers. Everyone who made phone calls spoke in a calm voice and interestingly, when asked, no one on the receiving end of those calls heard jet noise or panicked passengers in the background. Several callers pointed out the fact that this wasn't a hoax or tried to establish certitude by asking if the person they called believed them. And one flight attendant actually told a supervisor, 'Listen, and listen to me good.' Vera made quote signs with her fingers. Jim, no flight attendant would ever speak that way to a supervisor, even if she were being hijacked. Later, another flight attendant used those same words, 'listen and listen to me good.' Oh and another thing, almost all of them said that the hijackers were Middle Eastern or Iranian, as if there is no difference between Arabs and Persians. Yet nobody mentioned any identifying feature that would indicate their Middle Eastern background."

"Okay, Vera, those are all interesting anomalies, some of which I've wondered about myself. Can you draw any collective conclusions about them?" He asked.

Vera was deep in thought as she finished her coffee. She pushed her cup aside and stared out the window, almost not wanting to answer. She drew a long, deep breath, and then exhaled slowly while looking Jim directly in the eye. "After listening to Max last night and learning about all the gold and the financial craziness that went on that day, the only way I can make sense of all these phone calls is if I force myself to drop the official illusion that I have been fed for all these years and think based on the logical facts instead of the fantasy. When I do that, I come to only one logical conclusion: Every one of those calls was made on the ground and many of the callers were forced to use cue cards or notes with specific details they had to say. It's the only way I can explain the total lack of fear in their voices. They knew the planes weren't going to crash, since they'd already landed. And it's also the only way I can justify the total disregard for FAA hijacking protocols on the part of all the flight attendants."

Vera searched Jim's face for a reaction. When it wasn't immediately forthcoming, she couldn't help but wonder if she might have crossed a line into foolishness. She waited.

Jim looked down at his paper napkin and underlined some of the words he had written. Then he too found the spot out the window where thoughts seemed to become focused. He tapped his pen nervously on the table and then spoke, "You're probably right. Your theory does explain the phone calls, but it also opens the door to other questions we don't have answers to. For now, let's assume you're right. What do you think about the FBI showing up at the call recipients' homes within a half-hour of those passengers' calls and confiscating their caller IDs, and their messaging systems? The agents then insisted that no one could have received a call from a cell phone."

"You know as well as I do, Jim, that the FBI did not receive any information about passengers from the airlines in that short of time. 'The press be damned' attitude is an industry-wide standard, and in an event like this, the companies would've had to check and double-check passenger manifests, crew orders, and jump-seat authorizations for each of those flights. It usually takes more than a day or two for that information to be released to anyone, including the FBI, but especially to the media. You remember we heard that information announced only a few hours after the crashes. I recall thinking how unusually fast all that private information was released, and I questioned the airlines' ability to contact even the flight crews' next of kin. The FBI almost had to have had prior knowledge of who was on those flights, who made those calls, and to whom those calls were made. I would bet you they didn't get that information from either airline. There simply wasn't enough time. Look how long it took the media to receive that kind of information on the Vegas and Orlando tragedies. The powers that be had to quell the notion that cell phones were used because that was a huge oversight in their plan, but they were willing to take that risk because that was the only way they could get the information out through the media to the world about what they wanted you to think happened onboard those planes. I mean come on, without those cell phone calls, we would have never known about the nineteen Arabs, box cutters, Allahu Akbar, and all the other baloney they dumped on us within hours of the crashes. Is it any wonder that for the next decade movies and television showed people using cell phones on airplanes? Those images were put in front of the public to bolster the illusion in their collective conscience that such things were possible, it's called predictive programming. I learned about that in college. The professor explained that the government can easily have anything it wants you to think subtly woven into any television or movie script to brainwash you."

Jim nodded his head and then pointed his finger at Vera, "Okay for now, we will assume all calls from the planes took place on the ground, we don't know where or how, but we will assume the why. Let's set that aside for the time being and move on to another subject, but we'll keep this information in mind and test it against the next phase."

"What phase would that be, boss?" Vera asked, while looking at her empty coffee cup then searching for the waitress.

"My trouble has been with the pilots. Something you mentioned yesterday about not squawking 7500. It's highly unlikely that four or five hijackers would have controlled all the flight attendants simultaneously since they would have been scattered throughout the cabin, some in the aisles taking orders while others were in the galleys preparing the breakfast service, and one or two, no doubt, in the lavatories. That being the case, at least one of the cabin crew would have had the opportunity to call the flight deck and give the hijack code word. Once that happened, the pilots would have immediately squawked the hijack code to notify ATC and the company. All of the flight deck crew members were well-trained military pilots. Are you telling me that landing an F-18 on an aircraft carrier in the middle of the night in rough seas is easier than hitting the hijack code if you think your passengers' lives or your airplane is in danger?"

"So, why were none of the hijacking protocols followed by any of the flight attendants and why didn't any pilot in one of the four cockpit crews hit the hijack code to notify air traffic control?" Vera asked.

"Maybe they didn't know they were being hijacked," Jim quickly responded. "That is the only thing that makes sense."

"How could they not know they were being hijacked?" Vera's confusion resonated in her voice. "How could any flight attendant miss seeing a hijacker onboard?"

"Maybe the pilots thought the aircraft was suffering from a mechanical problem and were busy, maybe that's why they were not answering the interphone when the flight attendants tried calling," he said, thinking aloud.

Jim found himself staring out the window again. His mind

was reviewing emergency procedures that might have been going on in the cockpits that morning. His training and numerous hours in a flight simulator presented him with many different scenarios. It had to be something associated with the control of the aircraft. If there were something wrong inside the cabin, the flight attendants would have called or come into the cockpit to report it verbally. The plane's possible altitude and the duties of the pilots onboard the flights rolled through his mind like a training film.

Vera was mentally reviewing every scenario she had ever come across in her yearly recurrent training. Why wouldn't any flight attendant that day follow their training? Their in-flight duties would have had them barely out of their jump-seats that early in the flight. She reviewed the PA announcements she would have been making at that stage of the flight and what the crew in coach would have been doing to prepare the breakfast service. The flight attendants would have been busy preparing breakfast and there would be no reason for them to contact the cockpit as was reported in their phone calls.

Jim shook his head as if to clear his mind, "Vera, I have a sick feeling in my gut, and I'm afraid there's way more to this story. The only possibility, as crazy as it sounds, is that neither the cockpit crews nor the flight attendants knew what was happening to them and their aircraft."

Vera drew in a deep breath while taking in the significance of what Jim had just said. She started to process his statement, but knew it would require more strength than she felt she had at the moment. "Let's eat some breakfast and continue this conversation when we can get upstairs to our notes and our laptops. I feel like we're about to find some missing pieces to this puzzle."

thirty-three

Vera spent the rest of the afternoon organizing her research into piles on the king size bed in her room. It was easier for her to study one subject in-depth, then move on to something else, than it was to obtain an overview of many subjects. She was right in the middle of sinking her teeth into the flight termination system information when Jim knocked on her door. She welcomed him inside and challenged him to find a place to sit down. He looked around and calmly said, "Girl, you've been hijacked."

Vera let out a laugh and pretended to hold a telephone to her ear, "Captain, I'm being methodical, this has become an awful trip."

Jim's quick comeback was simply, "Well squawk, squawk, Houston, we have a problem."

At that, they both burst out laughing, until Vera had tears running down her cheeks. Just as they were beginning to compose themselves, Jim's cell phone started to buzz. It was a text message in code, indicating Max was in the lobby. Jim sent a text back telling him to come to Vera's room.

When Max entered the room and saw all the papers stacked neatly on the bed, he went over and shook Vera's hand and patted her on the back. He didn't even say a word, he didn't need to. She just grinned and shrugged her shoulders in Jim's direction.

"Max, we were just about to do some research on the flight termination system on those Boeings used on 9/11. Putting all of our experience and understanding together this morning over breakfast, we figured there was a good chance that a system like that might have taken over control of the planes remotely and the crews possibly didn't even know they were being hijacked," Jim explained. "That's one explanation as to why none of the crew members responded as they were trained. Had the planes been commandeered remotely, the flight deck would have assumed that when their plane didn't respond to their commands, it was a mechanical problem, not a hijacking."

Max interrupted before Jim could finish, "But you couldn't figure out how air traffic control would have missed them landing or how they wouldn't have seen exactly where the planes flew to if it wasn't into those buildings, right?"

Jim and Vera both looked at Max in amazement, "Yeah, how did you know that?" Questioned Vera.

Max stroked his chin, "Sit down, folks. I have a little story to tell you. Several years back, there was quite a stink about a software company called Inslaw. I'm going to guess it was some time in the mid 1980's. They produced software called PROMIS, which was originally designed to keep track of criminals for the Department of Justice. Somewhere along the line, our government gave this software to a friendly foreign intelligence agency. That foreign intelligence agency had what's called a 'backdoor' installed into the program. Once the secret entrance was in place, they began to install this software on computer systems around the world. You see, this PROMIS software was the most complex and intrusive software ever developed. It had been modified with artificial intelligence, data mining capabilities, and interoperability across any platform. This one single program could also operate and modify the source codes of other programs. I know that sounds complicated, but in short, it could perform magic tricks, in a sense. By using this backdoor, an operator could manipulate a computer screen remotely; he could make things that were not real show up as visible and cause other things that were real, to completely disappear. It could take an FAA computer screen, for example, and display fake planes in the air traffic patterns and make a real plane's radar blips disappear. That same software also had the ability to make NORAD's screens unable to view what the FAA or Air Traffic Controllers were seeing on their screens. Now, can you see how someone with this software might be able to mess with our national security a wee bit? It's the perfect spy software. That's the condensed version, but you can find all the information online quite easily. To continue, this software was installed on all the U.S. government computer systems, with the hope, or should I say with the promise, of closing the gaps in the incompatibility between all the different alphabet agencies. Now hold on to your pants, this might come as a shock to you. At the time of the 9/11 event, this software was installed on twenty-two U.S. government computer systems, including the White House, the Department of Treasury, the Department of Defense, the Department of Energy, the Secret Service, the Air Force, the Navy, the FAA, NORAD, the CIA, the FBI, both houses of Congress, the IRS, NATO, and many other companies, that make up what we refer to as the 'military-industrial complex.' I'm sure some of these corporate connections you have already discovered; Raytheon, Lockheed Martin, SAIC, Booz Allen Hamilton, IBM, ENRON and Boeing. Somehow someone managed to block or reroute communications between the FAA and NORAD and even managed to hack the communications systems of United Airlines and Air Force One. The President and the Vice President were unable to keep a phone connection that morning until almost noon. By then, it was all over but the cover up. What could the government do? Admit that they had installed this software that enabled a foreign intelligence agency to pull off this event? Hardly, they were either completely in on this conspiracy or they were blackmailed by their own stupidity to allow a foreign owned start-up company to install software that completely crippled our national security that day. Lord only knows what else they're capable of doing."

Jim interrupted, "What? Who was given this kind of top-level security? Why would our government hire an outside company to install software that could be commandeered by a foreign government and just how much control do they have?" Jim's mind was racing between the incredulity of the obvious national security breach and the questions that such a breach generated. "So, those radar blips the FAA and ATC were looking at could've been bogus, completely faked? Is that why there were nearly twenty reported hijacked planes showing up on some radar screens that morning, which created total confusion?"

Max's ponytail almost fell off he was nodding his head so fast in the affirmative.

"No wonder then, when the FAA contacted NEADS or NORAD, they couldn't find those first two planes on their military radar screens. That means that the flight paths—or any of the information we have seen from the FAA, could also be completely false," Jim proposed. "Both the FAA and NORAD ended up looking completely foolish and totally inept. I know there was an air traffic controller who reported the first hijacked plane was twenty miles south of Albany, New York, and that it was traveling at a speed of 600 knots, that's nearly 700 miles per hour. How could that not raise a red flag with any half-assed experienced controller? Hell's bells, that's the rate of speed a missile would travel, not a commercial airliner. To see a 767 flying at that speed, one would expect to get reports of structural damage. And how could NORAD not see it as a missile threat from a foreign country when they knew that only a missile could travel at that speed?" Jim could feel his frustration level rise as he spoke. He had been trained as a commercial pilot to rely and depend on NORAD's rapid response to any threat to his aircraft and to his country.

Max started in again, "That's just the tip of the iceberg.

We're talking about a huge corporate and government monster with tentacles that reach into nearly every aspect of our lives. Unfortunately, the principals behind this monster do not have nice things planned for humanity and especially for the United States of America. We're just the biggest stone in the road that's blocking their path to their ultimate end game. For them, our Constitution, Bill of Rights, gun ownership, and liberty are stumbling blocks and present them with their biggest challenge. They work covertly, pretending to be something they aren't, it's a deception and they are masters at the grand illusion. They have total control over both political parties too, so we are in serious trouble as a nation. Our supposed representatives in Washington D.C. that have not been blackmailed or controlled in some other fashion are very few and far between.

Max stopped talking and could see that Jim and Vera were taking in every word and begging for more. "Could one of you fetch me a coke or something? When I do this much talking, I get parched?"

Vera darted down the hall and came back with drinks for everyone. Max chugged half a bottle of Coke, wiped his mouth on his sleeve and started talking again.

"If you want to create total havoc in a country, what better way to do it than to start a war? In the situation we find ourselves in now, this monster is pulling all the strings. It's known as the Hegelian Dialectic; you create the problem, maybe a war or you cause one religion to hate another or you create and pull off what they themselves called a New Pearl Harbor, just like 9/11was designed to be. You create a conflict, and then supply both sides with weapons, fuel, and intelligence. While that war distraction is filling up newspapers and television news reports, you create laws like the Patriot Act or NDAA, both of which restrict freedom in the name of safety for the American citizen. That reaction is where the big corporations and politicians make all the money.

If we examine our country's immediate reaction to 9/11; the government spent billions of dollars on military hardware, it created new agencies like Homeland Security and the TSA, all of which usurped freedom from the people. Our own CIA, with the help of other foreign intelligence communities, created and transformed a group of Muslims into a world-wide boogeyman, capable of reaching out and striking any one of us without warning. Then to make matters worse, our media reinforced these ideas in television shows and movies which essentially brainwashed the American people to hate Muslims and blame them for all the world's ills. Hell, the government didn't even need to show us proof, they just showed that one plane flying into the South Tower over and over until it was embedded in our minds as fact. It was basic mind control and brainwashing taking place right there in every American living room."

Max leaned back in his chair until it touched the wall and kept talking. "Now, if you are an intelligence agency and you're going to arm the enemy, label them as a 'terrorist,' you sure can't get caught supporting them with U.S. taxpayer dollars now, can you? The CIA had several banks set up for this type of black operation activity where they laundered millions from arms and drug sales. One such bank was known as the BCCI, you might recall that name from the Iran-Contra scandal. These types of financial institutions don't ever really vanish, they just change their names and continue doing business and if things turn sour, Congress gives them a taxpayer-supported bailout. Nice work if you can get it. You don't have to study the 9/11 event very hard to find all the same corrupt players, the huge insurance companies, investment firms, banks, and of course, all the military contractors, and especially many of the same political figures from Iran-Contra. Okay, back to the story about the software. The company that had taken the PROMIS software to the next level was a relatively small start-up called Ptech, located just outside Boston, of all places. They, along with a much larger company, the MITRE Corporation, had been working inside the FAA headquarters on their computer systems for two years leading up to 9/11. The MITRE Corporation worked closely with the Department of Defense, the FAA, and the U.S. Navy providing simulation and testing technology, much of which was used for those military war games. Interesting item about this small start-up company, their financiers and programmers were reportedly members of an international network of organized crime, involved for decades in gunrunning, money laundering, terrorism, and narco-trafficking. You'd think that might be a matter of concern to the U.S. government, but it apparently wasn't. Now, when you find something as suspicious as a small, unheard of start-up company that's into blueprint architecture combined with artificial intelligence, buried deep inside government computer systems, you might want to take a closer look. Combine that with the fact that this company appears to have received financing from a wealthy Arab country and was managed by a guy with known ties to the Jewish intelligence agency known as the Mossad, you got yourself the makings of one hell of an exciting Hollywood movie. Except in this case, it was a horror film and it was real. This young start-up company was created somewhere around the mid 90's and by 1999; they were deep into the computer systems of nearly twenty-two U.S. government, military, and intelligence agencies. Those agencies are all extremely vital to our national security. Now, this is where it gets deep and dark and I might add, pretty damn dangerous. Anyone who figures this out and tries to get the word out to the public usually ends up dead.

"In 1991, there was a freelance journalist named Danny Casolaro, who started investigating this Inslaw Company and the PROMIS software—and how it found its way into the hands of this foreign government. His investigation cost him his life.

He uncovered a shadowy network he referred to as 'The Octopus' because it seemed to have its tentacles in everything from drug trafficking and money laundering, all the way up to political assassinations and the occasional coups d'état. The tentacles of this octopus were also tightly wrapped around our government and many of the corporations that profit from war. Danny is only one of many who have lost their lives to this entity. This octopus is the same monster behind not just the 9/11 events, but also the instigator of events that have transpired around the world like attacks on military barracks, embassies, and public transportation. And true to form, most of these events were blamed on the same group of people taking the fall for 9/11."

Max all of a sudden seemed more nervous than usual. He got up and looked out the window. The darkness made it difficult to see down to the dimly-lit parking lot. He stared for several minutes then returned to his chair without comment. He then picked up where he had left off. "This group, this octopus, as the journalist called it, is nothing to mess around with. It plays for keeps and it shoots to kill. They already have total control over the institutions that you and I grew up believing we could trust, our government and the main stream media. Their aim is control and I mean total control. We're talking world domination and total tyranny. I'm sure you heard an ex-president refer once to a 'New World Order'. Coming from a grandfatherly-looking President, it didn't sound all that alarming or threatening to our freedom. But this monster, this octopus, this cabal, whatever you want to call it, intends to garner total control not just over the citizens of the United States, but of the entire world. They first had to gain control over all the world's oil and natural resources. They pretty much have taken care of that with Iraq, Afghanistan, Libya, Syria, and their future plans for a couple other oil-rich nations. They have seized control over the flow of information in most countries already. They completely manage what news and information is broadcast, printed, and released to the public which allows them to stay well hidden and very well protected. They have control over nearly every central banking system in the world. The few countries that have managed to keep their banks free are under assault as we speak and are threatened with extinction through a managed civil war, or at least that is how it is reported to us. They run the pharmaceutical corporations and manipulate physicians to dispense drugs like candy to the masses in the western world. Hell, nearly 60% of the kids in our public schools are on some type of pharmaceutical. Needless to say, they are deep into the world of technology and have the ability to take any citizen, politician, or corporation down if they do not behave as instructed or if they start to rebel or open their mouths against this monster. Through the PROMIS software, now installed into just about every aspect of our world, they can manipulate or change everything from your IRS filings to your savings and checking accounts. They have the ability to frame anyone for a crime by planting child pornography on any home or work computer or both and to notify the proper federal law enforcement agency. You can wake up and find your bank account drained, even if it's a private numbered account in Switzerland that you thought nobody knew about. That has happened to a few politicians that were on the take. They woke up one day and their Swiss accounts were empty. All the money in those accounts was from illegal activities, so they were helpless to say or do anything. This software can monitor every single thing about a person, how much electricity his house uses, how much gasoline he usually puts in his car, how much he normally spends on groceries every month, and if they're watching him for any reason they'll be able to see any change he makes in his normal life patterns. If he starts buying ammo or more booze, whatever he does, they can watch and monitor. Now, if you're a Christian, you'll recognize the term mark of the beast, this is the 'beast' and in this case, the beast is an octopus. This is the world we find ourselves living in, where a covert international power structure super-cedes the interests of nation states and the banner of 'national security' is used to keep this network's secrets hidden from the prying eyes of both investigative journalists and the general public. This monster controls both political parties and has, through laws and many executive orders, set the stage for horrible things to come. In order to garner complete control over the world, they must take out liberty-loving America. In order to do that, they will have to disarm us so we can't fight their tyranny. They need to destroy what little is left of our Bill of Rights and Constitution. We're running out of time. Many on my research team thought that it would have happened by now; we aren't sure what slowed it down. It might have been the impeachment of the President and the changes that came as a consequence of this new Administration, we aren't really sure. But, my source in Chicago seems to be onto something monumental. We don't talk over the phone, we talk in person. Now that you know about the octopus, if you two want to talk about it, do it in person. Everything and everyone is being monitored, they just aren't doing anything about it yet, but gathering and storing loads of information on every one of us. If you are going to find a needle in a haystack you need the haystack."

"Now, one final thing, Orlando and Vegas were meant to send a message to President Sherman. They were direct threats. In Vegas, they used the flight termination system to remotely steer that aircraft directly into the hotel. That poor pilot didn't have a chance. He pulled back on the throttle of that 747 and could only watch the ride. They took over control right after throttle up and laser guided that baby in a forced stall right into the tower. Had Sherman been there, he would have been killed, but they thought by taking out his wife he would get their message. Apparently, he didn't respond the way they wanted, so they targeted his brother in Orlando. That was a remote-controlled device in a wheelchair, Jim just as you suspected. I guess the trigger man was a tad late on ignition and the President's brother and his wife survived. But something else is going down, according to my sources. There is a plan in the works much larger than 9/11. I'll drive to Chicago in the morning to meet my sources. They know every single thing we do," he laughed. "They might know what we are going to do before we even know we are going to do it. They don't scare me; I've decided long ago that if they accomplish their plan of total world domination and control, I don't want to live in that world. So, if this investigation costs me my life, as it has so many others who have dug down deep enough to find the octopus, then so be it. We grew up horrified by the stories of the Nazi's in Germany, the old Soviet Union, and Communist China. This is all basically the same threat, world domination and total control of the individual. This beast has turned people against each other for centuries. They have created wars, they have fed both sides intelligence, and they have made money implementing their plans. When all the money to be made from war is exhausted, they end the conflict and hire each other to rebuild the countries they had just destroyed. You know the Latin saying: Novus Ordo Seclorum, that's found on the back of the dollar bill? It means 'A New Order of the Ages,' don't be tricked into thinking this has some sweet peaceful meaning, it's all about total control and world domination."

Max looked down at this watch, "Holy hell, time flies when I'm with you two. You must have some kind of magic spell that I can't see coming. I was hoping to have you buy me another great dinner, but I need to get ready to head to Chicago. It's about a seven-hour, drive and I want to be there by mid-morning. Thanks for listening to me bloviate again. I hope I've been helpful to you. I'm afraid this next attack will trigger martial law, and when that happens, many folks will die. I'll keep you informed."

thirty-four

When the door closed behind Max, Jim spoke first, "Vera, did you hear what Max just said about the 747 in Vegas? It was taken over remotely. If that start-up software company he mentioned had access to all of those government computer systems, it could have easily displayed anything on the radar screens for air traffic control, the FAA and NORAD. In fact, they could have all been seeing something entirely different with those four planes. Come to think of it, NORAD was unable to see what the FAA and air traffic controllers saw that morning. I remember reading that NORAD couldn't see any radar blip at all for Flight 11; it was their excuse for such a slow response. Vera, do you realize the official flight paths that those planes took that morning could also be completely fictitious? Everyone has been using those official government flight paths as the gospel, trusting the FAA to have the actual flight data. If there's even a remote possibility that someone had the ability to manipulate the radar screens, it changes everything we thought we knew was real from that morning, including the final outcome of what exactly did fly into those buildings."

"You may be absolutely correct, Jim. That explains why NORAD thought Flight 11 was still in the air at 9:24 and was headed for D.C. That was almost 40 minutes after it supposedly hit the North Tower at 8:46. That would also explain what that retired military guy on our flight said about no 757 hitting the Pentagon. If that's the case, where in the hell were the planes taken, and what happened to the passengers and crews?"

Jim interjected, "If they put those planes on the ground, then those cell phone calls would have been able to have been made. And if they took over the jets remotely, they didn't need a tower, they didn't need permission to land, the FAA and air traffic control wouldn't have been able to see them on radar. Their transponders would have been over-ridden, those planes could be anywhere."

Vera interrupted, "This is crazy. I can't put my finger on it, but it's those calls, the timing and the almost-scripted messages from the callers that are troubling me. It just doesn't feel right. If those cell phone calls were made after the planes had landed, then where in the world would they have gone? Could all four planes have been taken to the same location?"

Jim added, "That's quite possible, but where? How much time after Flight 11 took off from Logan was the first phone call made?" Jim was busy pulling up maps of Massachusetts on his laptop as he spoke.

"Flight 11 took off from Logan field at 7:59, by 8:13 air traffic had lost communications with it and by 8:20, a flight attendant called her supervisor at Logan."

"Then they had to be on the ground by 8:20."

"A second flight attendant called into a reservations number at, it looks like; this is weird, at the same exact time, 8:20." Vera grabbed a pen and paper and began to do some quick math. "What altitude would a 767 reach fourteen minutes after take-off?"

"Depends on the traffic during climb out, but by then they could be as high as nineteen thousand feet or so, maybe a little higher. Either case, cell phones wouldn't be able to hold a signal at that altitude." His eyes were carefully scanning the maps in front of him as he spoke. "Didn't you tell me that those first two calls were nearly twenty-five minutes long? That would be nearly impossible even from an air-phone; those things had the worst reception."

"This book says the transponder appeared to be turned off either at 8:13 or 8:20, there's some conflict in times. If a hijacker got into the cockpit and turned off the transponder at 8:13, why was the flight attendant who called reservations seven minutes later, so confused about what was happening onboard? Listen to what she reported to the reservations agent, she said, and I quote: 'The cockpit is not answering their phone...' and then 'there's been a stabbing in business class and she says, 'somebody's got mace or something. We can't breathe in business class.' then she adds that she is in the back of the plane, but she doesn't show any signs of breathing difficulties or coughing. Again, she repeats, 'nobody can call the cockpit,' and then she concludes, 'we're in the air.' Could she have been sending a message? She definitely was not using the FAA hijacking protocols. Was this her way of letting her company know that this was not a typical hijacking, but something else? They could not call the cockpit or they could not communicate with the cockpit? Was that her message? Could someone have been standing over her and telling her what to say? They might not have been in the air at all. She could have been told to say that just to make it more believable. If there were hijackers onboard and they stabbed someone and got into the cockpit, why didn't one single passenger attempt to make a phone call if those two flight attendants were on the phone for nearly half an hour? There were almost a hundred people onboard that flight. The second flight attendant called at the same exact time as the first, which was not one minute after the transponder was turned off. She called a company line to her supervisor. She goes on to repeat that they 'cannot contact the cockpit' she adds that the hijackers are of quote, 'Middle Eastern descent.' This second flight attendant also tells her supervisor something else that is not important and not protocol, she says, 'they have moved all the passengers to the back of the plane.' Why would she say that and not say the most important details like how the hijackers managed to get into the cockpit? She did initially report that the hijacker was seated in 9B and later calls back to recant that claim. That would never happen, Jim, if any flight attendant reported a hijacker was in 9B, they meant 9B, period. They would only report a hijacker's identity or seat number if they were one hundred percent certain. In the event that the plane landed and was liberated by a Delta Force, they might take out the wrong guy. No way would any flight attendant make a mistake like that. These two flight attendants were on the phone to their company for nearly twenty-five minutes and didn't really give any useful information.

"Anyway, we are mostly interested in timelines here, sorry. I got carried away with the crazy details of these phone calls. It all seemed scripted to me, as if they were reading from Hollywood cue cards or being told what to say. Okay, getting back to the timeline, the transponder was turned off by somebody or somehow they lost communications and in less than one minute two of the nine flight attendants figured out that they 'might' be being hijacked? What were the other seven flight attendants thinking or doing, and what were the passengers doing? Why didn't one of the 76 passengers make a phone call from their air-phones or cell phones?" Vera questioned. She knew she was repeating herself, but these were the nagging questions that she couldn't get out of her mind.

Jim had been quietly listening to Vera as she verbally started to put the pieces of the puzzle together. "The key to this theory is that the plane had to be on the ground when those two phone calls were made. So where were they? Where would someone land a wide-body jet full of fuel? Where is there a ten-thousand-foot runway twenty minutes or less from Logan? And it would have to have the privacy to make those airplanes become invisible once they landed. Large hangars perhaps," Jim said and then muttered under his breath, "where, where, where? We're looking for a long runway about 80 miles west of Boston." Jim paused for a moment, "It's going to have to be a long enough runway to land a 767 heavy and someplace remote enough that it wouldn't be spotted. We're probably looking for a military airport that was no longer active or one that was used only on the weekends." Jim's eyes were scanning the Google Earth map on his computer as he spoke. "Hey! I think we might have something here." He zoomed in to get a closer view. "Vera, come and take a look at this."

Vera was moving in Jim's direction before he could finish his sentence. "What?"

"Right here, check this out," Jim told her as she pulled a chair up next to the desk.

"Let's turn the labels on and see what this is. It's about the right distance from Boston. They could've brought a plane down within twenty minutes easily to this distance."

Vera leaned in as Jim highlighted the labels. "Westover Air Force Base," they both chimed in at the same moment.

"I've flown over that base, I remember it was used as a C-5 Transport base, air reserves, I think. In 2001, it was likely active only on the weekends. It's possible, I suppose, if there was a Pentagon connection or some other government agency involved, the base, its runways, and those huge hangars could have been utilized on 9/11 to land and hide aircraft. And nobody would have known." Jim's voice slowed and faded as he grasped his words, if there was a Pentagon connection or some other government agency, "Vera, do you know how big a C-5 is and how large a hangar has to be to accommodate one? Think 747 on steroids."

Vera interrupted, "What are you saying? Do you think that plane could have been taken over remotely after leaving Logan, landed at Westover, and pulled into a hanger? Wait, this transcript, that first flight attendant said, 'He stood upstairs'. There are no stairs in a 767; they had to be in a hanger."

"Holy, moly! That base was on lock down on 9/11, much like all the other bases, but I recall reading that the Reserves at Westover were not just locked down, they were locked out from even entering that base for days. Now it's starting to all make sense. Vera, get on your laptop and go to airplane manager dot com."

"I'm there," Vera reported.

"Now click on the flight calculator tab," Jim instructed.

"Gotcha," Vera replied.

"Type in for aircraft type: heavy jet, winds: type in none, in the departure airport put in B O S and for your arrival C E F."

"CEF, I don't know that airport code," Vera replied.

"CEF is Westover Air Force Base," Jim informed her just as the results appeared on her screen.

"Twenty-one," Vera reported.

"Twenty-one minutes, that's pushback to gate in. Flight time could have been under nineteen minutes easily and this runway would have been a straight in shot. With no traffic on the ground, they could have been taxied into one of these five super-large hangers right here." Jim pointed to the satellite photo on his computer screen. "See, these planes parked here? They dwarf a 767. These hangars could easily accommodate more than one commercial jet."

"Let me get this straight," questioned Vera. "This flight took off to the north out of Logan, someone managed to remotely take over the flight termination system when they were well under twenty-thousand feet, probably when ATC lost communication at 8:13. The plane was remotely flown and landed at Westover, taxied into a hangar, and that would have taken under twenty minutes. That would explain why the flight attendant said, 'I don't know, I think we are getting hijacked or something.' If there were no hijackers onboard maybe just one or two guys to control the scene once they landed, the flight attendants wouldn't have known they were being hijacked. They would have only known that something was definitely not right. Oh my, Jim, do you remember when they first installed the flight termination system in commercial jets?"

"Yes, I do. Jeff worked with the pilots union against it," Jim added.

"I remember Jeff told me the reason the pilots were against it was that once activated, they would lose all communication with," Vera stopped, then continued at a slower pace, "with everyone—the cabin crew, the company, dispatch, other planes—with everyone. These first two flight attendants did say one thing that didn't ever make sense to me. Twenty minutes into an early morning flight, they wouldn't call the cockpit for any reason, unless they didn't reach cruise altitude, which would have prevented them from pulling out the meal and beverage carts. They would have all been strapped into their jump-seats waiting until they leveled off at cruise altitude. They would call the cockpit only if the plane had stopped climbing or if, oh my, if they had started a descent! Our feet know when we can get up; it becomes almost instinct after a couple years of flying. On a coast-to-coast flight, if the plane started a descent thirteen minutes into the flight, you bet they would be trying to call the pilots. That would have been the only reason any of the flight attendants would have called the cockpit that early in the flight. That plane most likely never reached its cruise altitude. That's why the flight attendants didn't know for certain that a hijacking was taking place, there was no visible hijacker making demands. If that plane was descending, the flight attendants knew it. They would have called the pilots to find out if there was an emergency and how they should prepare the cabin and passengers."

"Damn, if what you say is true, the pilots would have automatically thought their plane was having some type of mechanical problem, an issue that also prevented them from talking to the air traffic controllers, the other planes, the company dispatch, and the flight attendants. The flight termination system would have done just! Since such a thing had never happened before, they would never in a million years think that the flight termination system had taken over their plane." Jim stopped for a moment then continued, "They wouldn't have known it was a hijacking, so of course they would not have hit the highjack code. They would've been busy trying to figure out why the plane wasn't climbing and how to fix it. Then the plane would have immediately begun a descent, which would have really confused them as they went into final approach for a landing. There is no way in the world either one of them would have left the cockpit for any reason. They were experiencing an all hands-on-deck, fly-this-bird-manually-or-figure-out-how-to-over-ride-the-onboard-computer-system moment."

"What if that passenger in 9B really was a hijacker, as they first reported?" Vera questioned.

"What if he wasn't a hijacker, but someone there to handle the situation once the plane landed? Let's remember to look into who was seated in 9B," Jim implored. "Now, what about that second plane, Flight 175. How does it fit into our theory?"

"Flight 175 took off at 8:14 from Logan. The first phone calls were made at 8:52, which would've been thirty-eight minutes after take-off," Vera calculated.

"That would indeed fit the scenario," Jim nodded.

"And again, two calls were made at the exact same minute, one from a flight attendant and how odd is this, one from a passenger in coach. He called his father and said 'an airline hostess has been stabbed.'"

"A what?" Jim asked.

"He used the term 'airline hostess'. We've been called flight attendants since the late sixties," Vera laughed.

"How old was this guy and where was he from? I mean, I haven't heard that term ever used by an American. It's used in Europe and other foreign countries, but not here."

"Hold on, the book says this passenger was only thirty-two. Now that's weird since he wouldn't have been born when the term stewardess was replaced with flight attendant. We have never been called airline hostesses in his lifetime or mine," Vera said, thinking out loud. "He also called his father again, eight minutes later, three minutes before impact. This time he says, 'the stewardess has been stabbed'. He then goes on to tell his dad that the hijackers have knives and mace and that people are getting sick. And you will love this; he says he thinks 'they are going to be flown into a building in Chicago.'"

"What would make him think that? Nobody prior to 9/11 would've thought a plane would've been flown into a building and there is no way anyone on board that plane would've known what had just happened in New York."

"No kidding, that wasn't even fifteen minutes after the North Tower was hit. It's statements like his that lead me to believe he was being told what to say. Only the handlers onboard would have known the scenario that needed to be created. Details like this caught my attention a long time ago and made me question the official story." Vera was building a scenario in her mind that her heart was resisting. "They say things like 'the passengers have all been moved to the back of the plane'. Most all reported that the hijackers were 'of Middle Eastern descent'. They also claimed that the hijackers had used mace. But if you sprayed mace onboard, the entire plane would be choking."

"Not if the plane was on the ground and no longer pressurized," Jim interjected.

"Could these phone calls have been designed to methodically paint and bolster the illusion that we were all being led to believe on television?" Vera questioned.

Jim ignored her, "That might take care of the two flights out of Logan, but the other two flights came out of Dulles and Newark. Could it be possible that they were also taken over remotely and flown to this same base? Get back on that flight calculator, Vera, and punch in I A D as the departure and C E F as the arrival. Let's see if this theory holds true from Dulles. That was Flight 77 that supposedly went into the Pentagon, wasn't it?"

"According to this flight calculator, that flight would have taken roughly fifty-two minutes," she announced.

"And the first phone call that was made, who made it and what time was it made?" Jim asked.

"The first phone call was made, oh my, this is really odd. There were two calls made at exactly 9:12—one from a flight attendant who phoned her parents and the other from a passenger. And those calls were made exactly fifty-two minutes after their departure from Washington! It was reported that the flight attendant called her parents using her cell phone. Again, she did not follow FAA protocols and only told her mother that her flight was hijacked and that all the passengers were moved to the back of the plane. The passenger who called was Barbara Olson, the wife of the Solicitor General at the Justice Department. She reported also that the passengers had all been herded to the back of the plane and the hijackers had knives and box cutters. She is the only one to mention box cutters as a weapon. Why would nearly all the phone calls mention that the passengers were all moved to the back of the plane? The back section of both those airplanes is really a long distance from the front section, how would anyone in the back know anything about what was going on up front? If there were hijackers onboard, the FAA protocols instruct flight attendants to sit down and to not draw attention to themselves. No flight attendants would be running up and down the aisles in the middle of a hijacking." Vera was trying to make sense out of the scenarios.

"Well, if Flight 77 was hijacked to be flown into the Pentagon and they took off from Dulles, which is less than ten miles away, why would they continue to fly all over for nearly an hour?" Jim questioned. "On any other given day, military jets would have been scrambled within six minutes of the plane going off course or losing communication."

"According to this flight calculator, Flight 77 would have been tucked into a hangar with plenty of time to have those two people make cell phone calls. They must have had someone onboard that designated the two callers. There were fifty-three passengers and six crew members onboard. If that plane was really hijacked and was equipped with air-phones, why didn't any of the other passengers or crew members make phone calls? Someone must have prevented them from calling."

"If I recall correctly, it was that flight that hit the Pentagon or rather that they wanted us to believe hit the Pentagon. The last ten minutes of that flight would have been crazier than any roller coaster ride. The passengers would have had a very difficult time even talking. What time were her phone calls?" Jim was still taking notes as he spoke.

"Barbara Olson talked on the phone off and on for fourteen minutes until 9:26 and the crash was supposed to have happened at 9:37. Vera was scanning several pages of notes she had taken on the phone calls.

"It makes no sense that all the passengers would be moved to the very back of the plane, if it were in the air." Jim continued, "Putting all that weight in the back of the plane, in flight, would not have made it any easier to handle. It might have made more sense if the plane was on the ground, which would have allowed them to control the passengers more easily."

Vera piped up, "I'm telling you, it really sounds like they were briefed on the ongoing scenario and told what to say. That's why so many of the callers expressed they were 'in the air' or 'on the plane'. That passenger who used his first and last name when talking to his mother also asked her if she believed him and that is even crazier." Vera was flipping through the pages of both the official 9/11 Commission Report and the FBI documents Max had shared, "Now, here's something else strange. That passenger in 9B was a specially-trained Israeli Defense Forces intelligence guy. This FBI report says he was a dual citizen, an anti-hijacking specialist, a hostage rescue team member, a trained assassin and a member of Sayeret Matkal." Vera quickly typed Sayeret Matkal into a Google search and read, "Sayeret Matkal is also tasked with counter-terrorism and hostage rescue beyond Israel's borders. This Special Forces unit is described as one that would carry out strategic intelligence-gathering and other operations. It says that some of Israel's past Prime Ministers were also members of this special intelligence unit." She clicked on to another link, and read, "His friends claimed he was in remarkable physical condition and could both bench press and squat over 300 pounds. One of his buddies from the Israeli Defense Forces said that he could kill anyone with a credit card and a pen. The guy was seemingly unstoppable." Vera picked up the FBI report again and thumbed through until she found the pages that referenced him. "On page nineteen, of this FBI report, it tells that the wife of the passenger in 9B called her cell phone carrier and requested that a message be pulled off her cell phone records from a few days prior to 9/11. She told the phone company that a friend wanted a copy of the message. The agent at the phone company accessed her messages and was surprised to discover that the message on her phone was not in English. In light of the events of 9/11, she got concerned and looked into this woman's call log. She discovered that many of her calls were made to international destinations and that oddly enough, she did not make any outbound calls that fateful morning. This struck the agent as very strange, assuming that anyone whose husband was killed in that terror attack would have made numerous calls to friends and family the minute the news broke."

"Interesting," Jim listened carefully and asked, "is there more?"

"Oh, it's more than interesting," Vera said, as she continued to read from her computer. "His wife was from Belgium and moved to Israel when she was in her early teens. Don't all Israeli's have to serve in the military there?"

"Yes they do have mandatory military service, I believe when they turn 18 years of age," Jim responded. "What are the odds that this guy is first pointed out as the hijacker by a flight attendant, yet he is an anti-hijacking specialist, a trained assassin, fluent in Arabic and then he is the only passenger murdered? This just doesn't make sense to me."

Vera began to read more details. "A purser had been called by American Airlines crew-scheduling on September 9th and offered Flight 11 to be added to her schedule. They were going to deadhead her on the 10th from her home in Miami to Boston to take Flight 11 the next morning. When she got to Boston, they called her and told her that they had found another purser to take that flight and that she was not needed. By the time she got back home to Miami, sometime on September 11th, she found the most interesting message on her home answering machine. She told the FBI it was a heavily accented woman's voice and what sounded like two men in the background. What they said borders on Twilight Zone material. It made no sense and must have blown this poor purser's mind. The message said, 'If this had anything to do with Israel, there's gonna be a backlash against the Jews.'"

"No way," Jim grabbed the document from Vera's hand to read for himself.

"Do you suppose this message was left by the hijackers? And who is this woman with the heavy foreign accent? How would the hijackers or handlers have known that this purser had been assigned this flight only two days earlier? Do you think this message was left on her home phone to be found after she died? One more thing, according to the FBI documents, that call was left on her answering machine at 9:51, about ten minutes before the last plane supposedly crashed at 10:03. And the most perplexing thing to me is that it was a woman's voice. The official story never mentions any female hijackers. How would any hijacker or handler get a flight attendant's home phone number? You know how protected that information is. Could this woman with the heavy accent possibly be the wife of the passenger in 9B? That might explain why she wasn't making phone calls to friends and family that morning," Vera questioned out loud.

As Jim continued to review the FBI document, Vera was busy scanning through the timeline book for more details. "Jim, take a look at this, while we are thinking those planes had to have been on the ground to make cell phone calls, the official story gives some conflicting accounts. At 8:35, the military liaison at the Boston Center claims that he informs NEADS that Flight 11 is 20 miles south of Albany, New York, heading south at a high rate of speed. He reports its traveling at 600 knots."

"I mentioned that earlier," Jim exclaimed, "No way was a 767 traveling that fast. It had to have been something registering on radar as Flight 11, but I can guarantee you it was no commercial jet going at that speed. It's absolutely impossible."

Vera continued reading, "And here, at the 8:42 mark, it says Flight 11 and Flight 175 were in a near-collision. She pointed at the book as Jim peered over her shoulder and read: 'According to an employee at the FAA's Boston Center in Nashua, New Hampshire, Flight 11 and Flight 175 nearly crash into each other while heading toward their targets in New York. The unnamed employee says, 'The two aircraft got too close to each other down by Stewart International Airport, which is in New Windsor, NY, about fifty-five miles north of New York City.'"

"If those two planes were in a near miss-near Stewart International, at 8:42 and one of the planes supposedly hit the North Tower four minutes later at 8:46, how long would it take to fly a 767 from Stewart to Manhattan at the typical speed? And Jim, how could one plane be traveling out of Boston fifteen minutes ahead of the other plane and not be hundreds of miles ahead?"

Jim walked to the window, "Vera, what the air traffic controller saw at 8:42 near Stewart International was most likely what the other guy reported was south of Albany, New York, at 8:35 traveling at 700 miles per hour. What he thought was Flight 11 traveling at that unimaginable speed was not a plane at all; most likely it was a missile. And whoever had the ability to manipulate those radar screens that day was also able to label that blip as Flight 11. What they thought was Flight 175, was most likely a 767 refueling tanker, being flying remotely that was made to look like Flight 175 on radar. That's why all those eyewitnesses reported that the plane that hit the South Tower was a military-plane; it was all dark, it had no logo and had no windows. But, it could have been a 767 and would have been traveling at the normal speed. From Stewart to New York would have taken that plane about seventeen minutes or so.

Vera was adding 8:42 plus 17 minutes, "That is nearly perfect timing, that plane hit the South Tower at 9:03."

"Yes, to reduce its altitude low enough to hit that building, it would have slowed down by a few minutes," Jim was beginning to formulate a likely scenario. "This means that those gospel-laden flight paths from the FAA that everyone has believed could be trusted were just another piece of disinformation meant to throw everyone off the track."

"It's either disinformation or an out-and-out lie, Jim. If both those flights from Boston were really at or near Stewart at 8:42, wouldn't they both arrive in Manhattan at the same time?"

"Not if one was a missile and the other was some type of plane meant to look like Flight 175."

Vera started to say something, but was overwhelmed at the magnitude of their discovery. Could this really be true?

After a long period of silence, Jim asked, "The last flight was United 93. How does its flight time and phone calls work with our theory?"

"Flight 93 left Newark at 8:42—it was forty-one minutes late getting off the ground," Vera reported.

"That could have caused a problem for either hijackers or handlers," Jim interjected.

"Yes, it could have. Could this plane have been what was supposed to hit Building 7? Remember, it wasn't hit by any plane or even much debris from the towers and it fell down at free-fall speed and looked exactly like a controlled demolition. What if it was supposed to look like Flight 93 was the plane that hit that building? Since nothing did hit it, why did it fall down into its own footprint at 5:20 that afternoon?" Vera asked.

"Clearly that late departure messed up their plans. If it was scheduled to depart at eight o'clock, it could've been meant to hit Building 7 first, shortly after eight o'clock. Well, how long would it take to get from Newark to Westover if that's where this plane ended up?" Jim questioned.

Vera punched in the airport codes, "That is a twenty-five minute flight. That plane would have been on the ground and taxied into a hangar by about 9:10. Their last transmission was reported to be at 9:21, oh wait, now here it says a United dispatcher sends an electronic message to Flight 93, using ACARS. That message was acknowledged, supposedly by the pilot at 9:26."

"At this point, about all we have to go on is the time the cell phone calls were made. It's the only information we can trust," Jim added.

"Wow, only one minute later, at 9:27, a passenger calls his wife and reports: He is on Flight 93, the plane has been hijacked. He also says, 'We are in the air.' Vera stopped. "There it is again, 'we're in the air' that doesn't make sense, if it's a hijacking of course they would be in the air." Vera continued, "He tells his wife they have knifed a guy and that there is a bomb on board. He later tells her in one of the four calls he made to her, the hijackers have a gun onboard. There's lots of conflicting information in this book about where they thought this Flight 93 flew to and what was going on inside the cabin. But what is baffling is how could a passenger know within one minute that the plane had been hijacked? Certainly the flight attendants did not immediately announce a hijacking. Near the end of this flight, a passenger and a flight attendant both called at exactly 9:58. The passenger called an emergency 911 operator and said that he was calling from a bathroom and that he saw white smoke. The flight attendant called home and left a heart wrenching message to her family saying good-bye. Hey, Jim, maybe there is something online about her, check Wikipedia, type in Cee Cee Lyles 9/11."

"Here it is," Jim started scanning the story, "interesting, have you ever heard her phone call? There's a player here, let's take a listen."

Vera pulled up her chair to listen to the recorded message. "No, I haven't heard this; it's her recorded message from her home answering machine?"

"Did you hear that?" Vera leaned closer to the computer speakers. "At the very end of her message right before she hangs up, a woman's voice said, 'You did great.' Play that again, Jim and listen very carefully. I didn't hear anything that sounded like jet engines and this was less than five minutes before that plane was supposed to have hit the ground in Pennsylvania. Their voices are so calm. Why would the woman hijacker compliment the flight attendant at a time like this?"

Jim hit the play button again as they both moved closer to the speakers to be able to hear every detail.

"You did great," the woman's voice whispered at the end of the flight attendant's message.

"Who could this woman be?" Vera asked.

"Good question," Jim said, sounding even more puzzled, "but that's twice now we have a recorded woman's voice involved with these hijackings. Yet neither the government nor the media have ever mentioned a woman hijacker being involved."

Vera continued, "There were thirty-three passengers and seven crew members onboard. Only two flight attendants made phone calls, the other flight attendant called her husband and asked, 'Have you heard what's going on? My flight has been hijacked by three guys and some passengers are in the back galley filling coffee pots to use against the hijackers.' She makes that phone call at 9:50. Thirty calls were made from that plane by eleven or more people and most were originally reported to have been from cell phones. That makes total sense; those air-phones were so bad you could barely make one or two calls at a time. And another thing Jim, as you know, flight attendants would never allow passengers to take over in an emergency situation. And how crazy would it be for them to let hot water or coffee be brought into the cockpit, where the flight computer between the pilots could've been completely fried by the liquid? That in itself could have crashed the plane. Flight attendants are trained to be in control, no crew would've ever allowed that to happen."

"So, by 9:27, one minute after someone acknowledged the ACARS message, the plane is hijacked and a passenger in the back knows about it and is calling his wife from his cell phone?" Jim asked with his hands in the air.

"Yes, his wife said he called from his cell phone," Vera confirmed. "She said that his cell number showed up on her caller ID and that confused her because she was a retired flight attendant and knew that he could not call from his cell phone—while in the air."

"The handlers on the ground would have had about seventeen minutes to choose the callers and paint the scenario for them. And at that point, if each flight had a couple handlers onboard, they could have all been onboard Flight 93 in the hangar."

"Jim, let me reiterate, a common detail reported by the passengers and flight attendants was that the hijackers had used mace or something like that. Several of them reported that the passengers were becoming sick and vomiting. You don't vomit from mace or pepper spray. You don't suppose, do you, that the passengers and crew were all killed by some type of gas, after their much-needed phone calls painted the picture that the octopus, as Max called it, wanted the American public to believe?"

"If they killed the passengers and crew with some type gas; that would have only taken minutes and yes, the passengers would be vomiting if they used something like cyanide gas. With this last flight, they had until the supposed crash happened in Pennsylvania, to deliver to the media—all the details that were needed to cement the official story and paint their methodical illusion. They even created heroes that supposedly rushed the cockpit," Jim said, as he returned to the desk chair.

"And the airplanes, what happened to those four airplanes at Westover?" Vera questioned.

"Remember the comptroller at the Pentagon, who owned the company that manufactured the flight termination system? He also owned a company that refurbished commercial 767's and sold them as military refueling tankers. He just got some free airplanes to add to his inventory. They could have easily kept those planes hidden in the hangers and flown them out after dark."

"You can't tell me they just killed those people in cold blood and then what, incinerated their bodies?"

"Anyone who would allow people to jump a hundred stories to their death and then exterminate over 2,500 others trapped inside those towers, would have no compunction killing a mere two hundred and fifty more. Like Max said, these people are pure evil. Life is meaningless to them. They are driven by only two things; money and power and will do whatever is necessary to obtain both," Jim added.

Vera was nervously thumbing through several papers Max had stapled together, "Look at this from BBC, it's an article dated Sunday, September 23, 2001. It says, several of those nineteen hijackers are still alive and at least four of them are airline employees. Do you remember when the FAA and Interpol sent out those directives that airline ID and passports were being stolen from crew members?" She unfolded a second article, "There are up to ten of these hijackers still alive. Mohammad Atta's father said he spoke to his son on September 12th. He was happy, alive, and well." Vera continued reading, "He also said that his son worked for the Israeli Mossad and the journalist asking questions about his son, should call them."

Jim took the articles from Vera's hand, "Let's look a little closer at those passenger manifests. If there was a woman or two involved and the supposed hijackers are still alive, perhaps that guy in 9B wasn't really killed and was, as the flight attendant first reported, one of the hijackers. If so, we might be able to figure out who else onboard was working with this guy. The official report of the supposed hijackers is patently false and as fake as those FAA flight paths and the radar blips. With these details we have uncovered, the accused hijackers still alive, and these women on the tapes, we definitely have more discoveries to make."

Vera felt her stomach twist into a knot. "This is why I never wanted to know what really happened on 9/11. This is so awful, I can't believe what we are saying, but it makes so much more sense than the government's official story. People in our own government arranged this. The entire event, all the people, were just pawns in their game and they played the public as fools. And worst yet, if anyone questioned their story, they were made to look and feel like a terrorist or an unpatriotic traitor. If you follow the money, it's easy to see that not one Arab country has benefited from this event. The same cannot be said for individuals and corporations involved with this Hegelian Dialectic, as Max explained. This might be too much for me, Jim. I've just gone down the rabbit hole of my greatest fears and met the rabbit. He has convinced me why Jeff was murdered, and I need to come to terms with that somehow."

thirty-five

Jim hoped that a night of rest would do Vera good. It hadn't him, the discoveries of the day before had left his mind restless and his stomach uneasy. Every effort to sleep was effectively countered by another what-if scenario. He waited for most of the morning to pass before he called her room. Even from "Hello" it was apparent that sleep had escaped her as well.

"Are you at all rested?" He asked, not having to wait for her response to know the answer. Jim imagined how their discoveries had affected her. He could not fully understand what it might mean to her to come to the realization that Jeff had been killed because of what he knew. It was probably the same things Vera knew now.

"Jim, my soul hurts. It hurts from deep inside and is shaking my foundational principle of life. How could they have killed so many innocent people that day? Why did they kill my Jeff? Why?"

Jim may have known the answer, but it had no meaning now. He let Vera continue, hoping she would eventually find comfort in her words.

"I have something, Jim, something you need to hear. Give me five minutes and then come over."

"What is it, Vera, what do you have?"

"It'll become clear when you listen. It's a tape I have that I'd forgotten about. When I found it and played it, sometime early this morning—well, just come over, you've got to hear this."

"I'll be there in five minutes," Jim said softly.

When he entered Vera's room, she handed him the recording pen that she had collected from Grace's room. It had fallen to the bottom of her purse and might have stayed mixed in with the other loose articles had she not been consumed with their 9/11 discoveries and thoughts of Jeff's pointless murder.

"What is this, Vera? Why have you handed me a pen, yet told me I needed to listen to something?"

"Oh, that's so much more than a pen, Jim. It's a high-tech recording device that belonged to Jeff. It's voice activated and incapable of being detected. He bought it to counter those union thugs who used every device known to man, not to mention threats and bribery. I lent it to Grace to help her catch Khalid in the act of cheating on her. But, we have caught something much more significant. Pull the top off and plug it into your laptop. Listen with me."

Jim did as he was instructed, admiring the sophistication of such a unique little device. The software loaded instantly and he hit play. Vera sat down in the chair next to him.

"Shalom, Khalid, so nice of you to invite me over while I am in Paris for the next few days. We have much to discuss. Take me inside, I will sweep the room for listening devices and we can talk there. After Yitzhak's assassination, everything changed, and one can never become careless."

Jim stopped the tape. "I know that voice, I can't place it, but I know I've heard it. Do you know who he is?"

Vera didn't answer and motioned with her finger for Jim to restart the tape. He again hit play.

"It is time," the voice continued, "Sherman has made this necessary. He is not one of ours, and his altruistic Boy Scout approach to the world's problems is making it impossible for us to achieve our objectives. He has usurped our ability to lead the United States into wars and destroyed our beloved Hegelian Dialectic. When we knew he would not be in Las Vegas, we thought we could control him by taking out his wife. That proved pointless. So, we struck in Orlando, hoping to send another message to him by taking out his brother, but we executed poorly and got the bomb off late. His brother survived, and the President failed to comprehend who needs to be in control."

Khalid interjected, "You know my teams are prepared and await your final instructions. There is nowhere we cannot strike and nothing we cannot do. We have the sophistication now to make the rough edges of 9/11 seem like mere irregularities. Once you select the six targets, everything will seamlessly fall into place for a simultaneous display of our power. When that occurs, we will literally control everything. We will replace the money supply with a world currency, which is already in warehouses just waiting to be issued. The software we have managed to install on almost every significant computer system in the world, allows us to eavesdrop and modify, through its backdoor, any data point to our benefit."

Jim stopped the tape again, "Khalid has an Arabic name, but he is no Arab. He may speak Arabic, but that's not his mother tongue."

Vera nodded, "Yes he fooled me. I'm sure he's fooled everyone. He fooled Grace until she took her last breath. It's all part of the illusion, isn't it?"

Jim resumed the tape.

"But there is an added wrinkle, my friend Khalid. This time Sherman must go. Our man McClean is primed and ready to assume control. He has waited a long time. It took a lot of favors and nearly depleted our stockpile of incriminating photographs to get him appointed and then approved as Vice President, but we prevailed. We have planned many years for this day to come. Our control of the media is much tighter than it was a decade ago. In those days, we humiliated, chastised, and belittled anyone who called the official story of 9/11 into question. We applied pressure. Once the chaos begins, following these coming attacks, we will apply force. With Sherman out of the way and our beloved Democrats thinking they have regained power, martial law will soon follow, and we will finally confiscate their guns, their food, and their will to resist. Novus Ordo Seclorum is upon us and in the words of their patriot-act-president, 'you are either with us or you're with the terrorists'. And in our case, it's both."

"But this is only the beginning," Khalid yelled with profound glee in his voice.

"Indeed, Khalid, those infamous days will only be the beginning. For two weeks, devastation will reign in selected cities across America. We will unleash the biologicals we stole from Iraq, the Anthrax we still have from Fort Dix, the nuclear devices with Iranian signatures we helped them develop and even the genetically modified food toxins we helped create. The chaos will be so profound that martial law and the suspension of all rights will follow. Hell, McClean helped write the NDAA, so he will have no problem putting people in FEMA camps that refuse to turn in their guns. Soon the world will be ours and we will have total control."

The tape concluded in laughter as Vera reached over and stopped it.

"Is there more, Vera?"

"Only proof that Grace's suspicions were correct and not worth listening to," Vera replied as she pulled the tape device from Jim's computer.

Jim buried his head in his hands as he sat not uttering a word. This reality was more horrendous than he could ever have possibly imagined. It meant the government, the institutions, and the corporations in fact; the whole world had been successfully infiltrated by entities whose intent was world domination. The magnitude of this discovery made it impossible for him to think clearly. Every path his mind started to go down seemed to be blocked by the insignificance of any one person trying to prevent this coming catastrophe. He felt puny and irrelevant. He was afraid that even if he exposed this dark secret, no one would believe it. Finally he spoke, "They have destroyed us, Vera. We're impotent as a people, as a country, and even as human beings. Look what they have done. Look what they will do and who are we to stop them? They have become as the gods, yet knowing only evil."

Vera stood up from her chair, walked over to Jim, and pulled his hands away from his face. She looked him directly in the eyes and yelled, "No, no, we will not allow this insurmountable evil to prevent us from doing everything in our power to thwart their plan. I don't care who they are and I don't care what they've done, all I know is that I will fight until my heart falls out of my chest to stop them. This means we start by calling President Sherman and letting him know what we've discovered. Now, do you think you can do that or do I need to?"

Vera's directness snapped Jim back into the moment and he immediately realized that what she had said was both the right attitude and the correct course of action. Jim reached for the secure cell phone and dialed the President.

thirty-six

"Yes, we are together, Mr. President, in Vera's room actually," were the words Jim spoke after making connection. Vera strained to make sense of what was being said, she thought it very odd the way Jim greeted the President. With the exception of Jim telling him about the tape and a few 'yes sirs, Mr. President' and 'of course we will, Mr. President,' Jim remained relatively silent. Vera waited patiently for the phone call to end, incredulous that Jim hadn't shared all the details with the President. When Jim finally said good-bye, Vera stretched out her hands and inquired "Well?"

"Maxwell J. Hager and his contacts in Chicago met head-on with a rocket-propelled grenade while sitting in the Range Rover. There were no survivors."

Vera shrieked, "No, no, that poor sweet man! Tell me that is not true, Jim. Tell me they didn't kill him."

As the reality of the President's news sank in, Jim grabbed Vera and held her tightly. "It's true, Vera, and we are not safe here. The President is sending FBI agents to guard us until a private jet can be prepared to fly us to Washington. He wants to personally debrief us and he wants us there immediately. How quickly can you get ready?"

"I'm a flight attendant, Jim. I can dress in the hall and shower in the car, if necessary. Say the word and I'm ready."

thirty-seven

"I'm a little nervous, Jim," Vera whispered, as they touched down at Andrews AFB. "I've never met a President. Politics was never my thing, in fact, I hate to confess this, but I didn't even vote in the last election."

"You'll be just fine," Jim said, with a little smile. "That won't matter a bit to Joel, he wasn't even running in the last election, except for Congress and you weren't in his district, so he won't hold that against you."

"Yeah, but you know him personally. I'm just the tag along here, and I have no idea about proper protocol; should I curtsey, bow or give the dead fish handshake?"

"Trust me; President Sherman is a lot like your husband Jeff, which should make you feel very comfortable. He's smart, down-to-earth, and extremely personable. Once you get over the initial formality of being in the White House and sitting in the Oval Office, I have no doubt Joel will make you feel like you've been life-long friends. Besides, he's very interested in what you have to say, so I assure you he will be dialed in to you and you'll have his undivided attention."

"Now, that really makes me nervous. I'm afraid he will ask me things I don't know the answer to, and I'll look stupid."

"Hey, I invited you on this mission for your brains and your experience, not because you are the fastest suitcase packer on the planet. The President himself approved you and you know what that means."

"You did a full background check?" Vera asked.

"Right down to your sock size," Jim said, laughing.

She playfully punched Jim on the shoulder and said, "Oh you're a lot of help, buddy."

For security reasons, they were picked up by helicopter at Andrews and delivered right to the White House lawn. Once past the security gate, they entered into the West Wing and were ushered into a waiting area inside the executive office. They didn't have to wait long. President Sherman appeared almost out of nowhere. He shook Jim's hand with both of his and stood back to be formally introduced to Vera.

"President Sherman, may I present to you Ms. Vera Hanson?" Jim proudly announced.

"Ms. Hanson, you are as lovely as the nine hundred photographs in your dossier," the President said, with a smile extending his hand toward her.

Vera gingerly took the President's hand and performed something between a curtsy and a knee buckle, recovering just in time to see Jim choke down a laugh.

The President ushered them into the Oval Office and invited them to sit on the couches in the center of the room. Rather than take his usual position, the President sat on the couch across from them. Jim was right; Vera's nervousness subsided and was replaced by a feeling of reverence that overwhelmed her as she looked around the Oval Office. When she thought of all the decisions that had been made in that room and all the great men and women whose lives had directed the course of history, her insecurities were replaced with a sense of awe. The President was aware of what Vera was feeling. He had sensed it himself the first time he was invited into the room. Out of respect for her and for the Office itself, Joel allowed her to take her time. He even offered to answer any questions she might have, because he wanted her to be at ease when they began the debriefing. Once the President felt comfortable with all the emotions in the room, he began.

"I can't thank you two enough for all you have done and for your willingness to put your lives on the line for me and for the country. This entire investigation suddenly became more dangerous than even I suspected and that's why you are here now. I want to thank you for being able to ferret out information that perhaps only you could have found. That's why I asked Jim to take on this assignment and why I trusted him to invite you, Vera."

The President continued, "Let me tell you what I know, to set the stage, before we discuss your new intelligence. I know there is a secret organization that has operated in this country for decades. They manage to weave in and out of organizations and infiltrate whatever agency they want. They have politicians in their hip pocket, they don't lack for money, and they don't seem to be accountable to any one specific person. If there is one, they manage to keep him well-protected and hidden. There is more, but allow me to listen to you."

Jim spoke first, "When we began our investigation, we were focused on the events in Las Vegas and Orlando. We wanted to know if these were more than just random events or accidents. Surprisingly, our investigation led us to many details of 9/11. Now, as you know, Mr. President, I have been a proponent of opening a new investigation of that event for many years, but that's jumping ahead. Our visit to Salt Lake City definitely provided us with a method that could have been used in Orlando and we now have evidence that our suspicions were indeed correct."

"And this is confirmed on the recording you mentioned, correct?" The President asked.

"Yes sir, that is correct."

"Continue please, Jim."

"In Minneapolis, we spent many hours with my dear friend Max Hager, God rest his soul, and that time was invaluable. He laid out for us this organization you mentioned and referred to it as the octopus. It all goes to motive, sir. And their motive points to total control. That was their motive on 9/11, that was their motive in Las Vegas and Orlando, and that is their motive for wanting to take you out."

"Perhaps we had best listen to that tape. Tell me again how it came into your possession," requested the President.

Vera explained in great detail the events that led up to her finding the recording earlier that morning and then played the tape for the President.

In many ways, it was more difficult to hear the tape again, for both Jim and Vera. The inherent evil that seethed from the voice on the tape was chilling. The President maintained his composure throughout and when the recording was finished he asked questions about its authenticity. Vera told him all she knew and offered to give him the tape recorder pen. He was most gracious, took the pen and placed it in his suit pocket. "Is this the only copy?" He asked.

"Yes sir, it is," replied Vera.

"Mr. President, I seem to recognize that voice. I think it's from someone I heard speak at the United Nations just a few years ago," Jim interjected.

"I recognize that voice too, from Stanford, back in the seventies," The President added.

"Not a word of this conversation can leave the White House. Clearly, this octopus has eyes and ears wherever it needs them and we, at the moment, do not know who can be trusted. We will meet tomorrow morning with Jerry Reitz and the National Security team to discuss this further. I want both of you involved in that meeting. Preventing these attacks on the country is my only priority; everything else will be tabled or reassigned. I would like to invite you both to be my guests in the residence for the time being. I want your input, your thoughts, and your reactions to the discussions we will have regarding the taking back of our country. Much of what we'll propose will be met with resistance and we need to explore ways to mitigate both the resistance and the ensuing aftermath of the sweeping changes we'll have to implement. This octopus has been decades in the making, maybe longer; it won't be neutralized in days or weeks. You two bring a much different perspective than many of the people here in Washington. I need that point of view and the wisdom it generates. Can I count on you?"

Vera nodded and Jim responded, "Of course, Mr. President, we'll support and help you in any way possible."

"Good, now let's head over to the residence. Come, follow me, and I'll give you the cook's tour of the Executive Offices on the way."

The ease and grace with which the President had received their intelligence report was impressive. He was exactly how Vera expected a leader to be. There was a sense of calm surrounding his entire demeanor that was reassuring in the threat of total terror. His confidence in his ability to address this potential horror and to defuse its effect on the country was remarkable and gave Vera great hope. Having lost a spouse herself to these bastards, she knew the kind of emotion that could potentially interfere with resolving the dilemma and yet, the President's focus was on the country, not his own personal vendetta or safety.

When the elevator arrived on the second floor and opened to the residence, Jim and the President were engaged in an intense conversation about the loss of Max. It was obvious that the President at least knew of Max and had probably met him. Jim's long-time relationship with Max only added to the sorrow that both men obviously felt. Vera remained silent and followed slowly behind. As they approached an open area in the residence, Vera froze. She stood there pointing at a Secret Service agent, but could not get any words to come out of her mouth.

"What?" Jim asked.

When her words finally did come, they were practically stuttered. She grabbed onto Jim's arm while still pointing at the Secret Service agent and exclaimed, "That… that… that… man! He's the man in black from Paris, the one from the coffee shop. He tried to kill me. He's one of them. He might have killed Max. What's he doing in the White House?"

Vera could see Jim and the President glance past her and then directly at each other. The smiles on their faces confused her. When they began to laugh, she stood back and demanded, "What, what?"

The President took Vera by the hand until they were standing in front of the agent. "May I present to you, Vera, Gordon Garcia, the most trusted and loyal agent on my personal detail, whom I have known for years and who I can assure you, did not kill Maxwell Hager."

"But he tried to kill me and Kelli at Alki with his accomplices in that black SUV," Vera insisted.

Again, the President smiled. Vera looked back at Jim, who was chuckling to himself.

"Okay, what's going on here?" Vera demanded.

"Gordon, would you care to explain?" The President asked.

"Ms. Hanson, the President assigned me to look out for you. We knew when you had met up with Khalid in Paris the first time; your life was in danger. I went to Paris right before Christmas to make certain you were safe. More than once I was effective in eliminating some of Khalid's operatives both on the streets of Paris and in and around the hotel. One of the reasons you were moved to the penthouse after Grace's death was so that we could better protect you."

"But the hotel manager said it was because they all loved Grace and and…"

"The French can be most persuasive when properly encouraged," added the President.

"What about at Starbucks on Alki?"

"Ma'am, had I not stood right behind you and pointed my weapon directly at the driver of that SUV, he may indeed have hit you. As it were, he swerved at the last moment and missed you, but unfortunately nicked your dog. I'm glad to know she is okay now."

Vera turned around and glared at Jim. "Did you have something to do with this? I mean, did you know all along that this agent was tailing me?" She paused for a moment and then questioned, "Hey, when I was in Paris before Christmas, you weren't even on assignment for the President. How did he know about me and why would he even care?"

"Perhaps I can help with the answer to that, Ms. Hanson," offered the President. He pointed to his study and motioned for her to follow him. "Do you know anything about Facebook?"

"I have an account and use it from time to time, why do you ask?"

"My security does not like me to use social media for obvious reasons, but I twisted a few arms and managed to get a Facebook account I could use on special occasions. Would you like to see it?" He asked.

Vera looked at Jim, who had followed them into the study and was standing next to her. Jim's stoic look convinced her to just go along with the President. "I guess so, Mr. President," she said.

The President opened his laptop, turned it on, and clicked the Facebook icon. Almost instantly the Stanford logo with the tree appeared. The President didn't say a word; he just looked directly at Vera waiting for her response. When it dawned on her what had just happened and that the President was indeed Stan the Man, she burst out laughing.

"You're Stan the Man?" She asked, pointing to the computer screen. "But I was so rude to you," she blushed. "Wait a second, how did you even know I existed?" She looked at the President, then back at Jim. "You!" She said, pointing at Jim. "You must have told him about me, but why?"

"Well, I've known the two of you for a long time and I just thought, well maybe, you know," before Jim could indict himself further, both the President and Vera started laughing.

"So you're Stan the Man," Vera repeated, looking at the President in disbelief and shaking her head from side to side.

"Yup, and guess who sent those roses hoping to brighten an otherwise miserable stay right before I called the President of France to insist they let you out of that prison? If not for that call, you might still be rotting away in that swank penthouse."

Vera playfully punched Jim in the arm again. "Oh you," she said, "I should have known."

"Well," said the President, "I think this calls for some kind of a drink, a cocktail before dinner, served right here under the big red S."

thirty-eight

The meeting in the Oval Office the next morning came to order with the following in attendance: President Sherman, Jerald Reitz, Jim Bowman, Vera Hanson, Attorney General Rudy Rathburn, Chairman of the Joint Chiefs of Staff Admiral William Anderson, and Speaker of the House of Representatives Mr. Lawrence Mendenhall. The tape Vera had provided had been authenticated. Each member in attendance had been briefed and had listened to it in detail.

The President began. "Ms. Hanson and Gentlemen, what we are confronted with today is unprecedented in the history of this country. We are facing potential acts of terror on our own soil, the purpose of which is to far exceed any war we have ever faced, any crisis we have ever confronted, and any devastation we have ever experienced. The United States of America is the target of a takeover by an evil that emanates from the depths of hell. It knows no boundaries, it feels no guilt, it claims no responsibility, and its appetite for power and control knows no end. If it succeeds, only God has the power to put an end to its existence and to wield the sword of justice in our defense. Our job as stewards of this land and of this people, is to put an end to this cabal, to expose it for who and what it is, and to restore the principles that established the United States of America, that have been destroyed as a result of negligence and complacency, to the people."

President Sherman wanted to hear, without directing them, their initial thoughts as to how to proceed. In this crisis, groupthink was to be avoided and a consensus had to be forged, so he continued his silence.

Jerry Reitz was fist to speak, "Sir, I recognized the voice on the tape. He was a political leader of one of our most trusted allies in the Middle East. The information disclosed on the tape is most concerning to me for many reasons. Because they have been such a trusted ally of our nation, they have infiltrated our media, the Federal Reserve, and the banking system. They control most of the lobbyists that in turn, manipulate far too many politicians. They also control most of the campaign contributions as well as both political parties. The disclosure of their covert involvement in 9/11; making that a false flag attack and not an attack by radical Muslims, tells us that it was done to destroy our freedoms and to put this nation into war for decades, with an unknown entity that has been and will continue to be, impossible to destroy. Their complete control over the media alone is going to be very problematic for us."

Jim glanced at the President, "No wonder Max called it The Octopus."

The Admiral was the next to speak, "I believe our primary responsibility is to protect President Sherman in a way that will confound their plans and preserve his ability to provide total continuity of leadership, until we can systematically destroy this beast."

"Now that we know who they are and what their plan is, I want you all to use the utmost discernment as to with whom you share this information. It is paramount that such a person has his or her allegiance only to the United States, our Bill of Rights, and our Constitution," President Sherman added. "This leaves me in a very precarious position. I must uphold our freedoms, yet be forced to deny rights to certain people who intend to do harm to our nation. This will not be an easy task, but we can use their own legislation, such as the NDAA, against them. I am sure all Americans will understand this is what is necessary to restore our nation and to destroy this octopus and its plan for the world."

Attorney General Rathburn added, "This explains some things that were making no sense to the FBI, there have been several troubling incongruencies in our intelligence that we could not fully explain. Based on what I have heard on the tape, I believe now they will most likely strike, Las Vegas, Houston, Chicago, San Francisco, Billings, and right here in D.C. Our intelligence made no sense to me until hearing this tape. Now, I believe Las Vegas quite possibly could be targeted for some type of nuclear detonation. Houston oil refineries and pipelines are in danger from conventional explosives that will affect domestic oil supplies and national reserves. Chicago, quite possibly, is where they intend to launch a biological weapon, most likely in a large shopping mall. Much like the symbolic World Trade Center towers, San Francisco is in danger of losing the iconic Golden Gate Bridge. Billings, Montana quite possibly will be the target of a chemical agent to prove to Americans that even small towns are no longer safe. And D. C.'s primary target is you, sir. These attacks, I believe, are set to happen in short succession, with one or possibly two days between each event. By the end of a nine day period fear will reign and the country will be in total chaos. It appears that their grand finale will be your assassination, Mr. President. Someone or several people in this town are most likely very deeply involved with this cabal and its destructive agenda."

Jerry Reitz interjected, "Our number one priority, after your safety, Mr. President is to neutralize any nuclear device that might hit Las Vegas or any other major city. Our past experience and intelligence has shown that these devices pass through their embassies. We will put a radioactive fishnet around all their embassies and consulates, and if so much as a micro curie is detected coming in or going out, we will be able to stop it immediately. This nuclear device could weigh as little as twenty-four pounds. We are very familiar with their nuclear weapons and capabilities, even though they denied the IAEA access. And since we know who they are, we can more easily determine who they intend to blame."

"That's terrific, but what if we did more than that?" asked the President.

"What do you mean, sir?" The Speaker asked.

"What if we declared an all-out war against them? What if we risked political suicide by exposing them and their operatives in the 9/11 attacks, opened a new investigation into the events of that day, started snooping around Westover Air Force Base, and forced the media to air our findings, just for starters?"

"That would be potential suicide, Mr. President," replied Speaker Mendenhall.

"Yes, Larry, but I'm in a unique position. I wasn't elected to this job, so if I commit political suicide, I have no financial backers to disappoint, no constituency to let down, and no voters to answer to. I answer to the people of the United States and if I can begin to unravel this cabal, then I am protecting and defending the Constitution, which is the only thing that will preserve this country short of God himself. If we were to initiate such an attack—a preemptive first strike, if you will—what kind of support do you think we would have in Congress, Larry?" The President asked.

"If we could prove that we were preventing mass destruction, widespread devastation, and your assassination, we could produce just better than feeble support, if we are lucky. You're talking about going against the status quo, upending the apple cart, and running counter to the brainwashing this country has experienced for decades. It is almost impossible to counter the cognitive dissonance that has been foisted upon the people of this nation," Larry hesitantly answered, knowing full well what they were up against.

Vera stood up, hesitated, and then spoke, "That might be

true with the ruling class, but we the people know something is not right. We hate Congress, oh we love our own Representative, maybe, but the other 434 members of the House and 98 or 99 members of the Senate aren't worth a damn. We're in debt, we're in an entitlement death spiral, and unemployment still hovers near depression-era ranges. Political correctness and mob rule—via both media and social media have become the norm. Healthcare is an unmitigated disaster. More than half the country is on food stamps. Regulations are choking the lifeblood out of the economy and America, quite frankly, is no longer the country it was created to be. Unless we change what we're doing, we might as well be controlled by some evil tyrannical monster from the depths of hell. Death is death and how we arrive at death may not really matter. Personally, I prefer life and liberty, and to me that means making the hard choice, making the ultimate sacrifice, and leading with conviction instead of being chased by a fear of being convicted."

Vera sat down and could feel her heart pounding. Suddenly, she was struck with fear that she had said the wrong thing, had spoken out of school, and had voiced an opinion in the midst of the country's leaders that was neither wanted nor necessary. There was silence after she spoke, until the President softly began to clap his hands together, followed by Jim and then the others. All of them sensed that she had spoken as the voice of the people.

The President followed, "That is exactly the type of fear we must overcome, and it is the kind of spirit we need to engender and harness in this country. As the President, this is what I intend to do. We cannot allow even a hint that things are different than they seem to this cabal. The State of the Union address is in less than ten days. I have almost finished my prepared speech; I will do so and leak significant parts of it to the media. Of course, this won't be the speech I will be giving that night. Your job, Larry, is to make the world think that this is the speech I intend to give and you can stir up as much political controversy as you wish in doing so. Have fun with it and knock yourself out. Jim and Vera, we will need to have the two of you continue to consult with us. Jim, I want you to get Mari here as soon as possible. The three of you will be my personal guests in the presidential box the night of the address. That will be sure to stir the main stream media's angst. We will meet here every morning at 10:30 sharp, until the day of the State of the Union address. People will be added to this group as needed, but only under my personal approval. Are there any questions?"

The President addressed a few points of order and reconfirmed some specific actions. When the questions had subsided he simply said, "Good, now let us go and do."

In the ensuing days, the morning meetings became more and more focused as to the course of action the President intended to take. He brought in his private counsel on several occasions to discuss the legality of his intended executive actions. Once the President felt comfortable with his overall outline of action, he scheduled a meeting with the Secretary of Homeland Security, Jamie Napioli. That particular meeting was held in private with the Secretary, who upon hearing the President's intensions tendered her resignation there on the spot. Before accepting her resignation, the President said, "This cabal is the elephant sitting on the chests' of the leaders of this nation. It prevents us from moving forward as a country and its one we are never allowed to discuss. The fear it has instilled in us, combined with the satiating of our greed has destroyed our government, corrupted our laws, and nearly annihilated who we are as a people. If you want to continue to be a part of that, then I accept your resignation."

The following morning, the Attorney General arrived fifteen minutes prior to the appointed time. His entire countenance had changed from one of fear and trepidation to one of absolute resolve and unfeigned fortitude.

"I see a distinct difference in you, Rudy," said the President, as he warmly shook his hand and welcomed him into the Oval Office.

"Mr. President, I remembered I was born an American, I fought for this country, and somewhere along the line I must have been side-tracked; rest assured, sir, I intend to die an American."

"Welcome home my friend, welcome home," was all that the President said, but that somehow said it all.

The invitations that had been previously sent to members of Congress, the Cabinet, and the Justices of the Supreme Court were followed by an addendum signed by the President, formally rescinding his request for their attendance at the speech now replaced by his insistence that they attend. This unusual request started all of Washington talking. The history of the State of the Union, required by the Constitution, had taken various forms throughout the country's history. Washington addressed the Congress, but Thomas Jefferson thought a speech was too monarchial and simply sent a written speech to them. That tradition continued until Woodrow Wilson in 1913, decided to once again address a joint session of Congress in the Capitol Building. In recent years, most members attended the address, but many felt it was optional and made other plans. This year, the curiosity level had peaked with the insistence request from the President. It was confusing to Congress; but it made them publically vulnerable, which caused the President and his small group of allies to privately take heart.

When 8:30 struck, the deputy Sergeant at Arms of the House of Representatives pushed open the door to the House chambers and announced the Speaker of the House, Lawrence Mendenhall and the Vice President of the United States, Lon McClean. The two gentlemen took their seats on the platform directly behind the rostrum where the President was to speak. Jim, Mari, and Vera were already seated. Some of the members of Congress knew Jim and greeted him warmly. He proudly introduced the two women in his company to anyone who was still milling around awaiting the President's arrival. The level of anticipation was growing throughout the chamber. Vera nervously looked at Jim, who smiled and gave her a hearty 'thumbs up'.

At exactly nine o'clock, the Sergeant at Arms stepped into the chamber and in his familiar staccato voice announced, "Mr. Speaker, the President of the United States."

thirty-nine

President Sherman walked toward the platform avoiding the customary hugs and handshakes from well-wishers along both sides of the aisle. There was a determination surrounding his demeanor that could be felt throughout the entire chamber, which quieted the assembled crowd. When he reached the podium, rather than having to wait for the partisan crowd to suspend their applause, he was greeted with the silence of a pastor preparing to deliver a sermon.

"Mr. Speaker, Mr. Vice President, Justices of the Supreme Court, Members of the House and the Senate and my fellow Americans, no doubt many of you have encountered the excerpts of the speech you believe I will give tonight. Under ordinary circumstances, that would have been an address I would have been proud to deliver. We are not under ordinary circumstances; nothing about my presidency has been ordinary. I came to this office devoid of an election and I did not ascend to it having prepared myself through service in the Executive Branch. I was an average citizen who sought to serve my country through public office, like most of you, and won a congressional election in my home state of Washington. It was in the course of that service that I awoke one morning and with my hand placed firmly on the Holy Bible swore before God, judges, witnesses, and the American people, to protect and defend the Constitution of the United States of America. I had no campaign promises looming over me, no large financial backers demanding a quid pro quo. I entered this office with only one simple vow, to give my life defending this divine document that established and now defines our country. My wife has already given her life in its defense and I am prepared to join her should I be called to do so.

As citizens of this country, many of you feel there is something not right with our government. You feel that it does not matter who is elected to office, because the outcome will always be the same. It has caused you to lose hope, foster apathy, and withdraw entirely from the process of governing yourselves. I stand before you today, to tell you that you are not mistaken in your feelings. You may not have all the facts, you may not understand all the intricacies, and you may not be pointing your finger in the appropriate direction, but your feelings are accurate. To you members of Congress, many of you are well past feeling or caring. You know for a fact something is wrong and in some cases you are an integral part of what does not work for the betterment of this nation.

I come here tonight to confirm some of your worst fears regarding this country and the entire world. There is indeed a consortium, a cabal, if you will, whose sole purpose is to exert control politically, economically, socially, and morally upon the people of this world. The United States is the primary stumbling block in the way of their plans to rid the world of sovereign states. Their efforts are directed and focused on us as individuals, as states, and on our nation. We now have confirmed evidence that this cabal had developed and had begun to implement a plan to facilitate the literal nuclear annihilation of the City of Las Vegas. With the help of the National Security Adviser, Jerald Reitz and Admiral William Anderson Chairman of the Joint Chiefs, along with a selected team of Navy SEALs, we have neutralized that threat and assure you that Las Vegas is and will continue to be safe. This was only the beginning of their plan; other cities have been targeted for chaos. The end result of which is to establish martial law in this country effectively nullifying the Constitution and rendering the military and the public helpless in the face of a complete take over and an effective end to this country as we know it to be.

We, who love this country, will not allow this to happen and to that end I have implemented the following changes to take effect immediately, under my power as Chief Executive and under orders I have issued in conjunction with the Attorney General. These changes I will outline are as follows:

Dual Citizenship: Unfortunately, there are a number of people in government, some here in this chamber tonight and many more, who serve in top-ranking agencies and departments throughout our government who are, by birth or by design, full-status citizens of this country and some other country. We allow such duality in this nation and celebrate these people for their contributions, but beginning tonight no one with dual citizenship will be allowed to work in the government of the United States on any level. I will give them the opportunity to renounce their foreign citizenship or resign their position. If they refuse, they will be fired. If you are a member of Congress who holds a passport from another country, I encourage you to surrender it immediately, resign from office or suffer the consequences of the wrath of Americans through recall, impeachment or the voice of the ballot box. The book I placed my hand upon when I accepted this office, clearly states that you cannot serve two masters. That is true with respect to God and it is true with respect to country.

Loyalty Oath: In the morning, every member of Congress, every Federal Judge, and every member of the Executive Branch serving as a Cabinet Officer or higher, will be given a loyalty oath to sign. It will not be unlike the oath you swore to uphold when you accepted your current position, but it will now be visible to the American People and serve as a constant reminder to you, for it will have your signature reconfirming your allegiance and loyalty to this country and its Constitution.

9/11: Anyone who thinks that nineteen Arabs cavalierly commandeered four airplanes on September 11, 2001, and flew them into buildings as described by the official government report is at best naïve. Tomorrow morning, I will announce a reinvestigation of that tragic day in which the truth will be obtained and not obscured. I will appoint Jim Bowman to head this committee. We now have hard evidence proving that the events of that day were indeed orchestrated by this cabal whose tentacles stretched deep into the halls of government. The effects of which co-opted people who were either complacent, complicit or conspiring to weaken this country. The end result was to implement wars, to destroy freedom, to transfer control, and to enrich the organization whose evil knows no end.

For that cause, I am suspending the NDAA, the Patriot Act, and the TSA at airports. This will be done in an orderly manner making necessary plans for public safety. Who do we think we are that we can pass legislation that is in direct violation of the Bill of Rights and do so in an arrogant dictatorial fashion daring the courts to call fowl and subjecting our citizens to unreasonable searches and seizures, abandonment of due process rights, and prosecuting unwarranted wire taps and eavesdropping? These laws were the direct result of the fraud perpetrated on the American people by 9/11 under the pretense to make us safer. Are we safer today than we were on 9/11? Only if slavery is safe are we more secure.

Healthcare: I invite you as a Congress to pass legislation to repeal that abominable law, if, in fact you can call it a law. It was foisted upon the public in the most devious, despicable and deceptive fashion known to lawmaking. You may choose to make restitution for your error or not, but I will veto any attempt to fund and implement that putrid piece of legislation. In addition, I will suspend from prosecution anyone charged with non-compliance for any element of taxation in that law.

Lobbying: This organization who seeks to destroy this country manages to infiltrate your legislators through the front door of lobbying and greases their palms out the backdoor of corruption. You rely on them to tell you how to vote. You fail to read and understand the legislation you cast an affirmative vote for, you line your campaign war chests with filthy lucre, and you do it all in the name of freedom of speech. As of this moment, that behavior must come to an end. Your responsibility is to listen to your constituents and to allow them to freely speak. Lobbying by registered groups will be prohibited from contributing money to any campaign.

United Nations: The United Nations is an incestuous cesspool of criminals focused on forming a one world government with elitist domination. They infiltrate every organization, they suborn every lie, and they charge this country dearly for the privilege of doing so. I am withdrawing our ambassador to the UN, effective immediately and will deal with countries on a state-by-state basis. I refuse to sign any treaty with that corrupt organization and will work to remove their influence and power wherever their presence appears.

Media: Our main stream media has been complicit with this evil organization for decades, pushing out a message of nihilistic nonsense that has weakened the fabric of our families, destroyed the certainty of right and wrong, and turned established truth on its ear. They, under the first amendment, have a right to broadcast their version of reality. But we are not helpless in defending ourselves and our families from the concentrated influence of this seemingly singular voice. Media today is such that it reaches all people in a myriad of ways. We must combat this unified influence by making possible, through grants and tax incentives, opportunities for additional and varied voices to reach the people. Many such messages have occurred on their own accord; we can and we will provide ways for more of that to occur.

Tenth Amendment: The tenth amendment grants power to the individual states to legislate and control all aspects of government not specifically established in the Constitution. For some reason, we have decided that that the federal government has the right to implement laws that circumvent the right of states to govern their citizens. This is wrong and must be addressed. I invite states to participate in the committee hearings of all legislation that comes before this body. I cannot mandate this, but I strongly encourage you to pass legislation that allows the states access to have their voices heard in the political process. We have seen that when left to their own discretion, states do a much better job of effectively addressing and resolving their problems than we do by taking their money and extorting them into compliance. The founders fought against this kind of federalism and we must pave the way for its elimination.

And now, my fellow Americans, I have saved the most important and the most difficult for last. We, as a country, no longer control our money and haven't for over a hundred years. In 1913, Woodrow Wilson invited a private bank to replace our constitutionally-mandated responsibility to print and control our money and to provide for our own fiscal responsibility. As this private bank sought and obtained more and more influence throughout the world with its ability to manipulate currency, control debt, and manage monetary policy, countries and particularly the United State began to lose their sovereignty. Today, we bow before this cabal. They are our masters. We have allowed them to lead us down a path of false security right into their lair and now we face being devoured by this beast. We cannot allow this to happen. We must throw off the shackles of this monetary monster and war machine and reclaim our destiny as a country, as a nation, and as a people. We will not renew the Federal Reserve's charter with our country. This means the added burden of liberty will be placed squarely upon you, the Congress of the United States, and you will answer directly to the people whom you serve.

We stand on the precipice of decision. We can choose to be free, based upon the principles this nation was founded upon or we can be forced into the den of destruction, forever serving the masters of evil, who are consumed by their own lusts. Join me and rise above such evil. Throw off the scales that blind our eyes from the truth. Look to liberty and live. Follow me to freedom. May God bless each and every one of you and may God once again be sufficiently trusted in, to bless the United State of America.

"When a well-packaged web of lies has been sold gradually to the masses over generations, the truth will seem utterly preposterous and its speaker a raving lunatic."
Dresden James

NOW WHAT

In the months since Methodical Illusion was released I have been amazed at the number of people who have come forward both in support of the theories revealed in the book and inspired with hope, to bring the truth to light. Countless flight attendants, pilots, engineers, physicists, and researchers have approached me, all with the same thought, and said, "You have figured it out. You have found the missing piece to the puzzle." They, however, pale in comparison to the numbers of people like you, who have always known there was something wrong with the official story, and have asked me, "How can I help?"

Quite frankly, I look at all of you as my teammates as we move forward in an effort to shine a bright light of truth on this dark, deceptive and disgraceful episode in our history. I am buried in my new research that will prove these theories to be true and will follow up with a sequel to Methodical Illusion that will truly 'blow the lid' off the corruption and cover-up that has suppressed the truth all these years. In addition, I have been taking the time to do as many interviews as possible to focus attention on what really happened on 9/11 and trying to wake up as many people as possible.

What I would ask you to do is to spread the word, share the truth, and wrap yourself in optimism. Give the book to those who are still asleep and encourage them to read it. Email your favorite show hosts, asking them to conduct an interview with me. Focus on the younger generation who has been brainwashed by the lies and distortions of the media surrounding the events of that fateful day. Keep in mind that in many cases, this generation does not have experiences to effectively compare against the prevarications that we who are older do. They need your help, your patience and your understanding to bring them into the light. We need them and we need all who are willing fight against the lies, cover-ups and distortions of the day.

We are succeeding. I cannot tell you how many emails or Facebook messages I have received from husbands, wives, mothers, fathers, sons and daughters who have shared with me how the contents of my book have been the catalyst to helping a loved one move past the cognitive dissonance and embrace the truth. Together we can do this. While we look to our leaders to one day assume the Joel Sherman like qualities necessary for change, we have the responsibility to express the change in us, and share it with all who will listen. We will do this. We will not stop. We will not shrink from the burdens of freedom and in the end we will win the day.

Rebekah Roth

"Join me and rise above such evil. Throw off the scales that blind our eyes from the truth. Follow me to freedom."
Joel Sherman

Glossary of Terms

AA .... American Airlines
APU...Auxiliary Power Unit
ATC .... Air Traffic Control
ACARS ....Aircraft Communicating and Reporting System
BOS.. Boston's Logan International Airport
CAIR .... Council on American-Islamic Relations
CEF..Westover Air Force Base
CIA .... Central Intelligence Agency
Deadhead...................A crew member is flown as a passenger to work a flight.
DHS..Department of Homeland Security
DIA.. Defense Intelligence Agency
DOD..Department of Defense
DOE... Department of Energy
EWR..Newark Liberty International Airport
FAA..Federal Aviation Administration
FAR... Federal Aviation Regulations
FEMA...Federal Emergency Management Agency
FTS .... Flight Termination System
FBI .... Federal Bureau of Investigation
GPS...Global Positioning System
IAD .... Dulles International Airport, WA DC
IAEA... International Atomic Energy Agency
IDF...Israeli Defense Forces
IRS .... Internal Revenue Service
NATO..North Atlantic Treaty Organization
NDAA ....National Defense Authorization Act
NEADS .... Northeast Air Defense Sector
NIST ....National Institute of Standards and Technology
NRO .... National Reconnaissance Office
NSA..National Security Agency
NTSB..National Transportation Safety Board
NORAD .... North American Aerospace Defense Command

ONI.. Office of Naval Investigation
PETN................................. Pentaerythritol Tetranitrate, an ingredient of Plastic
explosives.
PROMIS......................................Prosecutor's Management Information System
SAIC..Science Applications International Corporation
SEAL............................. U.S. Navy special operations force Sea Air Land Team
SEC ....Securities and Exchange Commission
SUV .... Sport Utility Vehicle
TSA..Transportation Security Agency
TAPN .... Explosive chemical component
UAL ....United Airlines
UN ....United Nations
WTC...World Trade Center

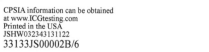

9 780982 757130